He's a Natural

A Bishop Bone Murder Mystery

By

Robert G. Rogers

D1738099

Also by Robert G. Rogers

Bishop Bone Murder Mystery Series
A Tale of Two Sisters
Murder in the Pinebelt
A Killing in Oil
The Pinebelt Chicken War
Jennifer's Dream
La Jolla Shores Murders
Murder at the La Jolla Apogee
No Morning Dew
Brother James and the Second Coming
The Taco Wagons Murders

Non-Series Murder Mysteries
The Christian Detective
That La Jolla Lawyer

Contemporary Dramas
French Quarter Affair
Life and Times of Nobody Worth a Damn

Suspense/Thrillers
Runt Wade
The End is Near

Historical Women's Fiction
Jodie Mae

Youth/Teen Action and Adventure
Lost Indian Gold
Taylor's Wish
Swamp Ghost Mystery
Armageddon Ritual

Children's Picture Story book
Fancy Fairy

Acknowledgements

Eva Abbo and Denise Wallace provided invaluable help in getting the book ready for publication. I thank them both.

Prologue

Hugh Jackson sat at his desk studying the speech he was preparing to give at a joint PTA meeting of several school districts. He pushed his papers aside, and took a few minutes to ruminate over the argument he'd had earlier with his wife, Julia.

"Have to do something about her. She's beginning to make waves." *But what should I do,* he wondered, as he poured himself a whiskey and coke. to relax with.

Divorce, he'd already concluded, wouldn't work for him. *What the hell would work? I don't want to marry Denise. She's okay in bed, but too strong willed for me. Maybe it's time for me to move on. No, I need her media connections. Hell, I need her other skills too. Got some problems to deal with, Hugh.*

He decided to let the thought incubate until he came up with a solution he could live with, one that gave him what he wanted as well as what he needed from time to time.

He'd taken off his tie and left his coat in the car to get comfortable. He enjoyed working on speeches he was to give. He loved them all, loved to hear himself deliver them and loved it especially when something he said got a good response from the crowd. So he worked diligently on every speech to include some lines to get laughs, and others to make people think, and to make 'em feel something about the things he was saying. All of that because, bottom line, he loved having the crowd under his control; getting them to do what *he* wanted them to do, namely vote for him, not what somebody else might want them to do, as in vote for them.

He laughed at the thought.

Denise Allen would be at the speech with her cameraman getting it on video for the television station where she worked. She was the news anchor for the station and very much in love with Hugh. He'd made sure of that. Each time they met, his goal was to make her feel like she was the most important person he'd ever met or ever expected to meet. She loved it, and loved him as a result.

Consequently, she became the key to his success as he was to hers. By following and promoting his career, the controversial and the non-controversial happenings that people wanted to know about, hers had flourished as well and she'd risen from being a newspaper reporter to the television anchor she had become. Her cameraman, Jason Garcia, had risen along with her. And he had fallen in love with her along the way, but had to live with frustration since she barely knew he existed, it seemed.

As Hugh had said to himself when he'd begun his rise in politics, "Nobody can be a success in today's world unless everybody knows what he's doing." So, he made damn sure Denise was around to make sure everybody knew what he was doing – all favorable of course.

Denise was somewhat younger than Hugh but she didn't pay that any mind. Love hits where it hits. Hugh didn't mind either. That's the way he'd planned it and was enjoying having her on his side and by his side, day and night, when possible.

Her plan was to cut significant clips out of his speech for insertion into news stories from time to time during his campaign. In effect, she'd be giving him free publicity for his campaign. He was running for the state Senate seat held by incumbent Aaron Nelson, a man who'd enjoyed being the state Senator but who had done very little since he'd been in office. Perfect for a man of Jackson's abilities to run against. "He's left plenty of ground for me to plow," Hugh had said to himself when he decided to throw his hat into the ring.

Hugh was currently the chairman of the board of supervisors of Lawton county, having achieved that position by blackmailing the prior chairman into retiring or risk exposure for taking kickbacks while in office. Everybody understood that the system worked like that, but if reminded, they had no alternative but to vote whoever was exposed out of office. It was their Christian duty.

Around nine o'clock that evening, he figured the speech was okay. *Mostly women'll be there,* he thought as he wrote it. So, he made sure to give women maximum credit for all the advances that had been made in education over the years.

He'd practiced it several times and had marked places to pause and smile or frown or to do whatever he felt was needed to give an "impromptu" emphasis on what he was saying. However, with Hugh, nothing was ever impromptu. It was always planned to achieve some effect designed to let him win the day. He was political to the core.

He called Denise to let her know he was almost finished. He knew she'd be waiting.

"I'll call when I'm leaving the office," he'd said.

He was thirsty and looked forward to a warm woman to snuggle up to. They'd have a late night bottle of beer while exchanging stories and then go to bed. He'd already told his wife he'd be out of town on business. She'd known it was a lie when he told her, and that he was sleeping with Denise, but didn't care. She'd long since adjusted to his wayward ways.

Until recently. Over the past few weeks she'd begun to indicate that she was going tired of it. Even suggested, ... no, requested, a divorce.

*****

Hugh locked his office and the outside door and headed to his car. It was somewhat dark outside but he could see his car. Nobody appeared to be around. He knew he was the last man in the office. Everybody else had left as soon as the clock showed five o'clock. He'd ducked out for dinner with Denise for an hour but came back to put the final touches on his speech that weekend.

Should'a turned on the outside lights, he thought, taking note of the darkness. But if he had, the lights would have been on all night, and he didn't want anybody complaining about anything he did. One vote could make a difference in his run for the state Senate, not to mention the next office he ran for, an office he had already begun to think about. *Never too early to look ahead,* he'd thought.

He cut between a couple of cars to get to his. Some people often parked their cars in the supervisor's lot for one reason or another, usually when they were eating out with friends and were all going to the restaurant in one car. They figured the lot would be safer than parking on the street someplace.

As he was emerging from his detour between cars, he reached inside his coat pocket and pulled out his phone to call Denise. He heard a shuffle behind him and was in the process of turning to see what it was when he felt a pain in the left side of his back – the sharp pain of a knife blade penetrating his body. He reached back instinctively before falling to his knees in shock and dying. The blade had hit his heart causing it to stop.

He fell forward, dead.

His right arm slid out in front of his body exposing the watch on his wrist. It showed the time to be a little after nine. The killer reached forward and took it off. A car was heard from someplace and the killer ran away holding the watch.

*****

When Hugh didn't show up by ten and didn't answer his phone, Denise drove to the supervisors' offices to see if anything had happened to him. She found his dead body a few feet from his car and called the police. She was crying when she called and remained distraught even after the police arrived, so once Chief Jenkins had spoken with her, he asked an officer to drive Denise home.

The officer called her co-worker, Jason, whose name she had given him, to keep her company that night. The love of her life was dead. She could scarcely believe it. She didn't go to bed that night. Neither did Jason. He sat beside her with his arm around her shoulders.

The Lawton Police Chief had answered the call because the dead man was a public official. The ambulance was there when he drove up but paused long enough for the chief to look at where a blade of some sort had penetrated Hugh's side. Blood had stained his shirt.

More studies by the police lab workers would enable them to conclude that a knife with a relatively long and hard blade had been used to murder the man.

Hugh's cell phone had ended up under his body. They'd find that when they took his body away.

"Murder," one policeman said. "Nothing taken though, as far as we can see. Maybe somebody came by and interrupted the killer before he could take anything." They'd discover the missing watch later.

Jenkins agreed. He stared down at Hugh's body. "Maybe his past caught up with him, if I had to guess." He thought with a quip he'd heard, *I've stood all I can stand, I can't stand no more. But, who? That's the question I have to answer.*

Chief Jenkins was in his sixties, about six feet tall and a little heavy around the waist. Seemed like he had time to eat but not enough time to exercise regularly and his wife cooked "good stuff."

His face was rough and broad with deep worry line that came from age and a hard life. Being chief of police had done that. But, for the most part, he maintained a good disposition, and was generally friendly – unless he was dealing with someone breaking the law or causing problems he was sworn to prevent.

After the ambulance had taken Jackson's body away, the chief picked up the man's cell phone and drove out to tell Jackson's wife, Julia, who dropped her head when he told her and cried. He stayed with her until someone she called "a friend" showed up.

"Riley Waston. Lives up the road," she said with a gesture between sobs. "He's … our handy man. Milks our cow sometimes. He did some business with my husband."

She called Riley and told him what had happened. He said he'd be right down.

She told the chief she'd also call her two children and let them know. It was late then, but she'd call the next morning.

*****

The next morning, the chief called a meeting of his staff to brief them. "We've got a murder on our hands, folks. Hugh Jackson, an important official was stabbed to death last night. Could be an attempted robbery, or possibly a hate crime, since nothing was taken. Either way, we have to get hopping." He assigned them things to do, preliminary things finding out about any recent run-ins Jackson had with anybody or any continuing conflicts that might have boiled over. Was he involved in any big money transactions?

After the briefing was over, he also called his friend and fishing buddy, Bishop Bone to tell him about Jackson.

"Well, ol' buddy, you practically predicted it," the chief said, reminding him of a conversation they'd had about Hugh Jackson when he was running for the Board of Supervisors of Beat 2.

Bishop wasn't too surprised. He knew talk was cheap, but now and then, it turned out to be the precursor to actual happenings.

"Son of a bitch!" he said. "Any suspects? I don't expect anybody hung around waiting to be arrested."

Jenkins laughed and said he didn't have anybody in his sights. "I'd be interested to get your opinions, if you have any," he said.

"Not off the top of my head," Bishop said. "Practically anybody he'd had to walk over to get to where he ended up or wanted to go would be on my list."

That's how the chief saw it as well. "Nothing taken as far as we could tell. He'd fallen on his cell phone. The killer must have heard a car or something and ran off before he could take anything."

"Or, it was a hate crime; somebody old Hugh had pissed off terminally. They weren't after anything but his life," Bishop suggested.

"Yeah. I had that thought too," the chief agreed. "Seems more likely but we'll check everything out."

"Be damned," Bishop said. "Why don't you drive out? We'll have a cup of coffee on the back porch and talk about it." He and Bishop often did just that over coffee or beer depending on the time of day.

"Warm me up a couple of them small croissants you eat and you've got a deal," the chief said.

Bishop laughed. "They'll be on the table with butter."

Jenkins said he'd be out in an hour or so to kick the case around and hung up.

The chief constantly complained about the coffee at his office. They'd make it at seven thirty and by ten when he was ready for a second cup, it was too bitter to drink. Bishop had one of those machines that ground the beans for each cup so the coffee was always fresh. And he kept croissants in the freezer for the chief, although he enjoyed them also. He knew the chief wanted a carb or two to eat with his coffee. They didn't do his waistline any good, but he enjoyed the taste.

*****

Hugh Jackson had been in the news most of his life, beginning with his high school days. Most people knew practically everything there was to know about him because in politics a politician's life is an open book. And Hugh was, what practically everybody knew, an extrovert and wanted people to know him.

Of course, Hugh made sure that what people knew about him were the things he wanted them to know; the good things – real or imagined. And most often his public posture was all-favorable because he was a politician in all things he did, and politicians were successful if the voters, or whoever else they dealt with, thought the best of them. So he always led with a smile and did his best to make 'em feel like they were special to him.

As Bishop had told Kathy when they were talking about Jackson, "He a natural born politician."

But not everybody liked him. Some people felt intimidated by outgoing people like him. "A loudmouth" he was often called by those who weren't, or couldn't be. They always voted for the other guy, but Hugh didn't mind so long as he had the majority, which so far he'd had.

But it seemed his luck had just run out. Somebody didn't like him enough to put a knife in his back and kill him.

His life, his luck, and the sowing of the seeds of his death had started years before. His psychological hang-ups came after his parents were divorced; the rest came when he was old enough to see something he wanted. By that time he was savvy enough to figure out a way to get it. And let the devil take the hind most if he had to bump into people doing it.

Chapter 1

Hugh Jackson was huge by most standards, and probably twenty or so pounds overweight, a lot of which had found a comfortable resting place around his stomach. But the comfort that came from eating and drinking well, and the ease with which he achieved what he wanted, seemed to be "ol' Hugh's" style. He stood six two and a fraction with broad shoulders. He'd played football in high school and junior college and was okay at it, even made All Star his senior year. But when it came time to move on, "okay" didn't cut it. He wasn't fast enough for recruiters from universities with competitive football programs to ply him with food and drink, money, and the tutors needed to get him past the courses he had to take to get some kind of degree before going on to play pro ball. And he wasn't scholarly enough to play football for colleges that still stressed learning as their raison d'état.

His face was wide and fleshy with smile rings that dominated it. He'd been smiling since he'd finished junior college. Most folks said he had a sixth sense that would let him know when somebody was getting close so he could start smiling. He was almost 50 and had been selling anything anybody could afford to buy since he graduated from the "JC." That's what the locals called the junior college in town. The town was Lawton, a small lumber town in south Mississippi.

He was married and had been for almost twenty-five years. The marriage had produced two children, one boy and one girl. He made sure he didn't have anymore. "Cost too damn much," he'd said. He'd put them through the local college, after that they were one their own, he'd told them. With their dad's ego and charm, which they'd inherited, they'd worked their way through Ole Miss. The boy ended up practicing law in the state capital. The girl became an accountant on the Gulf coast and mostly did tax work for people who didn't want to pay any more in taxes than necessary to stay out of jail.

The son was what other lawyers called a "transactional" attorney. He negotiated deals and prepared the documents for the parties to sign afterwards. Although he went to court occasionally, he was not considered a trial attorney.

Both children were married and both had children of their own. When they visited, it was to see their mother. They accepted the fact that their dad was more interested in his affairs than he was in theirs. The son often joked that when he talked about "affairs" in connection with his father, he meant it in the broadest sense, to include both personal and business affairs.

Hugh hadn't been so lucky in his childhood. His parents had divorced right after he was born. His mother, he'd later heard, didn't like men. He couldn't understand why she got married, but was glad since he came to be as a result. But Hugh pretty much grew up on his own and learned how to be self-sufficient. Consequentially, he hadn't learned anything about love and kept looking for it under the covers of willing women.

Hugh's wife was considered plain by most folks but nice and reasonably intelligent. She was a few years younger than Hugh. She put up with him and his perpetually wayward ways, it was said. Her name was Julia. She'd inherited her family's hundred and twenty acre farm which she loved managing. He hadn't said anything while they were courting, but as soon as they were married he pushed to have her put the farm in both their names so he could use it as collateral in his business ventures.

She refused. When her mother, the last of her family to die, deeded it to her to avoid probate, it had been on condition that Julia keep the farm in her name alone as long as she lived. "Some of these old men 're jes lookin' for a place they can stick their thang and anything a woman's got that they can steal," she told her daughter. Julia took the advice to heart and was glad.

After a few years, he accepted her refusal to put him on the deed, but he showed the farm on his financials anyway when applying for loans. So far, no bank had ever ordered a title search to discover that he didn't own it. They just assumed he owned it. Most men did own the land they lived on. There was still some feeling in the culture of Lawton that women were put on earth to serve men. Things were changing but some men still felt that way.

Julia loved her pets. She had cats, dogs and cows that came to the pasture fence where she stood and "lowed" at her to get a neck rub. An older neighbor, looking for somebody to talk to, came every day and milked the cows for her, in exchange for a share of the milk. His name was Riley Watson. He'd owned an appliance store in town.

She did her wifely duty with Hugh when he needed it, but as she told her friends, "I don't mind him getting it someplace else, which I'm sure he does. Saves me having to carry on like I'm liking it." Mostly she was reciting the essence of what her mother had told her, and what she'd seen during her lifetime - men hopping on and off after a five to ten minute ride and afterwards asking the wife if she enjoyed it. Most smiled and said yes, a lie of course. What they really enjoyed was that it was over.

Farming had never been Hugh's cup of tea. He could drive a tractor when he wanted to show he was a man of the people, even walk in "cow shit," he liked to say to himself, if needed, to prove that he was. He could be anything anybody wanted him to be when it suited him. Without a father to give him a role model, he used any male model that worked for him. *I have all those plays I did in school to thank for that. I put on the face I need to put on to confront my problems. Hell, it's easy.*

He "knew" he was superior to anybody he'd met and it didn't bother his ego one bit to act humble or to pretend to be impressed by somebody. It never bothered him that he was a total hypocrite. He was just playing a role. *It's just another damn play,* he'd tell himself about life's confrontations. *Not anything real.*

The only time Hugh was really impressed was when he looked in the mirror or heard himself talk.

When it came down to his bottom line, no matter what face he wore to get something he wanted, he was more a talker than a worker. In school, he was in every play with a part he could charm his way into. He volunteered to give speeches, using anything he could take from the Internet and modify to claim as his own. And, for sure, he debated every chance he got and more often than not, was on the winning side.

Like Will Rogers, Hugh never met a man he didn't like. And, he especially never met a woman he didn't like. Or could at least pretend to like long enough to get her undressed. Afterward, on his way out the door, he didn't mind telling her, "Let's stay in touch" and now and then he would, as long as she didn't show signs of looking for something permanent from him.

Out of school he had started selling used cars and did very well. All his cars were "almost like new." Not a one had been driven hard or abused, and all – thanks to a friend – showed low odometer miles. And, if anybody took issue with him, he was big enough to hold his own in a confrontation. Some buyers cursed at him but very few ever swung at him. And the few that did ended up wishing they hadn't.

After a few years of selling cars he had enough money – with the little extra he managed to wheedle from Julia and her mother's estate – to buy out an appliance dealer, Riley Watson, their neighbor who often helped Julia with her chores, even milked her cow. Milking, over time, often resulted in arthritis in a woman's hands. He told her he'd help her avoid that. It was obviously more than that, but he didn't say it.

If Hugh knew, he never said. Riley was too old for Julia, he figured and wasn't a threat.

Riley wasn't a natural born salesman and failed trying to run a business that depended on somebody who was exactly that. Milking a cow was a lot more fun.

Riley had barely been "gettin' by" in the store and had let it be known that he wanted to sell it. He was glad the day Hugh came to see him about buying the store. That meant he could retire, drink beer in the afternoons, go huntin' during the seasons and watch more football on the "telly."

Unfortunately for him, Hugh could tell that Riley was anxious to sell, so even after he'd tentatively agreed on a purchase price, Hugh reneged and offered less. The man cursed Hugh but took the reduced offer. Oddly enough, it was one of the few times Hugh was being partially honest. Julia had refused to give him everything else she'd received when her mother died. She did agree to give him some, but that was it and even then, made Hugh show her on the title of the store when the deal closed.

One day, Hugh asked her to sign some documents related to the store's operations and surreptitiously included a document granting him full ownership. But she caught it and ripped into shreds. She didn't talk to him for a week afterwards.

Watson wasn't sorry he'd sold to Hugh, but every time he drank his beer in the afternoons, he thought of Hugh and how much he hated the man for "chiseling" him at the last minute of the deal.

A few years after Hugh had bought the man's store he'd opened half a dozen other stores in relatively big towns up and down the state. With an eye out for people like him to run his stores, they all did well. When one didn't, the manager was replaced. Hugh could always spot somebody who was as full of "bull shit" as he was and willing to spread it around to close a deal. That's what those who knew him like to say about him ... behind his back.

Hugh traveled to China to negotiate a deal with manufacturers who could produce every appliance he needed at prices that would make his bottom line as fat as his ego was large. And his stores flourished and grew to a dozen in number up and down the state. He made sure he visited them all and gave speeches to anybody needing a speech in any town or county where a store was located. "Free publicity," he liked to say because he was always introduced as Hugh Jackson, the "biggest appliance" dealer in the state.

"The best in Mississippi and the biggest. And I intend staying that way," he would quip. And he did stay the biggest, especially after Sears began to cut back.

Finally though, his ego got tired of merely being the biggest appliance dealer in the state and cast about some something else he could do to boost his ego. And he found it in politics. The county supervisor for the district where his wife's farm was located had decided to retire and Hugh knew just the man to fill his seat.

"Me," he told himself.

Damn, every board meeting of the supervisors would be a time to let his ego shine, even if he had to pretend to be humble and act like a man only interested in the needs of the people of the county even though he didn't care a bit about their needs. He'd promise the world to get elected and afterward, he'd publically complain about all the people, namely the other supervisors, who prevented him from fulfilling his promises. *That's what politicians do,* he thought.

In the speech declaring his intent to run for the office he said, "My life is your life. If you're not happy or if you're in need, then I'm not happy and I'm damn well going to make sure your needs are met. I don't intend sitting on my butt and drawing money. And, I don't intend letting any of the other supervisors do that either. I'm running so I can work for you. And, that's what I'll do."

*****

Denise Allen, a young reporter for the local newspaper with ties to the television station, was the first one to interview him after he'd announced his candidacy. She literally had to chase him down in the field behind his house. He knew she was coming out for an interview and wanted to show he was a man of action.

Denise was one of those young women born with an innocent charm about her that was enhanced by her light brown hair and green-blue eyes. She was five and a half feet tall and stayed in great shape. Any man looking at her had an immediate urge to hold her in his arms and then some. So far, she'd managed to resist most of them.

The cameraman assigned to cover the interview was Jason. He didn't know that Denise and Hugh had met earlier to plan the "impromptu" interview. He was thin with a nervous persona, dark hair and eyes. He was about as tall as Denise. Knowing they'd be trudging through in a plowed field, both had dressed casually for the interview.

Hugh was plowing the field with his late father-in-law's old tractor. When Denise and Jason intercepted him, he turned off the motor and turned in his seat to face them both, smiling.

"Miss Allen and you, sir, what can I do for you?" he asked them.

"Jason," the cameraman told him.

"You look like you're enjoying working in the field. How can you take the time?" Denise asked. Hugh had thoroughly briefed her over a dinner a few nights earlier so he was as prepared for her questions as she was prepared to interview him in the field.

Hugh jumped off the tractor so Jason's camera could get a better shot.

Showing his most earnest face, he looked at her and said, "I love to work the earth. The earth is the root of our civilization. It is the soul of mankind." He waved his hand over the horizon of the field he was plowing. "It gives us life and I feel the surge of that life when I'm close to it, when I feel it in my hands. I'm working the ground you're looking at to help it fulfill its destiny. To help it give us food like it was born to do." Naturally he didn't believe any of that, but thought it would sound good. He had written and rehearsed it the night before.

"You've said if you're elected, you'll work to fulfill the needs of the people. Do you still stand by that promise?" Denise asked.

"I do! Every hour I'm in office, I will be like this ground I've been working. I'll be working to fulfill my promise to serve the needs of the people of my beat. I can't give them food, but I can give them a service that will make them feel almost as good."

The interview made the local news that evening and was in the morning newspaper. Hugh had seen to it. The story the young reporter and the video her camera backup had made during the interview was shared with the local television station as Hugh had asked. And, to make sure it'd be the lead story, he had taken all those responsible to the Country Club for dinner a week before.

He promised to meet and talk with every voter in his beat, as the supervisorial districts were called by the people in the county. And, driving an old truck he'd bought for the campaign, he set out to do exactly that. He owned a top of the line Ford car, but most of the people in the beat drove trucks, more often than not old ones, so, wishing to be one of "people" he went with the flow. He'd opted for the Ford for the same reason. Many successful merchants and professionals in town owned luxury cars. Hugh didn't want people to think he was making so much money "off them" that he could afford that kind of luxury so he stayed "humble."

He also dressed in "work clothes," usually old khaki pants or worn jeans with a short-sleeved shirt and older shoes. Most of the people he'd visit were working people. "And by God, so am I," he told himself with a laugh.

People who had been around the block a few times would comment to one another about how Ol' Hugh sure knew how to work a crowd. And so he did. He could work one on the inside, hands on, or on the outside with help from people he worked hard to convince that "he was the one." For those he worked on the outside, his so called "voter visits," he used Denise, the reporter, and her cameraman Jason. They always went with him to capture the essence of those "working" meetings.

Hugh couldn't help but notice the way Jason's eyes followed Denise's every move. He smiled each time she looked in his direction. And, he always managed a compliment not matter how slight when they finished an interview.

The boy's got a major crush on her, like he's gonna piss in his pants every time she looks at him, Hugh thought to himself with a smile. He also observed that *the boy* had good reason to be impressed. She'd caught Hugh's attention as well.

The "speeches" Hugh gave them were recorded and always made the newspapers and the local television newscasts. Hugh wined and dined the media people who could, and did, help him out – and he did it in style. Everybody who could help him win the election got his version of a pat on the back, usually dinner, and if a woman, flowers as well.

Of course, the "voter visit" stops he made with the reporter, Denise, were at the homes of people Hugh had known a long time, most of whom had shopped at his store at one time or another and had walked away with a "deal." Some of those were people life hadn't been fair to, the "salt of the earth" people, the heart and soul of the county.

Their faces bore looks of despair and weariness like death would be a welcome relief from what they'd been facing most of their lives. But they liked it when somebody, especially somebody as "important" as that man running for office, Hugh Jackson, wanted to pay them a visit. He'd get their votes and the votes of everybody in their families.

Even so, Hugh never took anything for granted. He arranged to visit those people himself ahead of his "media" visits, take a six pack or a couple of bottles of wine with him, depending on their preferences, and talk about the upcoming "surprise" visit. So those visits went well and got good press coverage. And all that hard work and press coverage was working – the polls showed him to be one of the front runners to replace the retiring supervisor.

*****

One afternoon in late July, Hugh Jackson drove to Bishop Bone's cabin half a mile off Indian Creek Road for a visit. After Bone bought it, he had totally remodeled it to bring it into the "modern world." Nothing had been done to it since it had been built way back when.

Hugh didn't know Bone personally, but had read enough stories about him in the local newspapers to figure he was a straight shooter and didn't beat around the bush. So this was one of those visits he decided it would be better not to alert his reporter "friend" about first.

He wasn't sure how the visit would turn out and didn't want to be embarrassed or upstaged. And, with any luck, Bone would be taking care of some bank problem someplace and would not be at home. If so, that visit, if it came up, would be one of those he could say he tried to make but didn't through no fault of his.

But Bone was at home. He was working in the orchard he and Kathy were cultivating. They had pecans, apples, oranges, pears, peaches, plums and figs. They also had blueberry bushes and were working hard to keep their pomegranate and persimmon trees healthy. For some reason they wanted to die, or acted like they were going to anyway. He was having the same problem with his grape vines. The vines were as green as they could be in the spring but tended to turn yellow during the heat of the summer. He couldn't figure out why and kept replacing them. The last batch seemed to be doing better. He'd adjusted the amount of water they were getting.

Anyway, that day Bone was in the orchard putting out fertilizer stakes and weeding. He'd installed sprinklers to eliminate the need to water the trees and bushes by hand but they all still needed "food" and pruning now and then.

Hugh saw Bishop in the orchard and parked as close as he could. He hopped out, smiling like he'd just won the lottery, and walked briskly toward him. Bishop saw him drive up in the old truck he'd been driving around the beat, campaigning in.

It reminded Bishop of an equally old soft-top jeep he used to drive himself. Finally though, when the roof got so bad he couldn't patch the holes in it and the engine began to sound like it was on its last legs, he decided to trade it in on a new one, a brown hardtop Wrangler.

He remembered when he drove it off the lot. He'd thought, n*ow Kathy won't be ashamed or afraid to go anywhere with me in my old jeep.*

Bishop watched as Jackson got out of his truck and began his walk toward him. He recognized Jackson from newspaper stories that always showed his pictures and from television reports when he was being interviewed.

Bishop had hoped Jackson would discover his "mistake" and wave as he drove away but that was not to be. Seemed he'd intentionally come to see him so Bishop let out a loud sigh and got to his feet. *Son of a bitch,* he thought, dreading the interruption.

*****

Bishop stood a shade over six feet, with almost no flab, a consequence of managing the land around his cabin. It kept him in good shape; that and playing tennis with Kathy. His face was rough and showed the beginnings of age lines. He was in his mid-sixties. He also had light brown hair that was showing some gray here and there and a thinning spot at the back.

He only shaved when he was seeing Kathy or handling an assignment from a bank, his "work" he called it. Bishop stayed busy representing clients, mostly banks. He did that primarily to have something to do, not because he needed the money.

Bishop had a decent income from investments he'd made after settling the complaint he'd had against a corrupt developer and his banker conspirator who, in effect, had chased him out of California and, at least temporarily anyway, ruined his life.

They'd framed him on a real estate deal he was handling. The legal battle dealing with that, one he'd initially lost, ended his career, not to mention his marriage. He retreated to Lawton to lick his wounds and try to recover. He'd been there years before on a business deal and remembered it favorably.

He was a lawyer, licensed in California where he'd gone to law school, and in Mississippi, which he regarded as his home ever since meeting Kathy. He'd never been happier.

While considering his next move after resolving his California problem, Bishop inadvertently got involved in the culture and town business of Lawton and found that he fit right into the life styles of the Mississippi people.

*****

He had heard about Jackson's vow to visit every voter in the beat so he had no doubts about why the man was there. Anticipating a political greeting - the big handshake and matching smile - Bishop removed his gloves to get ready. Sure enough, when Hugh was a couple of steps away, he stuck out his hand, broadened his smile and said, "Mr. Bishop Bone. I'm Hugh Jackson and I'm campaigning to be your supervisor. I wanted to drop by and say hello. You can ask me any questions you might have. I want to know what the voters of this beat have on their minds and any complaints."

Bishop sighed loudly and answered him. "Mr. Jackson, I know you. You have a successful chain of appliance stores. Good for you. And, I've seen reports of your campaigning on television. Looks like you're doing okay, but you're wasting your time talking to me about anything so you might as well keep going.

"I haven't been interested in politics since I worked on Seth Campbell's campaign for governor right after I got to town."

Bishop had intervened to stop some drunks who were assaulting Campell's daughter, Sonja. As a consequence, he came to know Seth Campbell and the friendship that resulted from that friendship and the political campaign opened many doors for him including the representation of banks with loan problems.

"Seth should have won but had to drop out of the race for personal reasons. A crying shame. He would have been a good governor. I haven't been interested in politics since. I represent banks and do what I can to solve their problems. The bank problems have a beginning, a middle and an end. In politics there's never an end. There's always a reason nothing ever gets done. A good one if you believe the politicians, which I don't. I can't stand the frustration of political stagnation if you want the truth."

"I understand completely, Mr. Bone. Politics can be a nasty business ... and politicians, well most of 'em anyway, aren't worth the powder it'd take to blow their brains out. If they had any brains."

"I don't know enough politicians to comment one way or another about that. You could be right, especially the part about the lack of brains, or you could be full of shit. Right now you're a politician yourself so who knows? But I don't give a rat's ass, Mr. Jackson, about any of it. As far as I'm concerned, politicians are public bull shitters trying to get elected to serve only themselves, not the poor shits they're supposed to serve. Have I made myself clear?"

"Damn!" Hugh said, still smiling. "I do like a man who speaks his mind. I find that refreshing as hell. And, I appreciate knowing your point of view."

But he was thinking, *I'm glad as hell I'm two steps ahead of the rest of the world. What if I had asked Denise to come with me? Listening to Bone, she'd be encouraging him to run for office. An honest man who speaks the truth. No political double talk.*

"I tell it like I see it, Mr. Jackson, not the way a politician says I should see it."

Hugh looked at Bishop for a couple of seconds and decided to change the subject to something he felt more familiar with.

"I couldn't help notice the gravel road I drove on to get here, Indian Creek Road. It was dusty as all get out. There're people on that road who tell me the dust gets so bad in summer their vegetable gardens get covered in orange clay dust and gets stunted. If it wasn't for a rain now and then, they wouldn't get a crop. That's a crying shame. Don't you think?"

Bishop shrugged. "I suppose. Not my problem is it? I'm far enough off the road so it's not a bother to me."

"When I'm elected, it'll be my problem and I'm going to do something about that road. I'm going to have it paved so the poor people living along it can grow vegetables not covered in dirt. Orange dust in the summer and potholes in the winter when the rains come. Trucks stay muddy and every time they hit one of them holes, it jars the hell out of them. Lots of seniors live on that road, Mr. Bone. I don't like to think of them getting knocked around like that. I loved my mother and father and I wouldn't want them to have to live like that." He was lying but figured lying was part of the political game.

"Well, sir, I plan to fix that road after the election. Should 'a been done a long time ago. And, you know what else? You might not know it, well you might, but lots of good folks in this beat still don't have public sewage. They have septic tanks. I think that's a disgrace. I intend doing something about that too. And natural gas lines need to be extended to every home. It's terrible for people to have to have their gas trucked in. Some people are still on well water in this beat. In this day and age, everybody should have good, clean, city water."

"Yeah. Good point. I hope you succeed," Bishop said with a nod.

"And, I bet you've noticed how your cell phone coverage comes and goes depending on where you're standing. I'm going to get on the cell phone companies' asses and make 'em fix all that. If they're gonna sell cell phones they damn well have to make sure everybody, at least in my beat, has coverage. My people are entitled to what everybody else gets."

My people, Bishop thought, *he's talking like he owns them. What a crock of shit.*

"Good for you. Is that it? Have we had our visit? I've got work to do." Bishop said and waved at the trees in the orchard. "I won't be voting but it has nothing to do with you."

Hard nosed bastard, Hugh thought.

"Yeah. You said. In effect you don't give a damn what happens to your government."

"I do, but I doubt there's a damn thing I can do about it. I just govern myself and my little patch of ground."

Hugh looked around, as if interested, and said, "Nice place you've got here. Done a good job with it," he said.

Bishop thanked him for that.

So, he thanked Bishop for taking the time to talk, shoved out his hand for a "leaving" salutation. Mostly though, he was ready to greet the open road he came on and mostly … to get away from Bone.

Bishop took it. The man's handshake was firm, to establish his domination as some men did. Knowing the man was a politician, or trying to be, Bishop had expected it and added a little extra to his to make a point as if to say, take your phony theatrics elsewhere.

Bishop watched the man's truck trailing dust from the road, drive out of sight.

"Didn't waste too much of my time. I don't think he'll quote me as supporting him."

Hugh wouldn't, but he was doing some thinking as he drove out of sight. *I'm glad that bastard won't be supporting any of the shits running against me. I'd hate to try and sell him a used washing machine.*

Now and then, he'd take one in trade, clean it up and sell it as "almost" new.

Chapter 2

That afternoon, Kathy came out to Bishop's cabin as she usually did. She managed the Lawton library which closed at five thirty. Like Bishop, she'd come to Lawton from someplace else. Also like Bishop, she had suffered through a divorce. Both had decided that marriage wouldn't make their relationship any better, so they maintained separate homes but spent their spare time together. Her home was in the city. His overlooked Indian Creek in the county.

She was neatly dressed in a light pink blouse, slacks and loafers. He had showered after working in the yard and put on a jogging outfit afterwards.

Bishop always felt complete when he saw her coming up the stairs. She had a pretty face with golden brown eyes and light brown hair that brushed against her shoulders when she walked. Bishop loved to see the glow in her hair when the sun caught it while they were outside. She stayed in great shape playing regular tennis with Bishop and looked younger than the fifties she was.

The time was almost six. Time to relax on the back porch of Bishop's cabin overlooking Indian Creek, which gave the road outside its name. The Creek was the size of a small river that flowed with green water unless it was the rainy season when it changed to yellow-orange from the belt of clay that ran through the county.

At night, Bishop turned on the lights he'd submerged in the creek at the bottom of his slope to illuminate the creek's water.

It was summer and hot, even in the early evening, so Bishop had mixed gin and tonics for their "happy hour" time and put out some nuts to munch while they watched the furry beavers on the far side of the creek. Their closing time was when it got dark. They'd damned a small tributary and formed a pond for their "village."

Most of them were working diligently to repair the damn that kept their pond from draining into the creek. A limb had worked loose and water was beginning to leak through the opening. Others worked just as tirelessly repairing their lodges.

While they sipped their drinks, he told her about Hugh Jackson's visit when he was working in the orchard.

"When he announced his intent to run, he said he was going to talk to every voter in the beat," she said.

"Well, he came by here today, and boomed out his political bull about how he's gonna improve 'his people's' lives by getting them better roads, and everything else. I told him he was wasting his time talking to me. I didn't vote. I do now and then, but I didn't want him staying any longer than he did."

"Good for you," she said. "I can't stand the way a politician carries on. You can't believe a word they say."

Bishop agreed. "As some folks around here say, 'he's a natural-born politician.' Do you think he'll win? I haven't kept up with the race."

She looked into the distance thoughtfully and said, "I think you said it, Bishop. But, I don't know how he'll do. He's the new kid on the block. There are a couple of other candidates who are giving him a run for his money. The leading candidate – well he and Jackson are very close in the polls – is Marvin Blackledge, a retired financial professor who taught at the JC."

"Jackson acts like he's the only candidate."

"He wishes. Marvin ran last time against the supervisor who has just retired. He came close to winning that election. The other guy in the race, with any kind of chance, is a football coach who is retiring from coaching. He's made a good reputation coaching but I doubt that'll get him the votes he needs to beat Blackledge or Jackson."

Bishop shrugged. He didn't know enough about the coach or Blackledge to offer an opinion but he knew Jackson and didn't care for him.

*****

For dinner, they had the chicken enchiladas Kathy had cooked the evening before. Bishop contributed the salad he'd bought from a grocery store and the beer. He was a novice in the kitchen and didn't try to deny it. If it hadn't been for Kathy, his dinners would be hamburgers or something from Denny's.

The next morning they had toast with jam and coffee for breakfast.

*****

Kathy was right with her opinion about the election. Blackledge and Jackson ended up in a runoff. Blackledge was the leading vote getter but didn't have enough to avoid a runoff.

Jackson's campaign was founded on his success in building and running a business. During his speeches, he liked to say, "I have hands on experience in running a business. And, running this county is like running a business. Blackledge no doubt can teach finance, but actions speak louder than words. I've done it. All he can do is talk about it. Who do you want managing your tax dollars, a talker or a doer?"

Blackledge countered with, "I've taught the men and women who run businesses up and down this state, and states around us, the financial ins and outs of a business, how to set up a budget, how to manage employees, how to control inventory. Not one of my students has ever complained about not being ready for the business world. And, not one of the companies that hired them has complained. I'm proud of my record. I can do for the board of supervisors what I've done all these years for my students. Teach them how to manage a business. That's what the board does, manages the business of the county.

"I've had over twenty years of management experience. How many years does Mr. Jackson have? None. Not one, when you get right down to it! I don't count selling dishwashers as running a business. How can he expect to run the business of this county?"

Hugh didn't take Blackledge's rebuttals lying down. He said, "Talk's cheap. It takes more than reading books to create and run a company. It takes more than reading books to know what the people of this county need. And, it'll take more than somebody who's never faced a financial crisis in his life to solve the problems this county faces and will face in the future. I have. I've turned around a dozen businesses. Made them all successful. You think that was easy. You think I could read a book and get that done. Hell no! It takes guts to handle that kind of pressure, to take failing companies and make them successful, and hire people in the process. How many companies has Professor Blackledge turned around? How many people has he made jobs for? I'll tell you. None!"

Hugh's campaign rhetoric cut Blackledge's lead in the polls from five percent to one percent. But Blackledge climbed back to a two point lead when the mayor of Lawton endorsed him. "I was taught by Professor Blackledge," the mayor said. "I can't think of a better man to represent Beat 2 of this county than Marvin Blackledge."

Hugh didn't like the endorsement one bit, but knew it was done all the time by people whether in his beat or not. A name is a name he knew, and names meant votes. The mayor was a name and he didn't think it was in his best interest to cross swords with the mayor of the largest city in the county. But it did put Blackledge further ahead in the polls with only a few days to go. Most people figured he was a "shoo-in" for the post.

But not Hugh. He never gave up anything he wanted until the last door closed. And it hadn't closed yet. *Still have time to come up with something.*

*****

Bishop and Kathy had watched enough of the evening news to keep up with what was happening.

"Looks like it's gonna be close," he told her. "But Blackledge should take it."

"It is," she said. "I agree. The Professor should win. The mayor's endorsement put him two percentage points ahead."

"I forgot about that. You're probably right. I'll take back what I said. It won't be that close."

Then the unexpected happened, at least unexpected to most people.

*****

The evening before the election, the local television news carried a story. It had begun earlier in the day when a well-dressed, successful looking man walked into the newspaper office and told a story. He introduced himself as Gilmore Jefferson and had the demeanor of an honest man.

The man told Denise Allen, "I've heard something I thought might be newsworthy. I've heard that Blackledge didn't exactly retire from JC. He was forced out according to what Bishop Bone said. Bone is somebody we all know and respect in the county. He and your chief of police, Chief Jenkins are good friends. So, if Bone says something, I figure I should listen."

Denise called Jason, her cameraman, into the room when the man said "Bishop Bone." Once he had the camera set up, she asked Jefferson to continue.

"I live in Beat 2 where Marvin Blackledge and Hugh Jackson are running. Nobody's talking much about it, but Bishop Bone said Blackledge left his job at JC under a cloud. I decided to let somebody know. I sure as hell wouldn't vote for somebody who left a job under a cloud. I'd vote for someone whose life has always been an open book. Jackson has always helped people. I believe him and I'm voting for him. Blackledge tells a good story, but that cloud he's under and his lack of hands-on experience make me shy away from him like I would from a cotton mouth moccasin. "

As always, when the interview was over, Jason told Denise what a "great job" she'd done with the story. She thanked him and called Bishop immediately to verify the man's story. But Bishop was in Jackson on bank business and didn't get the message she'd left him until he returned home that night.

It made him mad as hell to hear that somebody had misquoted him. He called both the newspaper and the television station and told them, firmly, "I don't know a Gilmore Jefferson and I have never said anything good or bad about Blackledge. I don't know the man personally. One person I know said he ran a close race last time he ran for supervisor of Beat 2 and I've seen his campaign signs. That's the extent of my knowledge."

Bishop's rebuttal and that of Blackledge were run with the late night news when most of the people were already asleep.

Blackledge also said there was no cloud. He was a few months from retirement but his wife had been suffering from the onset of Parkinson and he wanted to retire early to be with her. JC granted his request to be freed of his contract.

"Sitting as a supervisor wouldn't be a full time position like teaching and I've lived in the county all my life and know all its problems. And, I know how to fix them. This story by that guy, Jefferson, is a bald face lie. None of it is true."

Unfortunately for Blackledge, the newspapers had already been printed by the time they'd received the rebuttals. Both rebuttals went in the next edition.

Most of the people believed Blackledge's story and looked at the disclosure by Jefferson as indeed, a lie intended to smear Blackledge. But not enough saw the story and his rebuttals were too late to save him. When the votes were counted, Jackson had won by just under 500 votes.

Chief Jenkins ran an investigation of Jefferson. He couldn't find anybody by that name in Beat 2 or anyplace else in the county. The address he'd given was an old abandoned house on a dirt road in Beat 2.

A legal action was filed on behalf of Blackledge to void the election and to hold another vote. The judge hearing the arguments said, "I think both positions, Jackson's and Blackledge's, have merit, but I believe the proof offered to support a new election is too speculative to compel me to order one. The election results stand as reported." There was no appeal.

*****

Once the judge's decision was posted, a phone call was placed. "Thanks ol' buddy. There'll be a little extra in your pay envelope next month."

"I thank you. I enjoyed the limelight. Not often that I get any."

"If anything else comes along, I'll remember you."

"Thanks."

*****

On the evening after the decision was announced, Bishop and Kathy sat on the back porch of his cabin and talked about the election and the last minute devastating smear campaign against Blackledge.

"I guess you can see why I gave up caring about politics. It's dirty to the core. You don't know who to believe. You don't know how to vote. However, since I don't know anybody named Gilmore Jefferson and since I've never said anything about Blackledge, I have no doubt that the press release was a total lie. The judge should have voided the election and called for a new vote."

Kathy agreed. "I voted for Blackledge again because I'd heard his story one time already. If there had been any cloud over him, it would have come out the first time he ran."

Bishop repeated what he'd heard on the radio, the rebuttal by Blackledge. "Blackledge said the so called cloud was nothing. He wanted to be home to take care of his wife. I believed him."

She had heard that also. Unfortunately, by the time the truth was told, the people had voted. The ones asked said they weren't sure about him so they voted for Jackson.

"It's a shame," Kathy said. "Fine man like that losing the election because of a lie."

"Nobody named Gilmore Jefferson lives in Beat 2. There are half a dozen living in the state but none of 'em have ever been to Lawton county," Bishop repeated what Chief Jenkins told him. "The whole thing was a lie to get Jackson elected. I also heard that the Judge's wife bought a new washer and dryer from Jackson. I wonder what she looks like."

"I can tell you. She was a cheerleader at the school where Jackson played football. Not only that, she was a grade behind him. Close enough to know each other I'd imagine."

Bishop shook his head. "Makes me wonder about our culture. Have we lost all sense of morality? We do what it takes to get what we want when we want it. I wonder what happened to the Golden Rule?" He was talking about a verse from the book of Mathew in the Bible.

"Who knows," Kathy said. "Crazy world we live in."

Bishop agreed.

But wonder as they might, Hugh Jackson was the new supervisor for Beat 2.

*****

Hugh celebrated his victory by cutting 20% off the price of every appliance in his Lawton store and as a consequence sold more toasters, microwaves, refrigerators, freezers, known locally as "deep freezes", washers, dryers, dishwashers, garbage disposals and anything else in the store, in one month than he'd sold in the six prior months. And, the "installation" was free. He was well aware that men didn't like having to take out something and put in a heavy or messy replacement.

"Drinkin' a beer and watchin' somebody else do the work," was a lot more fun than putting alcohol and bandages on cut knuckles and cleaning black grease from under fingernails most men would have said if asked.

"I want to show my appreciation to the fine people of this county," Hugh had said when the price cut was announced.

*****

Kathy and Bishop joked about Hugh's sale on the back porch of Bishop's cabin.

"One of the library girls said people were lined up on the sidewalk to get in," Kathy said.

"I bet Hugh still made a profit. His background wouldn't let him loose money," Bishop said.

"That's what somebody said in the library; a man in there looking for a book. He was joking but sounded serious."

"I wonder how Hugh will do at the board meetings. He'll be like the bull in the china closet," Bishop said, "but, he'll be coming into a culture where the old guard rules and he'll have to sit there and take it. I doubt he'll like it much."

Kathy laughed. They'd talked about Hugh's personality during the election. "He acts like there's only one place for him."

"Yeah. At the top. The rest of them better get ready for him."

"Wouldn't you like to be at that first meeting?" Kathy asked.

He certainly would. "I imagine it'd be fun to watch. He'll probably play it cool until he can figure out a way to knock the guys at the top out of his way. I'd say he's as devious as they come."

He didn't know how right he was.

*****

The supervisors were seated to start the first board meeting of the new session. The existing chairman was re-elected to serve another 4 year term. He'd served two and a half terms. That was the case because a special election had been required to fill a seat after the death of the old chairman. The new chairman had more seniority than any of the other board members and was elected to finish out the deceased chairman's term. His name was Simon Oliver, a short man with one of those bottoms that somehow had greatly outgained the rest of his body.

Oliver had backed Blackledge in the election. In fact, he'd encouraged Blackledge to run, and had endorsed him. He was certain Hugh was behind the last minute smear announcement of Gilmore Jefferson but had no proof.

Hugh also put his name up for the position of chairman and got one vote besides his, the supervisor from the beat next to his. His name was Jerry Washburn. Jerry was also serving his first term and was a little overwhelmed by someone with power and panache, like Hugh seemed to have.

Hugh had convinced him that they should shake up the board by changing the chairman. Mostly though, he wanted the limelight and power that came with the position.

In addition to considering that Hugh was behind the smear of Blackledge, Oliver didn't take lightly the attempt by Hugh to unseat him. *The man lacks manners*, he thought when Washburn proposed Hugh's name.

He retaliated by assigning Hugh the task of re-negotiating Lawton county's agreement with Lawton to co-manage the maintenance of the city's streets. The old agreement would end in a month and needed to be renewed, if the city still needed it. It was a simple job he usually delegated to the administrator but wanted to make a point to Jackson. That point being that he was running the show.

"I understand you're a great debater so you shouldn't have any trouble dealing with the city," Oliver told him with a slight grin. "All that business experience you've had will come in handy. The Lawton street maintenance guy thinks anything we do for them should come out of our budget."

Hugh, realizing what was going on, thought, *more experience than you've had or ever will have. Dumb shit bastard. Sat on your fat ass all your life, telling other people what to do.* Oliver had managed the cafeteria of the Lawton county Hospital before he ran for the board.

"You'll work with the county administrator, Jeff Baxter," the chairman told him. With that order, he'd, in effect, knocked Hugh down a peg, making him work "for" somebody instead of the other way around.

That pissed Hugh off and he began thinking how he could unseat that "bastard," Oliver. Nevertheless, he didn't take issue with Oliver's simple-minded assignment. *I'll wait a bit.*

Hugh proposed paving Indian Creek Road, the road about ten miles long that cut through the middle of his beat. It was at the top of his list of things to get done. He'd campaigned on it. There were also a couple of other roads he'd promised the people living on them that he'd get paved.

"Takes money," the chairman told him, dismissively. "Tax money. You want to increase taxes. I could tell the voters you wanted to increase their taxes." He paused to take a hard look at Jackson who was staring back at him with obvious contempt for the put down.

Before Hugh could answer the man's attempt at intimidation, the chairman said, "Besides, people out there've been using that road the way it is since it was first cut. They wouldn't know how to handle a road without potholes. Let's move on. It'll get done as soon as to moves up the list."

In effect, he had cut off debate so Hugh's proposal never reached the motion stage and wouldn't be made public. That pissed Hugh off a second time. He had wanted to suggest borrowing money for the road, or adjusting the list the chairman had put together last term, so that he could move the road in his beat up the list by several positions.

Hugh cursed to himself and thought, *putting the new guy in his place. All dogs bite, asshole, and I've got some sharp teeth.*

The chairman moved the meeting along following the agenda he'd prepared. Mostly, he took care of mundane business, appointments, renewals of existing appointments and project approvals, mostly roads and bridges that had been pending since the last meeting.

Before he adjourned, he pointedly told Hugh, "Make sure you get on that job, Jackson, getting that city agreement negotiated and signed by the city before our next meeting."

Hugh nodded all the time thinking, *Power's gone to the shit's head* … He smiled to himself and continued his thought. *Gone to his head hell, it's gone to his butt. I figure I need to help old Oliver with that problem. He needs to get rid of some of that power. Maybe all of it.*

The board had long ago bought the old Post Office building to use for their headquarters. So, following the meeting, Hugh walked over to the office of the county administrator, Jeff Baxter, to ask about the city agreement. An idea about Oliver had begun to form in his head. He had to get rid of Oliver, and maybe Baxter.

He also made a note to make contact with the board secretary. The secretaries usually knew everything that went on in an organization. That kind of information was what he needed, or might need.

He already knew her name, Linda, and her birthday. The last name didn't matter. She'd get flowers. *Women love flowers. Makes 'em feel like somebody loves 'em,* he thought.

But first, he wanted to say hello with a smile and say something good to her. He'd learned at an early age that people liked it "a lot more" when somebody said something pleasing to them. So, especially when he was on the "hunt," he laid it on anybody he might need down the road. Most people stayed so tied up in their own problems, they didn't take the time to consider the impact their negative demeanors had on the people they had dealings with. That was something Hugh never did.

Also, since she was divorced, he figured she'd like a little male attention. He wasn't certain how far he was willing to go with that. She was a little old for him with gray in her hair and a bit much of a middle age spread but he could joke and hint, make her feel important.

Hugh laughed one time when a guest on a television talk show said he didn't know who he was anymore. He just went with the flow and ended wherever the flow took him. "Better than thinking," the guest had said.

"Hell," Hugh said to himself, "That's bullshit! I know who I am. I'm a man who wants to make it and make it big. I'm whoever I have to be to do that. Hell, I make the damn flow. I don't go with it. It goes with me. Nothing else is important."

Chapter 3

Hugh said his "smiling" hello to Linda, inquired about how she was and asked, with a sly grin, where "the administrator's office" was even though he could see the man through a windowed office.

She smiled and pointed toward Baxter's office. The door was open so Hugh walked in without knocking. The office was a "study" in simplicity, nothing ostentatious or expensive anywhere.

Anybody working for the government on the "people" level, that is, where people can see what their tax dollars are being spent on, was inclined to show modesty in all things.

On the wall hung his credentials. He'd graduated from "JC" and Southern, the third university in the state. It lacked the reputations of *Ole Miss* and *State* but graduates could still get jobs, just nothing anyone would call glamorous. A computer sat beside his desk. He was staring at it when Hugh walked in but turned to greet his visitor or at least to see if a greeting was required.

Hugh figured him for around fifty years old. Decent shape from what he could see. Wore glasses. Clean shaven. Hair cut relatively short. Face plain, ordinary, like he'd never had to sell anything and didn't have any interest in learning how.

Plain and ordinary, Hugh concluded. *And, no doubt taught by that well known and very reputable, Professor Blackledge who ran unsuccessfully for the open supervisorial seat. So, Baxter might not be all that friendly. We'll see.*

Baxter wore a white shirt and tie. The top button was open to show he didn't mind "casual." His coat hung on a rack near the door.

Hugh stuck out his hand. He'd already put on his big "let's have lunch" smile. "Hugh Jackson, " he said. "New kid on the block. Chairman Oliver gave me a job. Wants me to have a look at the agreement we have with the city to handle their overflow work. Their street maintenance they want to dump on us."

"Oh, yes," Baxter said, and reached into his out-basket for some papers he handed to Hugh. "He told me he was going to. I ran a copy of the old one for you to look at. The agreement runs out in a week or so, maybe a month. You may want to talk to the people in Lawton about it before you start re-writing it. They could very well have some new ideas about it. Getting their thoughts may save you some time re-writing it and … some money. Time is money, they say."

"I guess they do."

Hugh took the file and glanced at the front page. It had a simple title, *Lawton City/County Street Maintenance Agreement.*

"Good title, no doubt about what it is," Hugh said with a twist of his head. "But, you know, I would have thought the agreement would be the kind of thing you'd handle. I was surprised the chairman gave it to me. Not really anything… " He was going to say "challenging" but Baxter interrupted him.

"Yes. I did the last one," Baxter said, shrugging. "The city attorney drafted it. After I read it to make sure it didn't have us paying for their work out of the board's budget. I had our attorney look at it as well. The chairman told me to let you do it this time. Get you involved in what goes on in our neck of the woods."

No doubt. Mostly though, he wanted to let me know who's running this show, Hugh thought, then said, "Just for background, as I get involved and to help me get involved, I may want to take a look at the contractors we use, us and the city, on roads and bridges, building and maintenance. In fact, I'm sure I will. Do you have a list?"

Baxter's face took on a slight frown. It started out as a big one but he caught it before it got that far.

"Why do you think you need that?" he asked. "Nothing in the agreement about the contractors. No names at all. Seems like a waste of time."

"Could be, but if Oliver wants me to do the job, I want to get my hands into everything related to it. And, if it turns out to be a waste of time, it's my time to waste, right? But, it'll sure get me involved." He said that with a shake of his head.

Baxter frowned and said, "I can tell you, the contractors have all been approved by me and the board. Checked out, bonded, none have criminal records, no legal problems. Nothing really for you to look at."

"Still, I want to. I think it's within the scope of my authority anyway, don't you?" Hugh knew it was but was curious about Baxter's reluctance.

"Of course, I just wanted to save you the extra work. But, it you don't mind ..." he shrugged. "You'll find all our contracts in the file cabinets on the wall."

"I'd like a list of the contractors we've used in the last, say eight years," Hugh said. *The son of a bitch works for me. He can dig 'em out for me.*

Baxter looked away, shook his head, glanced at his computer and said, "Okay, yeah, I'll run you a list."

"Good. I'll be back in the morning to get started. I guess the city has somebody in Public Works I can talk to about the scope of work."

Baxter again looked puzzled but nodded. "Going at it ... well, if you don't mind me saying, the hard way. We thought you just take the old one, read it over and put in a new date."

"I've learned to check everything I'm responsible for," Hugh said, increasing the size of his smile. "Never liked anything bitin' me in the butt." He chuckled.

When Baxter didn't respond, he added, "By the way, I've heard or read that the supervisors are supposed to get involved in developing business and things like that in the county. What have we been doing? I haven't read about anything we're developing."

Baxter smiled knowingly. "Well Mr. Oliver isn't one to rock any boats ... cause trouble if you know what I mean. I think his approach is to let things develop from within the county and react to them."

"Instead of looking for ways to make things happen? Since we know ... maybe we do ... what's going on, we'd be in a good position to maybe come out with recommendations for new businesses or activities."

Baxter shook his head, obviously wondering where Hugh was going with what he was saying. "Yeah. I suppose."

"There is an Indian casino in his beat. On the lake. I guess he ... reacted to that ... gave his approval anyway."

Baxter shook his head. "Yes. They brought it in and we ... well, the board approved it after we'd studied it some."

"Good," Hugh said. "I think it's doing well."

"As far as we know."

"And I see that there are wide, paved roads to the casino. I guess we did that to help them out," Hugh said.

Baxter nodded and said, "We agreed to build a road from the highway to the casino. We also widened the highway with turn lanes to make it safer for traffic coming and going."

"Good idea. Saved them some money too. Have we done anything else?"

"Uh, we … I think we built some asphalt roads to some of the bigger chicken houses. That made it easier for trucks to pick up the chickens ready for processing at the plant. Chickens are a big employer in the county."

"Be damned. I'd have thought the processor would have been responsible for that."

"You have to look at the big picture, Jackson." He said that with a tone of dismissal and waved his hands at Hugh to emphasize it. "I suppose, like you said, we … the board was making things happen."

Hugh gave that a headshake and said, "Be damned. I guess you were. I'd also say all that road building to help private businesses makes it look like the chairman doesn't mind rocking a boat now and then."

"He didn't initiate any of that. The poultry processor asked for the board's help. So did the casino. We gave it. I suppose that was the boards' response. You could call it a reaction, I suppose."

"I understand," Hugh said. *Probably got a little kick back in the process. Something I want to check out. Yep, something for me to check out. Might give me some leverage when me and old Oliver next communicate about who does what around here and when. My damn roads. But first I have to take care of this chicken shit job he dumped on me. He just didn't think it through. Stupid shit. He may wish he had before I'm done with it. Sure gave me food for thought.*

After Hugh left Baxter's office he walked toward Linda's desk to resume the "friendship campaign" he'd begun when he walked in.

Linda, he noted, looked to be in her early forties or late thirties and well groomed, with no extra weight sagging conspicuously in the wrong places. And he took note of the fact that she had the usual feminine assets filling the proper places in her blouse.

Not bad looking, Hugh thought as he approached. *I won't be embarrassed to take her to lunch. In fact, I expect I'll get some envious looks from the guys who wished they could be me.*

"Linda," he said, holding out his hand and smiling. "Sorry I couldn't stop when I came in but I needed to talk to Mr. Baxter. I've heard so many good things about you already. From what the other guys are saying, you're the energy that keeps the board moving smoothly."

"Why, I thank you for telling me … Hugh, right? Hugh Jackson?"

"That's right. The new supervisor for Beat 2."

She said, "I followed your campaign. You and Mr. Blackledge got into it."

"We did. Typical political mud slinging. I try to avoid it, but when somebody throws it at me, I figure I have to throw it back. If you don't put a bully in his place, he'll keep doing it."

She said she understood.

He said, "Since I'm new, I'd like to get to know you better, Linda. I bet you can get me familiar with what I should be doing. Do you go out for lunch, ever?"

Usually she didn't but she could be convinced, she told him with a smile.

He promised they'd do just that as soon as he got his feet under him.

"Can I have one of those old fashioned hugs?" he asked as he ended his visit.

She stood, only slightly embarrassed, and hugged him hard.

"I love those good old Mississippi hugs, don't you?" he said and gave her an extra squeeze before turning loose.

She agreed with a big smile.

*****

Since he had time the next morning, Hugh drove past Simon Oliver's home for a long look. It was damned impressive. A single story, ranch style that looked completely new from the foundation up through the roof. The grounds were also in immaculate condition. Sprinklers could be seen here and there in the yard areas and the yard and shrubbery showed the benefits of regular watering.

On one side of the house was the satellite dish. Not only that, the driveway was concrete and no cracks showed.

Must have a ten acre spread. Horse and a couple of cows in the pasture. Pecan trees here and there. Maybe a few pears as well. I'd say old Oliver's doing okay on his supervisor's salary ... and some perks, I'd guess. Of course, he might have inherited it.

He later checked that out as well. Linda told him that Oliver had bought the house and land a little less than eight years before. Also, he learned that Oliver was negotiating to buy some adjacent land that bordered on a small creek.

The two supervisors who'd sided with Oliver during the first meeting were also doing well, perhaps not as well as Oliver but well enough.

Baxter's home was in Oliver's beat, also ranch style and in pretty good shape. Hugh drove by it as well. He couldn't tell if it had been rehabbed recently or if Baxter had bought it relatively new and it hadn't had time to deteriorate. Based on what appeared to be fencing around the home, it didn't look like he had as much land as Oliver. He made a mental note to ask Linda later. She would tell him she didn't know.

Maybe he doesn't want much land. More land means more responsibilities and more work. Old Baxter may consider himself lucky with what he has, so why borrow trouble with more land that could mean extra work.

Hugh also drove past the city houses of the mayor and the councilmen. Like Baxter, they all lived in relatively modest homes. The mayor's driveway and the fence between his and the neighbor's home need work, but nothing unusual showed, unlike at Oliver's spread.

Driving out of Lawton, he made a decision to have another look at Indian Creek Road to see if anything new came into his mind for his next fight over getting it paved. To do that, he would take the road past his home, well, his wife's home.

As he drove past, he noticed a truck in his yard. He recognized it. It was Riley Watson's truck.

"Son of a bitch," he cursed. "Too damn late for milking." He knew Riley often drove down in the mornings to help Julia milk. Not so much that she needed it even though milking was a tedious job, but more so because he had very few friends and looked at Julia as one. He laughed.

"Probably wishes he could still get it up," he said to himself.

He saw them in the pasture looking at her milk cow and rubbing its sides while they talked.

He laughed again, concluding that the sight proved his point. Riley needed a friend and Julia was it. "The bastard."

*****

Driving along Indian Creek Road, he did see a few places where the road bed has washed away, making it possible for a car or truck to be pulled into the ditch if the driver weren't watching carefully. "Lots of old people take it for granted that the road is safe. I'll use that as an argument next time the board meets," he said.

When he was back in the office, he made a note of his inspection of Indian Creek Road and sent out emails to the other supervisors with a copy of his observations. "Has to make a dent in ol' Oliver's diminished capacity as well as the other shit heads," he mumbled to himself. He knew that alone wouldn't get him where he wanted to go, so he moved to the next thing he had on his list to build a case for paving the road as he'd promised during the election.

To that end, he pulled the building permits for all the roads built in the county over the past eight years to see which company got the business and who signed the permits. Once he had that, he pulled the contracts with the county to see who'd signed the contracts. He also checked the board minutes to see who proposed building the roads and to see if a contractor was recommended by a supervisor.

After that bit of research, he figured he had all he needed to get "his" road paved. He also knew there'd be some blood-letting and it wouldn't be his.

During the time he was doing that investigation, he was also taking care of his assignment from Oliver to read the joint agreement with the city wherein the county board "helped" maintain the city streets, That was Oliver's assignment. Basically, Hugh made no changes. He did talk with the supervisor of public works for the city but that was just to make contact. Then, for the same reason, he talked to the city attorney.

At that point, he decided he'd finished his work on the agreement and gave the document to the county attorney to finalize and submit to the board at its next meeting.

*****

The last thing he did was invite Henry Hankins to have dinner with him at the town Country Club. Henry's company had done most of the road work, certainly the major projects, for the county over the past eight years. He'd also done some of the city's street work under the joint City/County Agreement. Hugh had told him it was to repay him for his support. Henry grunted something Hugh couldn't understand, but said enough to let Hugh know he was coming.

His company, Hankins Road and Bridges, had grown into one of the biggest companies in southern Mississippi during that time.

Hugh had joined the Country Club several years earlier actually, after he had his chain of appliances going. The Club was somewhat prestigious and not open to the public unless a non-member was brought in as a guest of a member.

Hugh was waiting at the front when Henry came in. Hugh had no doubt who it was. They'd spoken a couple of times during the campaign but he wasn't sure Henry would remember him.

Probably does though. I promised him the Indian Creek Road job if I got elected. He seemed somewhat pleased to hear that although it didn't look like it bowled him over. Tough nut to crack.

Most of the guests in the dining room were professionals of one sort or the other and while Henry was suitably dressed in a sports coat and pants, his face gave him away. It had a sun-colored red look about it, was deeply lined and didn't look like it had experienced a smile in a long time. Not only that, it didn't look like it would know what to do with one if it had. He stood with a nervous stance, like he was ready to do battle with anybody who crossed him.

He'd had his graying hair cut at least and was wearing glasses, Hugh noticed. *Probably bought them at Wal-Mart. Likely had to wear them today to read the menu.*

Usually in the field, Henry went without glasses just in case anybody would think less of him. That worry didn't apply to sunglasses so he wore those when he was working.

Henry was about six feet tall and appeared to be in pretty good shape with shoulders that punched out his coat, the benefits of working outside practically every day.

Tough looking bastard. Probably can kick some butt if the need arises. Might give me some static. We'll see, Hugh thought.

He reminded himself to be on guard.

Looking at Henry reminded Hugh he needed to lose some weight. He decided to cut out the sweet rolls at breakfast to start. Maybe start having a morning jog.

See what that does for me. Overweight men look friendly but people don't vote for them.

It was common knowledge that Henry could, and often did, work every piece of equipment used by his company in laying down roads somebody, or some company or government, had contracted years before. Now and then, if somebody pissed him off, he'd fire them on the spot and finish what they had been doing. And, if they gave him any static, he didn't mind answering static with some of his, his fists.

Hugh stuck out his hand, and, as always, added his trademark smile. "Mr. Hankins. Good to see you again. Glad you could join me."

"Yeah," Henry replied with a grimace.

Henry grabbed Hugh's hand and gave it a squeeze. *Like shaking hands with a brick,* Hugh thought with a chuckle that he kept inside.

They were greeted and shown to a table. Almost immediately, a waiter in a white shirt and dark pants appeared to take their drink orders.

Henry ordered a beer, his usual. Hugh, not wishing to create a conflict over something that had no money in it, ordered the same.

"You're working on the Flowers road?" Hugh asked. That was the name of the road Hankins had gotten a contract to re-pave with a layer of asphalt. *Should'a been the road in my beat. Indian Creek Road's been gravel as long as I can remember.*

"Yeah. 'Bout to wrap it up," Henry told him.

"I notice that you're the county's main contractor."

"My bids come in low and I do a good job!" Henry looked like Hugh had challenged him.

"No doubt. No one has ever complained as far as I know. Well, maybe some of the contractors whose bids didn't get accepted," Hugh said, agreeing with a smile.

Their drinks arrived. Hugh clicked his glass against Henry's and turned it up for a long drink. Henry did the same, except his was a longer "turn up."

A waitress, also in a freshly starched outfit, came to take their food orders. She was smiling like she loved her job and loved serving the rich bastards who ate there. In fact, if she never had to face another complaining, bitchy customer, it'd be a relief, but she kept that to herself until she got home.

Henry ordered a steak sandwich; wanted the "meat" done rare. Hugh decided not to follow suit. Too damned much food. He took the Club's BLT and asked for coffee with it.

Henry said he'd stay with the beer. He said he always had two at lunch.

"I've been given the responsibility to look into the county and city road work. A broad look. I've been talking with Oliver and Baxter about our contracts for the road work."

"Yeah?" His eyes widened a bit. "What're they saying?"

"They told me how things work around there," Hugh said suggestively. "You know what I mean?" Hugh's eyebrows raised a bit as he said it.

"Yeah? Hell, my bids come in low and I get the jobs," Henry said. "That's how things work. If you know what I mean."

Hugh smiled a response. "I think I do. Oliver and Baxter filled me in. A little more to it than that to get a contract, they said. You do bid low but wouldn't you know it, you run into problems nobody could have foreseen. Damned overruns that have to be funded. Following a hunch, Hugh had checked the files to see what he could find.

Henry opened his mouth to say something but Hugh waved him off and continued to talk. "Oliver and Baxter told me about those as well. Almost every contract, the same damn thing. You'd think now and then you'd get a break." Hugh nodded sharply and added another knowing smile.

Hugh had noticed the pattern of overruns when he reviewed the jobs Henry had been awarded from the supervisors. He thought one overrun could be understood, but not on practically every contract.

Hugh knew he was guessing that some hanky-panky might be going on but it was a guess born of experience. But, that was why he was being somewhat cautious with his suggestions. He knew that now and then, somebody in the business world was actually honest and believed in "The Good Book."

Henry put down his beer glass and said, "Yeah, well shit does happen. You must know that. You're in business. Appliances, right? Things don't always go like we want, do they?" Henry's head bobbed toward Hugh. He twisted a bit in his chair and picked up his glass for a big swig of beer. One more drink and he'd wave the waitress for another.

Yeah, Hugh thought, *shit like somebody holding out their hands.*

Hugh nodded. "Yeah, it does. I'll tell you, jes between us," He said butchering the English a bit as he leaned forward. "I've have to kick a little back now and then, jes like you, to get some asshole to do what I need getting' done. Ain't that the shit we're talkin' 'bout?"

Henry's eyes widened. He swallowed hard. "I reckon I know what you're sayin'."

"I guess you do. Hell, as you say, we're both businessmen, Hankins. Oliver … Baxter too, let it slip that some back scratchin' goes on in some of the county's contracts. You know what I'm saying. My house needs a new roof or some yard work. Hell, it gets done. We all love them overruns, don't we?" Hugh added more folksiness to his responses. It didn't look like Henry was impressed.

He did shake his head though, as if to show that he agreed, and stared at Hugh uneasily. "You … you're sayin' … . Hell, I get you, Jackson. Didn't take you long to catch on, did it? But, what the hell, I guess we can do business. As you say, back scratchin'. "

"Jes add a little more to the overruns," Hugh said. "To cover mine. Right?"

Henry shook his head but he didn't look happy. He was thinking. *Another fuckin' hand wantin' something'. Shit fire and save fuckin' matches.*

They ate their lunches mostly in silence. Hugh didn't press any further. He had what he needed. Oliver and Baxter were getting kick-backs.

Henry didn't shake Hugh's hand when lunch was over. Nor did he say anything. He just got up and left. He still hadn't gotten to where he liked being told what to do or being forced to do anything, especially anything involving money, his money.

Hugh figured that was about what he was thinking and laughed.

I'm thinking I know enough to get the fucking road in my beat paved. Old Oliver's gonna have to play ball with me. Baxter too.

However, as Hugh watched Henry stalk off, he realized that he might have gone too far with him. *I think I pissed him off. Not smart Hugh. Not smart. Maybe I should have played old Henry in two steps, not one. Damnit! I'd better come up with something to get off his shit list. He might figure he's doing enough back scratching as it is.*

I'll be smarter with Linda. I won't panic her the first time we talk … business. Easy does it, Hugh.

*****

He dropped into the county attorney's office after lunch. Jim Spradley was his name. He was a couple of inches under six feet tall, thin with a slim face. His hair had long since given up all its color and was completely white. He was at his desk studying something when Hugh strolled in without his usual smile. He wanted the visit to be a serious one.

After exchanging introductions, Hugh said, "I'm the new kid on the block. You probably know that."

The attorney nodded and shoved the papers he'd been looking at to one side with a sigh and a frown and a look that said, *nobody makes appointments anymore.*

"I had a couple of questions I wanted to run past you. I think I know. Well, I'm pretty sure I do, but better safe than sorry."

Without changing the expression on his face, the attorney shoved out his hands to give Hugh the go ahead to ask.

Hugh told him how he was going to be dealing with contractors regarding work in his beat and wanted to be clear on certain issues. "I don't think I can accept anything from any of the contractors we deal with, money or anything else that has value."

"It'd be a criminal offense if anybody offered you anything," Jim said, "Is that what –"

Hugh interrupted and asked, "And I'm guessing that I can't offer anybody I deal with, anything … for any reason?" The question was a no-brainer, but Hugh wanted to appear somewhat dumb, or at least ignorant of what was what. And, it could be he'd tell Oliver that he'd been by asking questions. *Might make him wonder what I know. Hell, I do know something.*

"That's right. Have you run into either problem so far?" The attorney, suddenly interested, leaned forward, his frown still in place.

Hugh chuckled. "Not yet. I'm just getting started. The chairman gave me a job. I gave you a document I prepared to extend our agreement with the city. That kind of got me thinking. I thought I'd make sure."

The attorney assured him he was right. No one associated with the board could receive money or anything of value or give out anything of value if it had anything to do with any board business.

Hugh thanked him and said goodbye. He hoped he'd tell Oliver about his questions after he'd left. *I'd like to see the bastard squirming.*

The attorney had already resumed studying the papers he had in front of him.

Maybe I should have checked the attorney's home as well. If it's ever at issue, I will. Who knows? Arrogant ass. All these people with their little bits of public power think they have the right not to be disturbed.

Chapter 4

At three thirty, Hugh parked in front of the Henry Hankins' construction shack on the outskirts of Lawton and got out holding two plastic glasses and a bottle of bourbon, Hugh's "make amends" offering. One glass was half filled with an amber liquid. It was tea but intended to look like bourbon. The other one was empty.

Hugh saw Henry's old truck parked in front of the shack. He had called the day before and the lady who took the call said that Henry usually got back to the shack around three every day to catch up on paper work.

There were no other cars around. Hugh was happy about that.

Hugh pushed through the partially opened door and walked in. Henry sat bent over a desk along the wall. His computer was on as well. He looked up when he saw Hugh come through the door. At first he frowned but when he saw the bottle of bourbon in Hugh's hand, the frown faded away, replaced by a smile.

"Ah, Henry," Hugh said, smiling as always. He shoved the empty glass toward the man who took it. "I hate drinkin' alone. I wanted to talk about Indian Creek Road and figured you might want to join me for some good whiskey." Recalling Henry's use of colloquial English, he had told himself to follow suit. *Don't want ol' Henry to think I'm uppity.*

Henry took the glass. Hugh poured it half full of bourbon. "Want some ice?" Henry asked.

"Hell no," Hugh said. "I don't want my shit watered down none."

"Me neither." Henry took a swig and wiped his mouth. Another smile came to his face.

Slight, but slight was better than a frown, Hugh thought. *Good start.*

"Damn good," Henry said. "You want to talk about Indian Creek Road, do you?"

"I do. Hell, it's been needin' paving since it was first laid," Hugh said. "Ol' Oliver sits on his ass and paves roads in his beat and his buddies' beats."

Henry shook his head without replying.

"'Fore I get into that though, Henry, I figured I'd better clear up something. When we had lunch the other day, we talked about … well, back scratching."

Henry frowned and thought, *Here it comes. Bastard's gonna tell me how much he wants. Or, what he wants. Jes like the others.*

"I don't take issue with what some folks do. Like Oliver … Baxter … some of the others, I reckon, but I don't go in for that. I told my people we'd get that road paved. I don't want any back scratching. You bid, and as far as I'm concerned I don't need any overruns. You get me?"

Henry's eyes widened. He looked surprised. "Yeah. I get you. You ain't gonna hold out your hand like some."

"That's right. I didn't run for office expecting any more than what the county is paying me." He laughed to himself at the lies he was telling but had no guilty feelings whatever. He was playing politics where anything was okay in the pursuit of a goal.

Henry shook his head. "Damn. Never thought I'd see the day. Mus' be a cold day in hell." He reached out to shake Hugh's hand.

Hugh took it and said, "Ain't no need for it, Henry, but I'm always glad to shake your hand. Anybody drinks good whiskey is a good man in my book."

"I reckon I agree. So, what can we do to get Jordan approved? Ten miles of dirt road, lots of dust. Ol'

Simon's been putting it way down on the list. He didn't like the guy you replaced. Didn't approve paving anything big in your beat."

"I'm gonna have somebody from the newspaper call you for a story. Denise Allen. Good reporter. She'll meet you at the beginning of Indian Creek Road to talk about the need to get it paved. I'd like for you to put in your two cents worth. You willin' to do that?"

"Might piss ol' Simon off some, but when you git right down to it, I reckon he won't have much choice. Mos' like, he'll still come around with his damn hand out anyway,"

"I wouldn't be surprised," Hugh said. "He needs you more than you need him. You know what I mean?" Hugh rubbed his thumb and index finger together with a knowing smile. That wasn't exactly true, but with a bit of wiggling here and there, it was close enough.

Henry shook his head.

"She'll ask you some questions about the road. Jes you remember we want to put pressure on the other board members to approve it. Them people living on that road 're tired of eatin' dust every day."

"Ain't it so," Henry said with a sly grin. "I'll give it my best shot."

Hugh looked at Henry seriously and asked, "Just curious, you send contractors out to do work on their houses, Oliver's and Baxter's, but what if they want money, the contractors? I know Oliver and Baxter wouldn't want a check from you. That'd be evidence. But, do they, Oliver and Baxter, ever jes want money?"

"Yeah. Now and then. What I do is take a sack of money and leave it at their front doors. That way, they figure there ain't nothing pointing back to me anybody can use against 'em. No kickbacks."

Hugh refilled Henry's glass and added some to his. He'd sip it slowly though, unlike Henry who could pack it away.

"What's the most you ever gave 'em?" Hugh asked, turning his glass up. He held it long enough to make it look like he was taking a big drink.

Henry rubbed his hair. "Hell's bells, let me think. I reckon I gave Simon twenty five thousand one time. Did it in parts, a week apart. Most I ever gave Baxter was ten. He lets me see the other bids so I'll know how low I have to bid."

"Good thinking. If anybody pokes around, they won't see shit," Hugh said.

"Yep."

"What do you figure Simon's taken off you over the years?" Since Henry was calling him "Simon" he followed suit.

Henry took another swig before answering. "Shit fire and save matches! I reckon I've gived him, money and all, close to a couple of hundred K since he's been chairman."

"He's doing okay," Hugh said. "I don't think I could sleep if I had that on my conscience."

"Yeah, I reckon. I jes take it for granted. Ever'body wants a piece of the action, as they say."

Hugh shook his head and took another pretend drink from his glass.

"What about the city? Anybody got their hands out there?" Hugh asked.

"Some, but most of what we do there is small pickins upside of what we do for the county. We hand out a bottle of booze now and then to anybody who looks thirsty. Turkeys show up on councilmen's front doors on Thanksgiving. The mayor gets one. That's how it works in Lawton."

"You know," Hugh said. "I was up there the other day. The mayor's drive way sure looks like it needs work. Why don't you just send a crew up there for some good will? I'm working on that joint agreement between the county and the city. Just tell the wife or whoever comes to the door, you had a crew with some downtime. You figured fixing the mayor's driveway would keep them from getting lazy. You had to pay them anyway."

Henry rubbed his head again. "You think?"

Hugh shrugged. "What could it hurt? It's not a kickback 'cause ain't no city job on the table. Jes good will for your next job in Lawton."

Henry shook his head and said, "Yeah. I could send somebody up there to take a look. If it ain't too much of a job, I'll see to it. Gotta know what it is first." He emptied his glass and poured himself another drink.

*****

A few days later, he would call Hugh to let him know that he was going to do it. From the tone of his voice, Hugh figured Henry considered the job to be good advertisement.

And, Hugh would just happen to be parked across the street when one of Henry's men knocked on the mayor's door to tell the wife what they were doing.

The wife tried to call her husband, but the "mayor was tied up" so she let Henry's men go ahead with the job. When the mayor got home that evening, he was surprised even though he'd eventually talked to his wife and learned what had happened.

He called Hankins Road and Bridge Construction and talked to Henry about it.

"Mr. Mayor, I had them old boys standing around with nothing to do so I sent 'em out to fix your driveway. Consider it good will for the city hiring me to fix your streets. Kept my boys out of trouble."

The mayor thanked him but it was not an enthusiastic thanks. He was concerned how it would look if it got out that a contractor for the city gave him such a "favor," good will or not. But he dismissed his concerns with the thought, "Hell, who's going to find out?"

He was partially right, but Hugh already knew and had a video of the pour in case he needed it.

*****

Their "let's be friends" meeting over, Hugh left Henry the bottle of whiskey on his way out. At the door, he told Henry, "The Allen girl will call after three thirty. I told her you were usually back here by then. She'll meet you when it's convenient."

"Hell, if it's about money, any time's convenient," Henry said that time with more of a grin than a smile.

Hugh knew it was a bit of a push to get Denise to interview Henry about the road, but he had been laying favors on her. He'd given her checks to cover some gas and other expenses she'd run up during the campaign. He also added a little extra for her cameraman, Jason. He was with her for practically every interview.

Also, he made sure she got flowers at the office when she put on a particularly good story. And, he had her down for gifts every holiday, whether flowers or candy or something else appropriate. He also took her to dinner from time to time.

"She shouldn't mind interviewing Henry," he told himself when he was back on the road. He chuckled. "And, old Jason won't mind coming with her." He thought of an old high school expression some of the boys used when talking about a pretty girl they wanted to bed, hell any girl they wanted to bed. *He'd eat a half a mile of her shit if it'd get him close to her glory hole.*

He admitted to himself that the expression was so crude he was embarrassed that he'd even thought of it.

He was right, of course, Denise didn't object at all to the interview of Henry. She'd do it and video the interview in case the television station wanted to air clips of it.

So he invited her to dinner to brief her on the road project, and its importance to the people. He suggested that she ask leading questions so Henry's response would be supportive of getting the board to approve paving it. Her staff would cut the interview together so it'd look like Henry was pushing to build the road instead of answering her questions.

He'd spoken to a couple of the more sophisticated people about it as well. She would interview them too. And by the time the story was aired as a human interest feature, it'd look like unless that road was built immediately, the world might very well come to a dusty end, which would have it's beginning on Indian Creek Road.

*****

Denise interviewed the people Hugh had named, the ones he'd talked to first. Of course, they wanted the road paved. She'd brought Jason along to record what was said. She strongly believed that a "picture was worth a thousand words." And, Hugh never passed an opportunity to tell her what a great job she was doing.

"Hugh promised to get the road paved," the first person she interviewed said. "I understand that the chairman put Indian Creek Road way down on the list of roads to be paved. Hugh sent out a newsletter after their first meeting that said as much." *And he made damn sure Oliver got the blame.*

"Are you going to write a letter to the board, protesting?" Denise asked.

"We are. I've called everybody I know and asked that they protest the chairman's action. Tell him that we want this road paved, now!" Hugh's newsletter had asked them to do that.

Like the others she interviewed, they all complained about the potholes in the road and the dust that never seemed to end during dry seasons. They also complained about the mud that dirtied their cars and trucks when it rained, not to mention how it got on their shoes and boots to be tracked into their homes.

"People have been using the road for years just like it is," Denise said.

"Yeah, but we've been trying to get it paved for a long time. Our last supervisor, we've heard, got on the chairman's bad side and he put the road way down on the list."

"I've been told that it's a matter of money. The county doesn't have enough to pave all the roads without increasing taxes."

"That's a crock, Miss Allen," the man said. "Sure it costs money to pave a road, but other roads have been paved. Roads that aren't as old as Indian Creek Road. Some in the chairman's beat. A lot of 'em. They cost money to pave too, but somehow the money was found for those roads."

That's basically how all the interviews went. Hugh had briefed all the people she interviewed so all were prepped to say basically the same thing. The reason Indian Creek Road had not been paved and why it was being passed over this term was because of favoritism and retaliation, nothing more.

Next for Denise and her cameraman was her meeting with Hankins.

*****

"I'm standing here on Indian Creek Road with Henry Hankins, the largest road builder in South Mississippi. People have been complaining about the condition of this road for years and yet, the paving of it seems always to be way down on the list of projects the county board of supervisors approves. Mr. Hankins, you've seen many roads, I imagine. Have you seen any as bad as this road?"

Henry looked out at the road then at her and said, "I can't rightly say I have. This road is in worser shape than any of the country roads I've worked on." Then, repeating what Hugh had told him to say, Henry said, "And this road is used by over a thousand people, some in this beat, the people who live here, and some in other beats. That's as much traffic as any I know of."

"And, yet, the supervisors refuse to improve it," Denise said, adding a mild bit of pontification on Hugh's behalf. "I've been told that people have suffered injuries using the road. Have you heard that?"

Henry, still using the information Hugh gave him said, "I have. At least two senior citizens told me said they'd hit potholes so hard they'd cracked their teeth. Had to get them replaced."

"What about other injuries?" Denise asked. "Someone told me about back injuries."

Henry shook his head. "That's the Lord's truth. I know one lady who has to use a walker now. Potholes caused her a back injury."

"And those people all pay taxes."

"I reckon they do," Henry said. "People have gardens that get covered by the dust from the road. Some poor people have to wash ever thing they pick. Some of it's not fit to eat, they tell me."

Denise looked at the camera and said, summing up, "That's Indian Creet Road in a nut shell. It's hazardous to use. People have suffered injuries. Thousands of motorists use it, and still the supervisors refuse to pave it. People who depend on their gardens for food, have to wash off what they can harvest, before they try to eat it. They lose a lot. Some vegetables just wither away, covered by road dirt. It seems to me, something should be done about that. Do you agree, Mr. Hankins?"

He sure as hell did. Though he didn't say, he wanted the contract to do the paving as well.

He ended the interview by saying, "Some say if it ain't broke, don't fix it. Well, that road's been broke for over ten years and nobody wants to fix it. Well, except for Mr. Jackson, the supervisor who just got elected."

"Well, Mr. Hankins, at least some of the supervisors claim the road 'ain't broke,'" Denise said, repeating what Henry had just said.

"I jes drove it and I can tell you it's damn broke."

She ended the interview by giving a summary of what Hugh and the people she'd interviewed had said. Most of the people she'd interviewed had been briefed by Hugh, and prompted by his letter campaign about the condition of the road they had to drive on every day to work.

And those people, she closed by saying, were letting the supervisors know how they felt.

To do that, she said, "The people of this county want this road paved and they're saying as much to the supervisors they elected to do just that."

In the background, Henry was heard to say, "About damn time something was done."

*****

Hugh took Denise to dinner at the Country Club that night and congratulated her for a great job. "If your story doesn't get that road paved, nothing will."

Even so, Hugh planned to make sure the story got it paved.

Her planned dinner with Jason had to be cancelled when Hugh asked her to go with him.

Jason had to fight off a disappointed depression for a couple of days afterward.

After dinner, Hugh asked if she'd share an after dinner drink with him. "Your place?"

She agreed.

When they got to the door of her modest home in Lawton, the first thing that greeted them was a huge vase of flowers. Hugh had sent them with a congratulatory note.

She hugged him.

He called Julia, his wife, and said he wouldn't be able to get home that night. She didn't seem to mind. She had been painting in her spare time and enjoyed it much more than she enjoyed having to stroke Hugh's ego. Julia didn't consider herself an artist actually. She just painted farm scenes, including the greenery she could see looking out her kitchen window. It was more a way for her to relax and not anything she intended to sell. She liked to say she wanted to capture the essence of farm life on canvas so "people wouldn't forget how it was."

Riley, when he was visiting, gave high praise to her works even though he was hardly anybody who knew much about paintings. However, he did know Julia painted them and wanted her to know that he cared.

*****

Denise's story about the condition of the road and Hugh's concern was aired by the local television station a couple of days later. From the calls the station received, the viewers appreciated the story and lauded her efforts to correct a bad road problem in the county. She laughed at that, since Hugh was the one pulling the strings on the story. Even so, she accepted the accolades and the pats on the back.

To make it up to Jason about cancelling her dinner with him, she asked him to come to dinner with her. His smile told the story. He was happy. During dinner he talked about relationships between people. She played ping pong with him about that but didn't encourage the implications he was making as he did. She wasn't interested in him as a man, just as a good cameraman.

Of course, to someone like Jason, the fact that she didn't disagree must mean that she was agreeing. It gave him hope that she liked him.

And she did like him, but only as a cameraman.

*****

A few days later, Hugh walked into the supervisor's offices to find stacks of mail on the conference room table. Linda showed it to him.

He wasn't surprised even though he acted like he was. The real story was all his. He'd hired a public relations outfit out of Mobile, Alabama, to write them, varying the content enough to avoid the obvious implication that it had been staged effort. Some of the letters were authentic but most were bought and paid for. Hugh didn't intend to let Oliver win the day against him.

If the bastard doesn't vote to approve the road at the next meeting I'll have go public. And enjoy the hell out of it, he thought.

Might anyway. Probably will have to sooner or later anyway if the dumb bastard causes me anymore trouble, he thought.

He hadn't decided what to do with the information he'd squeezed out of Hankins about the kickbacks to Oliver and Baxter the day "they drank" bourbon together, straight, or when to do it.

He told Linda to put the mail in canvas bags and leave them in the corner of the conference room for the next meeting.

The quantity of mail received in support of the road was reported by the newspaper and by the television station.

Linda said the chairman, Simon, hadn't seen it. Baxter had and seemed impressed and Hugh assumed Baxter would tell Simon.

Hugh laughed to himself. *Put some pressure on the bastard. Teach the son of a bitch to mess with me.*

*****

Kathy and Bone sat on his back porch and ruminated about the news Hugh had created. It was all over town, but Kathy had to tell Bone who didn't keep up with anything but his bank assignments and his little piece of ground along Indian Creek.

Kathy was saying, "A girl came into the library today. I heard her talking to a friend about it. Apparently that television story triggered a wave of mail to the supervisors. She said they had sacks of it."

Bishop laughed. "I wonder who Hugh got to write them?"

"One guy they interviewed for the television story asked people to write in. Maybe they did."

"Maybe. And, maybe hell just froze over. Knowing the kind of guy Hugh Jackson is, I don't think he'd leave anything to chance. Could be a few did write in but if they got sacks of mail, I'd bet Hugh was behind it. And most people around here just don't get involved with anything but their own problems."

"That road is a problem."

Bishop wagged his head. "I guess it is. When I drive it, I have to watch what I'm doing. But I'll still put my money on Hugh as the one pushing for it. Let's see if the board approves paving the road."

"The reporter said they had turned it down when Hugh proposed it at their first meeting. The chairman, Simon Oliver, used taxes as the excuse."

"He endorsed Blackledge when he ran against Jackson, as I recall. I expect Oliver has a political memory, as in long, and maybe turned Hugh down on paving the road out of spite," Bishop said as he sipped his beer and stared over the creek at the beaver pond where the furred creatures worked to keep their pond the way they needed it to be for their home.

"You think?" she asked.

"I'm guessing but I've been around people like Hugh Jackson and Simon Oliver long enough to know that it's very possible," Bishop answered. "I'll be interested in seeing what happens at the next board meeting. Hell, we haven't had this much excitement around here in years. Hugh is like that bull in a china shop, we talked about. He bumps into people, left and right, to get what he wants. Makes people mad."

"I can imagine."

They had BBQ chicken with salad that night. Beer washed it down.

*****

Oliver called the board meeting of the supervisors of Lawton County to order. His face was grim. He knew he was under attack by Hugh Jackson.

"I understand we have sacks of mail," he said with a disapproving frown and a gesture at the bags on the floor.

"Your doings, I assume," he added looking at Hugh. "I saw the television story. All those interviews and old Henry Hankins spilling his guts out about that fucking road. Had your fingerprints all over it."

"Indian Creek Road," Hugh interjected. "You won't find my fingerprints on any of it. What you're looking at is the people talking. They're telling us they want us to do what we were elected to do."

"Yeah, I bet. The road is in your beat, Jackson. That's the road you promised to get paved during the election. I see your work behind those interviews and these letters."

"I promised to get that road paved. I don't deny that. And, the people want it paved!"

"I wish money grew on trees so we could," Oliver said with a scoff. "The road is on the list to be paved."

"And has been forever. I'm making a motion that we give it priority, Mr. Chairman. Move it to the top of the list to answer the public's concern for the safety and wellbeing of the people who live along the road and for the poor people who have to avoid potholes to protect their cars and trucks. Not to mention their bodies. People have suffered severe injuries driving that road. It needs to be paved and I've so moved. Is there a second?"

His colleague from the adjacent beat, Jerry Washburn, seconded the motion. He'd supported Hugh's failed attempt to become the chairman of the board.

During the discussion that followed, Hugh continued to rehash everything Denise had reported in her television story.

Simon looked at Baxter and asked, "Do we have the taxes to pave the road in question just now?"

Baxter, who had already discussed the road with the chairman, gave the answer he knew Oliver wanted to hear. "No, sir. We'd have to raise taxes."

Oliver told him to go back to his office after the meeting and prepare a rough estimate of what it'd cost to pave the road and how much of an increase in taxes it'd take to do it.

"That's crap," Hugh said. "Total crap. Another one of your bullshit tricks to avoid doing anything. The paving of that road has been pushed back time and time again. It's time to pave it now. If that means postponing the work on other roads, so be it. I'm proposing that we put out a request for bids to pave it now. The people have spoken." He pointed to the sacks of mail on the floor. "We serve the people. Supposed to anyway." He pointed at Oliver and Baxter. "The people elected us to tend to their needs. Well, by God, they need Indian Creek Road paved and are telling us just that." He pointed at the sacks of mail again. "And I say we give paving that road a priority. I say that we pave it now!"

"Yeah, we got lots of mail. As I said, your doings, most like." He looked again at Baxter and said, "Get me an estimate of what it'll cost and how much we'll have to raise taxes to pave it. We'll let the people know who's behind the tax increase at the next meeting." He turned to stare at Hugh.

"Two can play the public game, Mr. Jackson," he told Hugh with a snap of his head.

"Be damned. I didn't know that doing what we were elected to do was a game to you, Oliver," Hugh said. "Maybe it's more than a game to you, when it comes right down to it. It sure as hell isn't a game to me or to the people who live out there. It's a serious problem that needs fixing. And, it's our job to fix it."

"We'll take it one step at a time, Mr. Jackson. I've asked Baxter for more information. I propose we postpone a vote on your motion until the next meeting. A second please."

One of his cronies seconded the motion. The vote to postpone was 3-2 in favor of Oliver's motion.

"You've just made a mistake," Hugh warned them. "We have all the information we need. And, we know what we need to do. We just need to do it."

"Moving on," the chairman said without responding the Hugh's last remark. "Next item on the agenda."

Hugh and the beat supervisor who supported him, voted no on all the items, noting that their votes were protests against the board's decision to put off doing their duty.

Denise had shown up with Jason to attend the meeting but Oliver ruled that the meeting be private because of the controversial matters on the agenda.

Afterwards, however, Hugh appeared on camera and told how the chairman had refused to do his duty to the people and how he wanted to increase taxes to pave Indian Creek Road. "That road is a disgrace to the county and is a hazard to all who use it. We were elected to solve problems like that. Our esteemed chairman, Simon Oliver, and some of the other supervisors are somehow afraid to take action to do that. Well, I tell the people of this county that I haven't given up. That road will be paved."

When they had finished and were driving away, Jason, feeling a bit jealous at the way Denise seemed to be following Hugh around, said, "I think the guy's a phony. As full of bullshit as a Christmas turkey."

"What?" she responded. "No way, Jose." She laughed. "You're just jealous you're not him."

He was, but he wasn't going to admit it.

"You've got to be kidding. I'm glad I'm not him. What I say, I mean."

She nodded her approval but was busy thinking about how to put the follow-up story of the unpaved road together including how the board had just turned down Hugh Jackson's motion to pave it.

*****

Later, Hugh walked into Oliver's office and sat down.

The Chairman looked up from his desk. When he saw it was Hugh, he said, "I'm busy now. Ask Linda to make an appointment for you." He resumed studying the papers on his desk.

"I think not, Mr. Chairman. I think I'll tell you what's on my mind right now."

Olive looked up. A frown came on his face as he evaluated what sounded like a threat from Hugh.

"What?" he asked. There was caution in his voice.

"Glad you asked, Mr. Chairman. So, I'll tell you. I drove by your ... shall I call it an estate. Lots of land, house in great shape, freshly painted, new roof, landscaping that could win prizes. You've done well."

Oliver slowly nodded his head to agree but the frown stayed on his face. A look of concern was added to it.

"My old house could use some paint, even a new roof, so I got to checking around and wouldn't you know, I found the outfit that painted your house and the bunch that put that new roof on."

"I was pleased with their work. I think you will be too," Oliver said and picked up some papers to signal that he was busy.

Hugh ignored Oliver's obvious effort to get rid of him. "I sure will be if I can get the same price you got," Hugh said, smiling. "You got yours for nothing as far as I can tell. The painter and roofer were playing it cool Simon, but I finally got it out of 'em. You didn't pay them a thing. How about that? How in the world did you manage that?"

"Yeah. They owed me for a job they never finished. I'd already paid them for it."

"No shit! The roofer and the painter? Hmm. That's not what they told me. You know what they told me?"

"No. Whatever it was, was likely a lie 'cause you were threatening 'em like you do, now that you have the power of a supervisor. What lie did they give you?"

"Be damned. I didn't have to threaten them much, Oliver. I just told them about the law. The one about bribing a county supervisor. I had to assume what they did was a bribe of some sort. I didn't know about that work they owed you for."

"Get on with it Jackson. They lied to you. I'm tired of listening to your horse manure. It smells." He reached for the papers he'd been reading.

"They lied huh? You know what they said, after I told them about the law for bribery and how many years they could get for it? They said Henry Hankins paid them. I kind of put two and two together and it came out this way. Ol' Henry's been getting most of the road contracts, the big ones for sure, in the county. Always bids low and get the contract and every damn time, he's had overruns. Ain't that a note to take to the baby Jesus?"

"What's this leading up to Jackson? Are you saying we give Hankins the contracts and then let him pad the contract with overruns?"

"I think that's exactly what I'm saying. But, I'm not surprised you could figure that out. I doubt you had to do much figuring. Not only that, I'm ready to go the DA with the story unless you approve paving my damned road without any increase in taxes. Get me?"

Oliver stared down at his desk. His face showed no emotion unless despair was an emotion.

"Hankins won't back your story," he said.

Hugh opened his mouth to say something but the chairman waved him off. "However, I've been some heavy thinking about all that mail and the things you've said and I think we've been wrong about that road. I'm going to recommend that it be put at the top of the roads we need to get done."

"And no new taxes?"

He shook his head. "No. We'll just have to wait on a couple of the other roads we had scheduled to do."

"Good. That's all I have for now," Hugh said. "However, I also drove by Baxter's house. Tell him to shut his mouth and do what I tell him. I know he's been getting kickbacks, just like you. And, I'll tell you something else. I can prove it." He waved a file folder at the chairman. The papers inside had no relevance to kickbacks but he knew Oliver didn't know that.

He stood and said, on his way out, "And, from now on, when I make a motion, I want you to support it. Understand?"

The chairman's face turned red. He knew Hugh had him by what some folks around the county called the short hairs.

Hugh hurried out the door. The smile he'd walked in with was still in place, only bigger.

Chairman Oliver announced the board's decision to put Indian Creek Road out for bid. He also added that it would be done without an increase in taxes. The announcement made it sound like it was his doing but everyone in the county knew it was Hugh Jackson's work.

When Oliver got home that evening, he poured himself a stiff toddy and sat cursing Hugh Jackson with such loud vehemence that his wife had to leave the room. She finally came back however to tell him to "get control of yourself, Simon. It's just a job."

He laughed at her naiveté. *Doesn't know shit about the real world. Still thinks the Bible controls all. Hell, its money that controls everything.*

Nevertheless, he calmed down enough to have dinner and a second toddy, something he rarely had. But the day was one he had rarely had either.

He told his wife the next morning that he'd dreamed about killing Jackson. She was aghast.

*****

After Oliver's public announcement, Hugh called Henry and thanked him for his help. He did the same for Denise Allen and sent her more flowers, which she loved.

Jason took note, shook his head and cursed but said nothing. He was beginning to realize that Denise had developed a major crush on the two-bit con artist. It made him mad. He made up his mind to continue to make Denise see him as a real person who truly loved her for herself not as somebody who could help him, like Hugh Jackson.

Damnit it hell, he thought as he watched her fawn over the flowers. He'd just have to continue trying to make her see what a fraud Hugh Jackson was. *I'm the only person who truly loves her for herself, not as somebody who can help him get something. Hugh Jackson, the bastard.*

He ended the thought with a silent curse.

Chapter 5

Bishop and Kathy hosted Chief Jenkins and his wife, June, at the creek house for a steak dinner. The chief's first name was Clyde but most people just called him "chief or Jenkins."

Bishop had been out of town for almost a week on bank business. Three banks had multi-million dollar loans in default and he had been asked to "work 'em out," meaning getting them back to some kind of "paying as agreed" status. He'd submitted proposals to the banks to do just that and was waiting for all of their responses.

The borrowers were all reputable but their businesses had not done as well as had been expected and they needed time to re-organize. Two of them had missed principal payments to reduce their loan balances but were making regular payments. Bishop negotiated with their attorneys to pledge more security in exchange for extensions of time to make the principal payment. The two banks involved in those two loans approved the "work outs" as presented without taking Bishop's recommended settlements to their loan committees.

The third borrower had paid his loan down considerably but his business income had dropped because of a competitor who'd opened his doors with lower prices. He needed to extend his maturity date and a reduction in his loan payments to reflect his reduced income. With no decent alternative, the bank would have to agree. But, the bank would take a second on his home and on a vacation home overlooking the Mississippi River as negotiated by Bishop. With that kind of leverage the bank felt secure and the borrow felt an intense pressure to make certain he never missed another payment. He'd already asked his father for help should it come to that. Fortunately, it never did.

When he got home, he and Kathy had felt like celebrating so they invited his old friend Chief Jenkins and his wife to the house for an always welcomed barbeque. Kathy had bought four steaks from "grass fed beef cows" for the occasion. They had that with salads and beer and talked about the news that was kicking around the county. Including the news about how Hugh Jackson had somehow managed to get the board of supervisors to approve the paving of Indian Creek Road without raising real estate taxes.

"I wonder who he had to threaten to get the board to go along," Jenkins said with a chuckle as he sliced into his streak. "I know ol' Simon had been stalling on that road for a long time. He and Jackson's predecessor didn't get along. That guy rubbed Simon the wrong way and Simon blocked every motion he made to improve that road. He and Jackson seem headed in the same direction."

Bishop agreed. "Sounds like it."

Kathy said, "I also heard that Hugh had tried to unseat him as chairman at the board's first meeting. That must have irritated Mr. Oliver. Also, Mr. Oliver was backing Blackledge who was running against Hugh."

Bishop nodded his head and looked up from his plate. "Sounds like politics as usual to me. Great steaks, Kathy."

She smiled. "Thank you, Bishop. I thought you all would like 'em. I think they taste great too. You and the chief did a super job barbequing 'em."

Bishop then looked at Chief Jenkins and said, "I figure Hugh for an operator, sly and slippery, more finesse than brute force, a natural born politician. As in anything that works, goes."

"No doubt, but I don't know about the finesse part, Bishop. Did you see his campaign ads. How he ran the ball at JC, tearing through the line, knocking the players left and right when they got between him and the goal line. He looked pretty brute force to me. Maybe if finesse doesn't work right away, maybe he pulls out his iron fist."

"Could be, Clyde. I didn't see the ads so maybe you're right. I was basing my opinion on my face-to-face meeting with Jackson. Of course, he might have shifted gears when he was talking to me. That's why I figure he somehow put, what I call, under the table pressure on Simon to 'change his mind' and vote to move the road to the top of the board's list."

"Yeah well, you're pretty good reading people, Bishop. Who knows? Hell, ol' Simon, as far as I know, is as pure as the driven snow," Jenkins said. "I don't see how Jackson would have anything on him to use as pressure."

"I don't know enough about any of them to make a guess. I've seen Hugh Jackson a few times on television, and the one time I mentioned when he came by here one day trying to bullshit me into voting for him. His efforts fell short," Bishop said.

Kathy pointed out that the letters people had sent to the board was perhaps the factor that moved the board to vote for the road. "I heard there were several bags of letters."

Bishop laughed. "In California, unscrupulous operators hire somebody to write the letters. Nobody ever checks to see if they're genuine. In fact, everybody assumes they're not and proceeds as if they weren't there unless they're getting something in return."

"You think Hugh did that!" June said. "I can't believe anybody around here would do such a thing. Do you?" She looked at her husband and asked.

"I've never heard it being done around here, but Bishop's talking about California. I don't doubt that they do it out there. In that neck of the woods, anything goes. Whatever gets them across the line first, they do."

Bishop nodded his head. "I can't say it's ever been proven, but lots of people say that's what goes on."

"If Hugh used that kind of pressure and it got out, he'd never get reelected to anything. We don't put up with phonies around here."

"No, we just shoot them when they're not looking. And, you get to chase the shooters down," Bishop said.

Jenkins laughed. "Yep. You got it in one, Bishop. And, right now, I'm betting Hugh might better be watching his back side. Pushing people around like he apparently does, maybe anyway, makes 'em mad."

"That was my thought too, Chief," Bishop said. "Folks I've run into around here are independent and from what little I know about Simon Oliver, he looks ineffectual, but I bet he has an ego. He's a politician and they all have one and when it get steps on, like Hugh must have done, probably put Hugh at the top of his sh–, uh, his 'to-do-bad-to' list."

"I doubt Simon's the first man Hugh has pushed into doing something he didn't want to do," Jenkins said. "He may have a lot of men out there just waiting for their chance to get even."

"And, if they can't do it above board, they might think about doing it below board," Bishop said. "I just got back from California and saw it first hand in a case I called *The Taco Wagons Murders*. One guy was shot because he screwed somebody and ended up dead because of it."

"Yeah, you told me," Jenkins said. "Damn near got yourself killed too in the process."

"That's right, but I was ready for them, even the one you saved me from at the Reservoir," Bishop said. He was referring to the run-in Bishop had with a Mississippi borrower nursing his big ego.

Jenkins grinned and said, "Could be, Bishop, you may be one of those people who push people aside if they get between you and where you need to go. Like ol' Hugh."

Bishop laughed. "Good one, Chief. Damned if I don't think you may have nailed me good, but at least I do it for a good cause."

"Yeah and that's a big difference. Keeps you in legal bounds. Anyway, I hope Hugh's not about to make more work for me, knocking people left and right to do what he wants to do. Having you stir the leaves like you do is as much enough extra work as I need."

"Right now, I'm not stirring much of anything. People are being reasonable."

"I'll Amen to what Clyde said," June added, nodding at her husband. "He says you make enough trouble to keep his whole force busy. Has to come out here now and again to get you calmed down."

"Now June'y, we don't tell our family secrets," Jenkins said with a laugh. "However, Bishop does keep us busy."

"Well, I think the chief likes to exaggerate, June," Bishop said with a grin. "He just looks for an excuse to come out here and take my best fish home."

"Don't forget the beer," Jenkins said with a smile. "I take some of that home too."

"Yeah. We do finish off some of that while you're catching my fish," Bishop said with a smile.

Kathy and June laughed in agreement.

"I'll put my second Amen to that too," June said. "Heads for the bathroom as soon as he comes in the house."

They kibitzed about Hugh most of the rest of the evening and watched the fish jumping out of the creek catching bugs.

"It was great," the chief and June said as they were leaving. "Food and company."

*****

Henry burst into Baxter Davis's office, mad as hell and waving a document. It was the board's request to bid on the Indian Creek Road project. "What's this shit? You haven't called me."

In the past after a request for bids went out, he was called to have a look at the other bids before a final selection was made. This time, he wasn't called and it was almost time for him to put in his bid.

"Ah, Mr. Hankins," Baxter said, "We've had to change our way of doing things after the campaign you and Mr. Jackson put on to force the board to pave Indian Creek Road. Mr. Oliver told me that we could no longer let you look at the other bids. Against the law, he told me."

"By God it's always been against the law! And, shit, I've always paid you guys for it! Ain't I?"

"Well, I can't get into that," Baxter said. He glanced through the windows of his office and saw Linda at her desk, clearly within ear shot of their conversation, especially since Henry was practically shouting. "You'll have to take that up with Chairman Oliver. I just work here. I don't make the decisions."

"The fuck you don't. You're the one I've been dealing with. You and Oliver but mostly you. 'Sides, I don't give a rat's ass 'bout fuckin' around with talkin' 'bout who you work for. Till now, you've been lettin' me see the other bids!"

Baxter shook his head and looked down at his desk. "Mr. Hankins, I can't help you. I don't have the authority to let you see the other bids. Chairman Oliver says it's against the law. I'm sorry but that's the way it is. I can't change the law or what the chairman tells me."

"I want to see them other bids, like I always do," Henry said, waving his hands at Baxter. "Keep on like you'a doin' now and I might jes have to kick yore ass six ways from Sunday. 'Sides, Jackson promised me the contract if I helped him, like I done."

Baxter frowned and said with anger in his voice, "Jackson's never told the truth in his life. He lied to you," he said, looking hard at Henry then, continued.

"Mr. Oliver said no! You don't get to see the other bids. Wait a second, I'll tell you exactly what he said since you're throwing your weight around. He said, 'we're not going to let crooked bastards like Henry Hankins or Hugh Jackson push us around and knife us in the backs. They're both as crooked as rattle snakes.' He also said … let me get this right … he said 'if somebody put you and Jackson in a bucket of' – excuse me, but this is what he said – 'a bucket of shit, and dipped a pitcher out, you wouldn't be able to tell one pitcher from the next.'"

"What? You shit face. You ain't seen the last of me. I ain't gonna take this shit laying down. They's prongs on both ends of that pitchfork you shovin' at me. And that bastart Jackson neither. Promising me the contract. By God, I mean to get it."

"You might want to re-think that Hankins. Giving kickbacks, even if nobody can prove anything – and, by the way, you can't, can you? – is against the law. Just the claim that you did it will automatically exclude you from bidding on all county contracts in the future. And hollering like you're doing won't help either."

"I reckon we gonna see 'bout that."

"Reckon all you want, Hankins, this meeting is over," Baxter said. He picked up a stack of papers and walked out of his office to give them to Linda.

Henry watched with a puzzled look on his face for a few seconds then stalked out.

As soon as he was outside, Henry called Hugh and told him what had happened, cursing him as he did. "I want to know what the hell is going on, Jackson! I ain't likin' being knifed in the back. You promised I'd get that contract! By God I'd better get it!"

"Quit your damn rantin' and ravin' Hankins. I didn't knife you in the back. I thought it'd be like always. You'd bid low and get the fuckin' contract. I'll call Oliver and see what the hell they're doing. He's a spiteful asshole! Paying me back, I'm guessing. Cutting off his nose to spite his face, if you ask me."

"By God, you let me know what he says. I want that contract and I mean to have it! Hell, I know a lot of shit 'bout what goes on and I reckon if I tell it, it won't do anybody any good, including me, but I'm pissed off enough to throw the baby out with the bath water."

Hugh laughed to himself at the quip and said, "No shit! Let me make a call."

Instead of a call, he drove to Oliver's house after he'd gone by the supervisors' offices and was told by Linda that the chairman was at home.

*****

Hugh rang the doorbell. Oliver's wife answered and after he'd greeted her, she let him in. "He's back in his study," she said and led him back.

When Hugh walked in the door, Oliver looked up, surprised. He hadn't expected to see Hugh even though Baxter had called to tell him that Henry was on the "war path."

"Let him rant and rave. In the end, he won't shoot himself in the foot," Simon had told Baxter. "He'll most likely drink a glass or two of whiskey and sleep it off."

He'd soon find out that he was wrong.

"Ah, Mr. Oliver, Chairman of the Board of Supervisors, taking the day off," Hugh said. "Good idea. Guess who called me, Of course, you already know. I'm sure Baxter has told you everything that's happening."

"You're talking about Henry Hankins," Oliver replied. "We're not going to deal with crooks. That's what Baxter told him. It's what I told him to say. No more under the table stuff."

"How about that. We're all turning honest in our old ages," Hugh said. "I guess we've skimmed enough for now."

"I'm not going to debate that with you. I know what you said. I've thought about it and frankly, you can't prove a damn thing. I've talked to the people involved and we're all clear. There were no kickbacks. So you can take your threats and shove 'em up your ... ass, Jackson. Sorry to be crude, but I expect you understand that better than most. You and Hankins, since he wants to play ball with you. He'll see how far that gets him."

"Right now, he's pretty mad," Hugh replied. "Mad enough to throw the baby out with the bath water. Says he'll call the DA and tell him what's been going on."

"It'll be a wild claim," Oliver replied confidently. "We've had 'em before ... from contractors who didn't get the bid. They run to the DA and claim fraud or something like that. They end up on the shit list and we're still here."

"Be damned. Sounds like you done got it all figured out," Hugh said. "Mind if I sit down. All this bullshit I'm hearing's making me tired."

"Sit if you want. As far as I'm concerned, this conversation is over. You can tell Hankins to go see the DA. I've already called him. Told him we got another nut case claiming he got screwed. The DA's heard it all before. All elected officials get falsely accused now and then. This won't be the first time for me. The DA's had a few himself."

"Be damned. You're covering your tracks pretty good. You know ol' Henry ain't got a college education like you. He don't talk good like you do either." Hugh deliberately switched into the local dialect as he began to tell Henry's story, well, the one he had made up on the way there.

"So, Henry'll sound pretty dumb when he walks into the DA's office. I imagine the DA will get a good laugh when Henry starts talking."

"I'd guess. So what? Are you finished?" Oliver waved his right hand at Hugh.

"Ah, the point of this story. You want me to get to the bottom line, is that it?"

"If you don't mind. I don't like my time wasted by a bullshit artist like you. You're getting your road. So if you'll excuse my crudity, go fuck yourself. I imagine you can understand that."

"Oh, goodness me. You're talking my language, I think. Yes I do get it. Well, let me get to the bottom line. As I said, ol' Henry ain't got book smarts, but he's got some street smarts. So, when he brought the brown bags to your front door, the ones with the money, guess what, he had one of his workers taking videos of him doing it."

Oliver's jaw dropped.

"And, guess what else. That worker hung around to take a video of you picking up that bag and looking inside. And, that was right after Henry took money out of his bank accounts. Oh, and I should say, he did the same thing when he left Baxter his brown bags. Almost every time he left one."

Oliver's face turned red. He looked down. His thoughts were in a jumble. *How in the hell can I get out of that?*

Hugh continued, "I'd say the DA will have a hard time laughing about that, won't he. He might not win the case against you 'cause it might look to a jury like something you'd see on television. Who knows what they'll think. But you know what, I bet he'd have to take it to trial. And, you know what else? Ol' Henry will testify against you and his bankers will testify and backup what Henry says. I'd put money on the table to back my bet that the DA will let Henry off if he testifies. Wouldn't you? And I'd bet the voters, regardless of how the case turned out, wouldn't elect you to be dog catcher after that."

"I'd ... like to see the, uh, ... video," Oliver said.

"I bet you would. Henry said the only person who'll see 'em is the DA if he doesn't get this road contract."

Oliver nodded and let out a noisy sigh.

"Oh, one more thing, Henry said you and Baxter insulted him. One or the both of you called him a crooked bastard. Henry says Baxter has to go right now. I told him I'd see if you'd give Baxter a few weeks to find a new job, in light of the business y'all have done in the past," Hugh said, smiling.

The look on Oliver's face was one of shock and dismay. His face had turned white. "He wants me to fire Baxter? How can …, who will … Damn."

He's buying the video story.Doesn't know what he's going to do. Hugh allowed himself to be pleased.

He had made all of it up after he'd talked to Henry. He'd also told Henry not to talk to a soul, especially Oliver or Baxter if either one called him.

"Or else, he gives the brown bag videos of his trips to Baxter's house to the DA. What he does with yours depends on the Indian Creek Road contract."

Hugh was thinking, *one step at a time. First get rid of one asshole, Baxter. Next I'll get rid of the asshole I'm looking at.*

Oliver mumbled something that sounded like he'd talk to Baxter and sort things out. Hugh left and called Henry and reiterated his order not to talk to anybody about anything. "If anybody calls, you tell them to call me. That'll shut 'em up. But, call me if and when Baxter calls you to drop by his office for a visit. That'll mean you'll get to look at the other bids."

That happened the next day.

Hugh was pleased with his victory.

*****

And, as usual, Hankins got the contract to do the work on Indian Creek Road. He sent Hugh a bottle of bourbon, which made Hugh laugh. He reported the "gift" to Linda for inclusion in the board minutes. No one objected so he kept it.

He also reported the gift to the county attorney, who sent an email to the board that it was okay, just the consequence of Jackson's public effort to get Indian Creek Road paved.

Hugh had dinner with Linda and got the story from her about Henry's shouting match with Baxter. Henry had said she must have heard everything. After dinner, Hugh made a written report for his file. After all, step two would soon be coming up.

Henry started on the road right away. He didn't want anything or anybody to come in at the last minute and say he couldn't.

He had one "overrun" on the contract about a third of the way through and the board didn't approve it. Hugh and his friend voted to approve it, but they were outvoted.

Henry had to eat a very small loss which he didn't mind. In fact, he laughed about it. He'd still made plenty on the contract since nobody got a kickback on it and his people had work.

*****

Baxter found a job with the Hinds county supervisors as an assistant administrator. He wasn't out of work more than a week. The existing administrator was expected to retire at the end of the current term and Baxter had enough experience to replace him.

Hugh had a chuckle when he heard, but didn't care. Baxter wasn't his problem anymore.

Baxter was gone by the end of the month. Hugh was surprised at his replacement. Oliver, wanting to have the last laugh, hired Blackledge to replace him.

Wants to show me he's still the boss, Hugh thought and cursed about it, but there was little else he could do but wait until it was time to take step two. Even then, he'd have to be careful. If he took Oliver's place as chairman of the board and immediately fired Blackledge, the voters would see it as an act of vengeance and might vote against him the next election.

Henry will be on his own after this though. He'll have to work his bids the old fashioned way, honestly.

He had called Henry to let him know. "Not a damn thing I can do about it, Henry," he said. "Ol' Oliver wants to have the last laugh." He told him the story about the videos he'd given Oliver to make him give in and let Henry have the Indian Creek Road contract.

Henry laughed. "Damned if you ain't a sneaky son of a bitch, Hugh Jackson. Hell, I may make enough off the Indian Creek Road contract to retire anyway."

He didn't, but the times he'd had the inside run at county contracts had ended. After that he had to bid like everybody else. But, hell, he knew how to do it. And, as he told Hugh, he was getting ready to retire anyway.

"I reckon I might jes sell this mother and retire," he told Hugh, referring to his company, the next time he and Hugh had a drinking get-together. "Me 'n my ol' lady'll git into our motor home and tour the country some."

*****

Remnants of the story about Henry Hanks and his conflict with the board as well as Hugh's involvement got around. About half of what was being said was true and half of it gossip but people looked at it like they do. "Where there's smoke there's fire."

Hugh heard the stories and laughed. "Getting close to Step two. I may let it slip to somebody that brown bags were left in front of Oliver's door. Who knows what that would sound like after it had been gossiped around the county."

*****

Bishop and Kathy also got a laugh out of it. "Hugh doesn't like to lose, does he?" Kathy asked next time she and Bishop had a happy hour on his back porch.

"I'd say not. He's like a bad snake. If you hit it, you'd better make damn sure you killed it."

She laughed.

Jenkins called Bishop later and said, "Damned if you aren't right. I've heard the gossip making the rounds. I'd say old Hugh is indeed a finesse man. He took Simon Oliver and the board to the cleaners. Got his road and wouldn't you know it, the contractor who went on television to help him get it, got the contract."

"As you say, people like Hugh make enemies. Most of the time, people just accept their 'whippin' and get on with life, but sooner or later, somebody will decide enough is enough."

"Yep. And I'll have a murder on my hands."

"And lots of suspects," Bishop said with a laugh.

"Maybe it won't happen anytime soon."

Yeah, Bishop thought, *and maybe it will. Hugh looks like he's a man with a mission. He wants to be king of something. A supervisor won't be enough.*

Chapter 6

Hugh got his way on other roads also during the next eighteen months. Oliver put up token resistance, but in the end let the board vote to improve the roads proposed by Hugh. The board had to borrow money to improve some, but they had plenty of tax money coming in to cover the loans. And, as the roads were improved, more people built houses and paid more taxes.

Hugh also added two more appliances stores in the state and even bought a fast food restaurant that was barely hanging on. He began advertising the sale of "healthy foods" like veggie burgers and anything that had been advertised in the media as being good for people.

He featured himself, name and face chowing down on what he called his "Hugh Burger" made from only healthy ingredients. "Eat one of my burgers and ..." he laughed on camera and added, "live forever."

He didn't mind a full body show in the commercials because he'd lost the flab that had hung around his waist by jogging every morning for thirty minutes. He also went on a diet at the same time.

Overnight the restaurant became successful. Some people wanted him to expand, but there were so many ravels he had to pull and watch over managing the restaurant – actually managing the man he hired to manage it - he decided one was enough. In fact, having to face the many details of running a restaurant, made him consider selling that one.

And, eventually, he did just that, sold it, at a good profit of course. It was summertime, the best time to sell a restaurant, when people wanted to get out of their homes and enjoy the outdoors.

But Hugh, as was his nature, stayed restless … bored was what he called it. He looked around for something else to do, another challenge, something else to buy. He saw that the state Senate seat partially in Lawton County was coming up for election in a few months. That got his attention. What's more, the seat was in his supervisorial beat. That meant he could start his run with a constituency that had already supported him in his election to the board of supervisors. Part of the district wasn't in his beat, or even the county, but that'd be his challenge.

"I did it before when I ran for the board seat. I can do again for the Senate seat," he told himself.

The state Senate seat looks good for me, he thought.

He had a good record as a supervisor and the sitting senator, Aaron Nelson, hadn't done much more than show up, draw his pay, and vote as he was told by his party's chairman. Since he hadn't done anything, he hadn't done anything bad so could claim a good record, which most voters accepted.

He was well liked, but with his do-nothing record he wouldn't stand a chance when pitted against a ruthless guy like Hugh who always ran on ten cylinders and who was more than willing to point out someone's failings. In fact, he enjoyed opening his campaign like that. Put the other side on the defensive right away.

Make 'em play to my rules.

And Nelson has more failings than winnings, Hugh thought. *And hell, it's my public duty to let the people know.*

He figured he needed backing and the extra money that would come with the backing so he began to think. *Where in the hell can I get it, without giving up anything?* That was a challenge in itself, a big one.

He had Denise interview him about running. He acted like he'd never considered it but responded like it was a good idea and one he'd be looking at. That was a start and a good one.

Simon Oliver got a kick out of the interview. He dearly hoped Hugh would run for something else and get the hell out of his little fiefdom.

"Hell, I'll even contribute some money to his campaign."

Oliver would soon find out more about Hugh's plan and discover that Hugh's senate race would cost him more than a contribution.

*****

Bishop saw the interview and commented on it to Kathy over dinner at their favorite Mexican restaurant. "Hugh Jackson is always in the news," he said. "He and Denise must have something going on. She seems like she's always there when he wants her to be."

"You think he already wanted to run for the state Senate?"

"Yes. I think he's always in the news, one way or another. He always seems to be interviewed by that reporter, Denise, about something. I doubt he leaves anything to chance. He's a shrewd politician. Always on the lookout for another place he can go."

"Now the state Senate?" Kathy asked.

"Yeah. Look for something else he'll be doing to get publicity," Bishop said. "The guy never seems to get tired and he's always thinking, apparently."

"Plotting you mean," Kathy said.

"Yes," Bishop laughed.

"Hard to believe anybody could be that conniving, but he does looks good. I mean physically. He had been a little overweight but he's lost that. That helps a politician, looking good ... at least with the ladies. They see him, Cary Grant handsome, bursting through the line, carrying that football for a touchdown or the equivalent in something public."

"You're right. And, I doubt he sees anything he does as conniving. Just an opportunity that has been waiting for him to grab," Bishop suggested with a chuckle.

"I wish I were as suspicious as you, Bishop. Maybe I could see behind what people are doing... their real motives."

"I'm not always right. I just go with my experiences. From what I've seen, most people, at least a majority, live by that Golden Rule the Bible talks about, do unto others.... But not all of us have evolved to that point. We let our instincts tell us what to do. I think that's Hugh Jackson. If he wants something, he goes after it. Like the cavemen did, before the Golden Rule."

"Well, good thinking, Bishop. I hadn't thought of it like that, the Golden Rule, but it sounds right. You talked about it once before ... when we were talking about Hugh. And, regarding your gut feelings. Like the chief says, you're right more often than you're wrong. So I wouldn't bet against you this time."

Bishop laughed. "We wait until the next episode with Jackson. He'll do something. Who knows what it'll be?"

They didn't have long to wait.

*****

Joe Martin, who in social circles called himself by a Choctaw name, Talako which meant eagle, announced that he was forming a new Indian tribe. He said in his announcement that he was not related to Phillip Martin, one of the original tribal leaders.

At Hugh's suggestion, Denise interviewed him for the story. Martin lived in Hugh's beat. The interview took place at the mobile home where he lived. Hugh had met with Martin and had encouraged him to form a new tribe of Indians. "It's time to do something about the discrimination Native Americans have been facing."

Martin agreed.

Martin was a few inches under six feet and in good physical shape. For the interview, he'd dressed in the worn clothes of a laborer. He had dark hair, sharp facial features, and a prominent nose.

He said they would call the new tribe the Freedom Tribe. That tribe would bring together all those Native Americans who were living off reservations in Mississippi and trying to compete for jobs in "the white man's world."

Denise said something encouraging to him for his goal and determination to do something to correct the inequities Indians had been facing.

He thanked her and continued. "There's still lots of discrimination out there. That's one thing I want to eliminate. The Freedom Tribe will give us the clout to be on equal footing with everybody else."

That was how Martin described what he was doing with the new tribe, the Freedom Tribe. In his announcement he said that was the name most people favored.

Hugh watched from the sidelines. However, he had thoroughly briefed Martin on what he should talk about during the interview. He'd also briefed Denise about the same thing. He wanted the interview to go smoothly without problems.

In his next public announcement, also carried by Denise, Martin said that over three thousand Native Americans had signed a petition to form the tribe with him as its first chief. He said they had acquired, or were in the process of acquiring, land fronting the Lawton River in Lawton County. The land was in Hugh Jackson's beat, Denise pointed out. That gave Hugh a reason to be involved in Martin's efforts to form the tribe that would create a business, a casino he figured, to help the tribe members. *Lots of money in a casino*, he thought.

Martin and his backers said they planned to develop the land into some kind of business that would benefit the Native Americans, and their newly formed tribe in particular, give them employment opportunities. They were studying various options, he had said. No specific mention was made about a casino at Hugh's suggestion.

"Wait until you're ready to move and have investors lined up before you release that information," Hugh advised him.

Martin did say that he wanted to give all Native Americans who were struggling to survive a new identity and an opportunity to acquire self-respect. He promised all those who joined the Freedom Tribe an equal opportunity to work decent jobs, so they wouldn't have to be relegated to what he called "grunt" labor.

The new Tribe had made an application to the Indian Association that more or less governed Indian activities in Mississippi, to be approved as a new tribe. The formation of a new tribe was relatively rare, but had been done although Hugh hadn't known that when he got the idea. All he knew was that no one had said it couldn't be done. That was enough for him.

A newly formed foundation called Justice for All, headquartered in Atlanta, Georgia, announced that it was fully supportive of the Freedom Tribe and launched a state wide campaign in Mississippi to gain approval of the tribe's request to be recognized. A corporation came out of the woodwork and funded the Foundation's campaign to support the tribe.

Hugh publically supported Martin's plans to form a new tribe and to develop business opportunities for it. After all, the tribe had its offices in his beat and supporting an underdog, as the Native Americans were, wouldn't hurt him at all in the polls when he ran for office again. He had been encouraging Martin privately already, and was behind Martin's announcement to form the new tribe of Native Americans. He'd also privately contracted the Foundation to help Martin's efforts. The corporation he'd secretly formed provided the funds for that help.

In a televised announcement, Hugh claimed that his support of the Native Americans was within the legislative mandate of supervisors in all the counties of Mississippi.

"We are supposed to support all efforts to improve the life styles of the people in our beats," he said. "To that end, we are required to encourage economic development in our communities and I do. Besides, I want to help them help themselves. That's the American way.

"Someone said, give someone needing help, a hand up, not a hand out and you'll make 'em strong. I won't be part of anything that makes people weak," Hugh said in closing.

Hugh had brought in supporters to applaud his announcement. *Make the viewers I have the county behind the Tribe's efforts to do something for themselves,* he thought to himself.

*****

Simon Oliver didn't say anything publically, but he did express some reservations privately. At that time, the goals of the Native Americans hadn't been spelled out.

Hugh heard about Oliver's private concerns and began thinking that it may be time for him to initiate step two. Just then it didn't matter, but Hugh knew it might matter down the road when the new tribe's plans were revealed.

"Son of a bitch is probably worried he won't have any control over the new tribe, 'cause it's in my beat," Hugh said. "He doesn't know the half of it. Control isn't what he should be worried about."

*****

Before all the activity with the new tribe had begun, Hugh had set down to do some thinking about his career. He realized that without a source of money he couldn't do shit politically, except sell shares in himself. And *that* he didn't want to do. He'd lose control over what he could or couldn't do. "Politics is a money eating machine," he told himself. "So, how can I get some?"

He knew he could use the income from his stores in any run he undertook, and did use quite a bit, but was reluctant to think he had to put all of it on the table. That income, he knew, fluctuated with the economy also and was not, he figured, reliable.

He wanted income he could count on, somebody else's, and decided that gambling was always a good money source. People gambled no matter what. They all felt the next dollar they put down was the one that'd get 'em "out of the poor house." And, if that one didn't, as was usually the case, the one after that one would. Of course, it never did.

He started by setting aside money from his stores to support his "gambling" plan, quite a bit, but he felt it'd pay off with a good profit when the plan got underway.

Then he looked around at what he faced. He knew about the casino on a lake in the county that belonged to an Indian tribe. And it was doing well from what he'd heard. It was in Oliver's beat.

That's probably why the son of a bitch has been expressing reservations, Hugh thought. *He's worried the new tribe might be thinking about developing a competing casino.* He laughed. *And it will when I tell them to. Martin doesn't know he'll be coming up with that plan to help the members of his new tribe.*

However, Hugh figured the Lake Casino was not as close to the Interstate as it needed to be to attract a lot of interstate traffic and out-of-state money. That's when he started looking around and letting his mind explore the possibilities.

He'd read someplace that Native Americans had a kind of "in" with the Gaming Commission in the state – *probably guilt from the way our ancestors treated them when we were settling the country* - and he'd also read that applications for casinos located along water ways, especially navigable waterways, got favorable consideration.

He saw that the "lake" was fed by the Lawton River. It went in, kept the lake filled and drained out over a damn on the other side. The river wasn't exactly navigable as far as big boats were concerned, but "navigable" wasn't a word set in stone. A boat could navigate up the river and Hugh had the video to prove it. That video would go along with the new Tribe's application for a gaming license when they got that far with their plans.

After he had everything in place, Hugh asked all his managers if they knew anybody who had a connection with the Mississippi Gaming Commission. One of his managers had a brother-in-law whose son worked for the commission. Hugh arranged to meet with the brother-in-law and the son to talk about the merits of giving Native Americans a "hand up" by way of a gaming license, should a tribe in his beat be interested in a new casino.

"I've heard talk about some Native Americans who are interested in developing a new casino in our county. They want jobs for the Native Americans. I think that's a damn good idea," he said.

He embellished on it, talked about the rec areas for families, everything good. He even suggested a place where people could meditate, even pray. He liked that part.

Part of my job, he thought with a laugh. The brother-in-law and son agreed with him.

He didn't put any money on the table in support of the license, but let them know that the Native Americans were likely to be grateful if their application for a casino license were to be approved. If necessary, assuming the Native Americans got a license, he'd let them know about *quid pro quo.*

When he reached that point in his thinking, and had all his ducks in a row, he didn't know any Native Americans he could talk to about a casino so he figured he'd have to create some.

That was when he hired the public relations firm in Mobile to search out the names and addresses off all Native Americans living off reservations in Mississippi.

It took a bit of doing, but they located thousands of them including Joe Martin, or Talako as his mother called him.

Hugh interviewed him about forming a new tribe. Of course, Hugh would do all the work, behind the scenes. He already had an option on over five hundred acres along the Lawton River. It hadn't cost much since real estate wasn't in great demand in Lawton County.

Hugh figured if the casino plan worked out, with it so close to the Interstate, there'd be enough land for a shopping center and condos or apartments for the Native Americans who'd work for the casino. He even figured on some kind of recreational area for families along the river.

Even though Hugh had an option on the land, he'd done it in such a way that his name wasn't on anything. What he'd done was form an Alabama corporation with its shares held by another Alabama corporation with a Mobile bank account.

He retained an attorney to represent the first corporation and had likewise retained the senior partner of the Mobile public relations firm to be the front man for that corporation should one be needed. It was the same firm Hugh had used in connection with the letter writing campaign in connection with his efforts to get Indian Creek Road paved. That campaign had established their working relationship.

Hugh's name, as far as the corporations were concerned, was only known by the firm's senior partner. In that way, Hugh figured he could support the casino as a supervisor without being accused of having a vested interest in it.

"Family values," he said to himself about the recreational area for families, with a laugh. "Hell, they'll like that."

Martin liked the idea of a casino that would benefit the new tribe. Hugh briefed him before he was interviewed by Denise. It'd be his idea, Hugh told him. However, Denise knew Hugh was the moving force and as always was in his camp. She agreed to help Martin he when stumbled. A casino was one of those things not many people could argue with. It would not only help the Native Americans, it'd also benefit the county.

More voters for me, Hugh thought.

*****

When the time came, endorsed by Hugh, Martin announced, in an interview video-taped by Jason, that the tribe was planning to develop a casino along the river, was generally well received by the county people. It would be called the River Casino.

Those that didn't gamble worried about bringing in another "evil' into town but liked the idea that the Native Americans were doing something to help themselves. Some were secretly pleased. Another casino meant another opportunity to hit it big and see the old time "pop stars" come to town for a last hurrah. And, casinos always had great buffets.

*****

After Denise aired the Martin interview, she and Hugh went out for a celebration and continued it afterward at her home. They had long since abandoned the thought that they had an arms-length relationship, he being a news source and she being the news reporter. He frequently slept overnight at her home and they even, now and then, took weekend jaunts together.

He put some money into upgrading her home to make it more livable. She had just been using it as a stop-over between stories she was working on and hadn't been sharing it with anybody seriously until Hugh began sleeping over.

He used the "love" word with her frequently and she'd asked why he didn't divorce his wife and marry her. She had used the word more often than he had and thought about it more often than she used it.

Responding to her question, he'd said, "In politics, a divorced man has a black mark against him. When I get where I think I'll be for the rest of my life, I'll divorce Julia and marry you. For now, sweetheart, we'll have to be content with an affair. Lots of politicians do it and get away with it."

"For a while," she noted when he said that.

"We'll have to be smarter about it than the others," he told her.

Although she didn't like it, she did agree with his assessment about divorced politicians. And, as a news source which she always had the inside tract to cover, thanks to Hugh, she'd received many promotions … and more money. She'd become the anchor newscaster for the local television station and had brought Jason with her.

Jason hadn't given up his quest for Denise even though he could see that she was smitten over Jackson. He didn't know the half of it.

*****

At first, Julia spent the lonely nights Hugh was "away on business" eating a dinner in front of the television which she watched until it was time to go to bed. But one day she said something about Hugh's habits to Riley, who'd come down for a visit. After she'd complained about Hugh, he came down more often and watched television with her after having the dinner she prepared for them.

They'd often share a beer while they watched television. She didn't much like beer, but drank half a glass with him to be sociable.

He never spent the night and always left after the ten o'clock news.

Riley enabled her to survive the nights Hugh was with Denise. Julia had begun to suspect something like that was going on but had no choice but to live with it. The idea of having an affair with Riley, who was too old for her anyway, never entered her mind and he never suggested it.

*****

The Lake Casino people put pressure on Oliver to come out against the newly proposed River Casino, Native Americans or not. The people with money behind them didn't want anybody rocking their money boat. They also called Hugh for a meeting since the proposed casino was in his beat.

Hugh and the other supervisors met with them, informally, and listened to the proposal made by the spokesman, Stuart Flint, for the investors. It was clear in all he said that they didn't want the new casino to be built. Helping the Native Americans who had formed the Freedom Tribe was not their concern. In short, they didn't give a damn about the Native Americans, other than the ones they put up the money to help with the Lake Casino. And they really didn't give a damn about them either, but liked them publically to get the Lake

Casino approved and up and running. The people with the money actually ran the show behind the scenes, but Flint headed it for them publically.

Flint was a hard faced man, a little stout, but physically impressive in that he looked like he could, as the ones who knew him would say, "kick ass" if anybody got in his way. After their first meeting, Hugh agreed. When he introduced himself to Hugh and the other supervisors who attended the meeting, he shook their hands with a strong grip. But Hugh wasn't afraid of the man. He was used to dealing with "tough guys" in his world. One more wasn't going to worry him.

"We'd like the supervisors to publically oppose the new casino," Flint said. "It'd hurt our business and wouldn't help the community at all. People will be put out of work if our business gets cut back. And if the Gaming Commission turns 'em down because of your opposition, there might be a little bonus at the end of the line for ... the board ... or maybe we should say the board members. Do I make myself clear?"

Hugh said he understood and told him that he would consider what he had said very carefully. "Your proposal has merit," Hugh said with his usual smile. Of course, he didn't mean a word of it. He wanted the new casino built on the river and wanted five percent of the gross income to support his political ambitions.

That would be his investment in the project, he told himself, when he considered the five percent he'd get without giving away any of his political freedom.

Martin hadn't been told what Hugh's corporation would want for the land, but would as soon as they came to the point of talking about it, when it came time to actually build the casino. Hugh hadn't told him or anybody he was in anyway connected with the corporation.

And down the road, if the proper amount of "tax free" money were to be put on the table, Hugh knew "his corporation" would be happy to take the money and walk away from the investment. But all those little details had yet to be worked out.

"All in good time," Hugh told himself.

Denise asked Hugh for an interview so he could express his opinion about the River Casino. Hugh told her he first had to meet with Simon Oliver and then he'd give her an interview.

Time for step two, he thought with some satisfaction. *Time to wake the sleeping dog. And this dog has teeth and is ready to bite. Oliver doesn't know it yet, but will very soon.*

Laughing as he did, he barked.

*****

So Hugh went to see Oliver and took a brown bag with him. It was a good day for a confrontation, or as he recalled a line from a movie or a book, "a good day for a hanging." The sky was overcast and drizzling rain off and on. Overall, a dreary day. *Perfect for a hanging. Oliver's.*

He knocked on the chairman's front door. His wife invited Hugh in and took him to Oliver's study where the chairman sat behind his desk staring at his computer scene.

Oliver looked around with a puzzled look when Hugh came through his office door, He asked Hugh why he'd come. A social call was not likely given their history. Hugh sighed loudly and plopped down in one of the soft chairs facing the man.

"I've come to discuss a serious situation with you." Hugh waved the brown bag in front of him so Oliver could see it. "Henry Hankins came by the house a few days ago. He told me he wanted the new casino built. He thinks he'll come out of retirement and bid on all the road work that's gonna be needed. Lots of it. New roads connecting to the Interstate. Lots of clearing's gonna be needed. It'll be a boom for the local economy. Just the sort of thing the board should get behind."

"Well, I'm gonna oppose it," Oliver said. "Stuart Flint came by to see me. He says it'd be in my best interest if I publically opposed it. We don't need it. One casino for the county is enough. That casino helps the Indians. Did you know that? You've been running around shooting off your mouth about helping Indians."

"The *best* casino for the county is the one we should back, and the River Casino will be the best. How can anybody be opposed to a business that helps more Native Americans? Lord knows, they can use a little help. The new casino will give it. Besides, I think it'd be in your best interest if you supported it."

He shook the brown bag in his hand at Oliver. "Henry gave me this. You know what it is?"

Oliver shook his head, but he had a pretty good idea what the bag was all about. His stomach began to feel a bit queasy.

"Henry told me about all the evidence he has 'bout you forcing him to give you kickbacks from the road contracts over the years. It's in this bag. He said I could give it to you when you resign and retire."

"What? Retire! What the hell are you talking about? I'm not ready to retire!"

"Yep. Retire. I think you are ready. You have to resign from the board, Henry says so, and I agree. I guess you could claim you couldn't support the new casino and instead of campaigning against it, you decided to resign and let the other board members decide what they wanted to do about supporting it. I think ol' Henry is giving you a deal. He could release the videos and the pictures and the bank statements he says he has, to the public and the DA."

Oliver opened his mouth to say something but Hugh waved him off and continued.

"Let me finish. I don't see how you could avoid being charged. Sure look bad for you. I imagine you'd spend time, probably in Parchman. Rough prison, I've heard. Probably the hardest place to do time in the country. A prisoner has to pay money to keep from being attacked by other prisoners. I suppose your wife could send you money each month." He rubbed his chin, smiling all the while.

Oliver's lips moved as he mumbled something. He was too stunned to speak clearly. "... wants me to resign, you say. I reckon you're behind it."

"I guess I didn't object when he told me what he wanted you to do. He said he'd given you plenty over the years. You'd get to keep all of that and you could burn what's in this bag. Live the rest of your days in peace," Hugh said.

Oliver looked down at the floor and began shaking his head. He half mumbled, "... been on my mind. Hanging over my head. Been wondering when it was gonna hit. Damn. Can't trust anybody these days."

Hugh stifled a laugh at Oliver's oxymoron and said, "Well, you don't have to worry about corruption anymore – yours, ours, or anybody else's. I guess the shit hit your fan the day Henry made a decision to put your history on the table. He says you can be a free man. Look at it like that."

"Hmm. Yeah. I ... I guess I'll have to talk it over with my wife. She's been after me to travel some. Take it easy, enjoy some life. I'll let you know tomorrow. When do I get the ... the bag."

"As soon as you hand in your resignation. Henry said I could give you the bag. He's a mean son of a bitch, if you ask me. I'm glad he doesn't have a hold on my balls like he does yours."

Oliver shook his head wearily. "I'll let you know tomorrow."

That ended their meeting, Hugh's second step. With Oliver gone, assuming he resigned, Hugh was certain he'd be elected chairman and the board would vote to support the new casino and their approval would influence the Gaming Commission, that and the fact that it would be an Indian casino.

The next day, instead of contacting Hugh, Oliver announced publically that he was retiring. He didn't feel he could support the new casino but had reservations about how he felt and felt the fair thing to do was retire and let the board decide and the people. The people could decide if they wanted a new casino.

As soon a Hugh heard the announcement, and the board got Oliver's letter of retirement, he took the bag by the ex-chairman's home and gave it to his wife.

*****

Oliver took the cd out of the bag and played it. When he did, he got the shock of his life. The scene was Henry Hankins staring at the camera. He said, "Hugh Jackson and Simon Oliver, I guess I done kicked both your asses. I got the Indian Creek Road contract and I reckon I'll get some more if I decide to un-retire. I ain't got no evidence that shows anything. Go get drunk and have a laugh. I did."

Of course, Hugh had done it all. He wrote Henry's statement and arranged to videotape it.

Oliver was upset, but he'd already resigned and had made the public announcement that he was resigning and why. And after he thought about it he wasn't too upset. Hell, he was up in years and his wife had been after him to retire and travel. He had enough to live well, thanks to the money Hankins and some of the others had "given" him. And, if nobody had any proof, he could use it without worry.

He took a beer and sat on his back patio and thought about it.

That son of a bitch Jackson did this. I don't give a shit what Hankins said on the video. Had to be all Jackson's doing. I hate that bastard. I wouldn't piss on him if he was on fire. And, I wish he was on fire. Hell was made for people like him.

Hugh also sat on his back porch, well his wife's, with a beer. He was smiling. Oliver was out of his hair for good. He'd be the new chairman and he'd publically announce the board's support of the new Freedom Tribe and their plan to develop the river property into a casino project that would benefit not only the county but the new tribe as well.

Stuart Flint called Hugh and offered him an option. "Take some money and shut the fuck up about the new casino or … I'd say you don't want to know the other side of that conjunction. We don't want you fuckin' with our money machine. Got it? Our red skins are doing okay," He said, deliberately slurring the Native Americans. "Even if the bastards do run around telling me what I should do with my casino."

I didn't know it was Flint's casino, Hugh thought. *I thought he was just the manager. Well, so be it.*

"They don't need the competition of a second casino. Understand? And, neither do it! Got it!" he shouted into the phone.

"Hell yes, I understand, Flint, but this is the real world. I'm surprised that you don't know that, being a man of the world, well, the underworld. So no, I'm not taking your fucking money. The Native Americans, not red skins, need help, and I want to make sure they get it. I'll make note of your threat though. If anything happens to me, I bet the DA will call you."

"Won't help you much though will it?"

Hugh figured Stuart was doing what he'd always done, threaten people to get his way. *My way is better. I get what I want with a smile and a lot of bullshit.* He laughed.

The state government, thanks to the pressure put on them by the Justice for All Foundation, gave tentative approval to the new Freedom Tribe. After that, all the tribe had to do was get the gaming commission to approve their request for a gaming license and a casino and that came after the Lawton County Board of Supervisors publically announced its support of the casino.

The mayor of Lawton was scheduled to be interviewed by the media about his position on the tribe and their plans for another casino. He had been saying around town that he didn't support it. His campaign for mayor had been supported by the Lake Casino. But before he could hold a public news conference to say no to the new casino he received a mail packet with an envelope of pictures. The pictures showed Hankins road crew installing the mayor's new driveway. A note said,

"If you don't say anything about your free driveway, we won't."

So he didn't oppose the new casino, saying instead, "The existing casino and the proposed casino are in the county. I think it would be inappropriate for me to take a position on a business venture under the control of another governmental agency."

The people at the Lake Casino didn't like it, but he stood by his position. He had no choice. He wanted to be re-elected. If the pictures he'd received were made public, he might not be.

The Gaming Commission approved the Freedom Tribe's application for a new casino. And investors lined up to put money into it.

Henry got a contract from the board and the tribe for all the road and surface work as soon as everything was in place. The tribe had only received a general promise about the land – it was available according to the attorney representing the corporation holding the options. But when they sat down at the table to discuss it with the attorney they were shocked.

The attorney demanded five percent of gross income for ten years to turn over the options on the land to the new Freedom Tribe. They had been led to believe that the land had little value. They felt five percent of the gross was gouging and much more that the land was worth.

But Hugh wasn't backing the casino for his health. It had always been about money for his next political venture. Down the road, Hugh expected to be offered several million to release the corporate right to the income, the five percent the corporation was going to demand for the land. *But that will come later,* he thought,

after the thing is up and running and raking in the
money.

The investors weren't pleased when they heard the demand of the corporation holding the options on the land. They objected. Loudly. And not only were the investors objecting, the landowners were also.

*****

The typical objection being made by the landowners was, "The holder of the options to buy our land wasn't dealing in good faith. They knew a casino was being planned."

They wanted more money for the options but Hugh's attorney's held firm and the landowners had no proof that the corporations had any knowledge about the proposed casino. In fact, the options were signed long before there was a new tribe and even longer before a casino had been mentioned. The attorney, acting with Hugh's instructions, contacted a broker to get the options and issued checks to pay for them. So, it was all legally done.

The corporation was out of state, as was the attorney representing it. Hugh's name was nowhere to be found. As he liked to say, "none of my fingerprints are on anything."

Even so, the landowners were unhappy to have been "screwed" like they were. Some began an investigation to find out who owned the corporation.

The investors who had lined up to develop the new casino were also protesting. "The bastards are trying to screw us," Barry Greenfield said of the holders of the options. Greenfield represented the casino investors.

During one negotiating session the investors decided to totally buy out the rights held by Hugh's corporation in the land. The demand for five percent of the gross was too much for them to accept.

"Get rid of the seller of the options once and for all," the investors had told Greenfield. So he made an offer to do just that. He said the investors would pay the holder of the options a million dollars with no "percent of the gross."

Hugh's corporation told Greenfield it wanted six million for all of its rights, including the percent of the gross income the corporation had been demanding. The offer from the investors had come sooner than Hugh had expected, but it wasn't a total surprise. If he had been in their shoes, he would not have wanted somebody taking five percent of the gross either. Not only that, his corporation was asking for audit rights as well in case the casino began to play games which, knowing human nature as he did, he figured it would.

Greenfield's comment was, "We're not going to pay it! That's final. And, for sure we're not going to allow an audit of our books and records."

Hugh's attorney told them, "If that's your answer, you'd better be looking for another piece of land along the river. I can tell you right now, you won't find it."

Greenfield asked Martin, aka, Talako, the eagle, what he thought about it.

He told Greenfield, "I didn't promise anybody anything," he said. "As far as I'm concerned, it's up to you how much you pay. I pretty much know this. If we back away from the offer to sell by the corporation, we aren't likely to have a casino."

Greenfield said, "The attorney we're dealing with is saying you have indirectly approved the obvious gouge he's proposing. Talk to Jackson. See what he says about it."

"I didn't know about it until now," Martin said.

Happy with the position with the casino that he'd been promised, Martin decided he no longer needed Hugh Jackson's help and didn't ask for Hugh's opinion. Not that it would have mattered. Martin made the decision himself. Pay the money. They'd make it up over time. The investors would accept the proposal after negotiations.

So in the end, Greenfield agreed to pay three and a half million over a three year period with five hundred thousand dollars at the close of escrow. They signed an agreement to that effect. But, Greenfield didn't do it gracefully. Before he agreed to pay anything, he had someone track down who was behind the corporation making the demand and found – by paying money – what he believed to be Hugh Jackson's name.

He called Hugh's attorney to let him know what he thought he'd found out and threatened to make a public disclosure if Hugh didn't get reasonable in his demand.

Hugh laughed at Greenfield's threat when the attorney told him. He didn't see how anybody could have found out his interest. He told the attorney, "I don't give a rat's ass what they disclose. Nothing illegal was done and my name isn't on any documents. I just want to help the Native Americans as the supervisor of the beat where they're planning to build the casino. All the corporation wants is money for its interest. The investors are pissed because the corporation is asking what the land will be worth once that casino and everything around it is built. They know that, and I don't think they'll be able to back out now. They're up shit creek without a paddle, or should I say, without land for a casino." He laughed. "But, they do have some money and I want my share."

The attorney agreed. Hell, he was getting a good fee for fronting Hugh's corporation.

Hugh had been bluffing to a certain extent. He didn't know how Greenfield found his name, and, notwithstanding what he'd said, he did care if the public found out. With his "greed" disclosed, the voters sure as hell wouldn't vote for him to be a senator or anything else.

"But hell, the investors 'have the bit in their teeth' and want the land more than they want the problems of a public disclosure without any real evidence," Hugh told himself. "They want that damned casino up and running and want the money they're going to make when it is."

To make the deal, Hugh had the attorney to drop the price and the land was transferred to the investors for a lump sum payment up front and the balance over time.

Even so, the investors wouldn't forget how they were scammed by the corporation Greenfield said Hugh controlled, anytime soon.

Flint's investigators also discovered that Hugh Jackson was the one most likely behind the corporation selling the land to the tribe. He cursed a blue streak and threatened to get even down the road. "That two bit, crooked son of a bitch," was how he described Hugh.

Hugh was satisfied with the resolution. All he'd done was put a few dollars behind his option to buy. He'd also contributed money to the Justice for All Foundation and had paid the public relations firm in Mobile some money for its help, specifically the senior partner, but he felt like he'd come out way ahead.

He knew he'd made some enemies – more than some – but didn't figure they'd do much about it. They'd be too busy, he figured, developing the casino to take revenge against him, even if they knew for sure he was behind it all.

Bottom line, the taking of revenge, he figured, would delay the opening of the casino and more importantly, delay the time they could start raking in the big bucks. *And nobody is going to delay putting money in their banks,* Hugh thought.

He knew though that his opponent in any future political race could count on a lot of support from all those he'd "pissed off." He also was wary that somebody would most likely leak information about his "alleged ownership" of the corporation. But he'd covered that pretty well he figured, and knew he could easily deny any involvement. It'd just look like his opponent was running a dirty campaign.

Chapter 7

Once formal approvals for the new casino were in and people were working to get it developed, Hugh announced his plans to run for the state Senate seat and, thanks to his work on the casino, had the money to fund the campaign without selling himself to money backers.

That could come later when he wanted big bucks for his next political move, but he'd wait until then to decide if he needed to sell anything. He was thinking that being governor would be a good thing for him as well as for the state. "Hell, I'm for the little people. The voters," he told himself.

And who could say where he could go from there.

Denise was the first to break the story of his decision to run for the state Senate with full television coverage.

Joe Martin accepted a paid position with the River Casino and hired as many of the tribe as possible to work for the casino. In reality, he was more of a figurehead than a manager of anything, but that was okay with him as long as he got paid. The investors ran the show and made the money. And the investors made sure the Native Americans with the tribe got enough to keep them quiet. So all were happy.

*****

Chief Jenkins drove out to see Bishop when the story about Hugh running for the state Senate seat aired. He was already laughing when he got out of his car. Bishop was waiting with the beer. Before they settled down at the creek to fish, they sat on the cabin's back porch drinking beer and laughing some more about Hugh Jackson.

Bishop told him, "I don't know if it was Kathy or me, but one of us said that Hugh was a natural born politician. I think I said it. I doubt he has a scrupulous bone in his crooked body."

"I think you're right on Bishop. I've heard it said that he was the one pushing to form that Freedom Tribe of Indians."

Bishop nodded. "Yeah, I'd guess he was behind the whole ball of wax from the git go, the Freedom Tribe *and* the casino."

"I wonder what he got, money wise, out of the deal?" Jenkins asked. "Knowing Jackson, I doubt he did it for his health. The word around town is that the people with money in the Lake Casino weren't happy about the new one coming in. Didn't want the competition."

"Yeah, I figure he got something for his support, dollars. He was ramrodding the project ... supporting it anyway. Guys like Jackson don't come cheap. Probably born wondering how to get his diapers paid for by somebody else."

"That's what I figure too. Don't you wonder how he got rid of Simon Oliver? Simon, as I understand it, hated Hugh's guts. They clashed from day one. I'd have thought he would rather die than let Hugh take over the board like he did. Let alone taking over as chairman of the board. Looks good when you're running for a higher office as in the state Senate seat."

"I'd say. Looks like he's a man of action. A man who gets things done. Voters like that. Most voters would like to be like that too but just weren't born for it like Hugh," Bishop said.

"Reminds me of another talk we had. Sooner or later, old Hugh's gonna run into somebody who's gonna get his shotgun out and even the odds some."

Bishop laughed. "You can't blame me for that, if it ever happens. I only met the man once. I thought he was about as crooked as a rattlesnake then, but now I think I misjudged him. He's a lot more crooked than a rattler. And, I think you could be right. Most people kill rattlesnakes to make sure they don't get bit."

Jenkins sighed and agreed. "Hell, let's catch some fish and let the good guys and bad guys work things out. Killing's not the only way to solve conflicts."

But, Bishop thought, *it sure is quicker and simpler. Especially if you don't get caught.*

After an hour of fishing and bitching some more about Hugh Jackson, Jenkins took what both had caught and went home to fry them. Kathy came out and had dinner with Bishop. They covered the same ground that Jenkins and Bishop had covered. But they didn't talk about killing rattlesnakes, just about politicians.

Kathy was pretty sure Hugh would be elected to the Senate. Most of the people who came into the library had high praise for him.

Aaron Nelson, the sitting senator, was meeting with his advisors and appointees at that moment to discuss the possibility that Jackson might win and how they could prevent it.

*****

"I guess you all know by now that some asshole wants my seat," Nelson said. "And I guess you all know what happens if he gets it. All of you will have to find other jobs. He'll have his own buddies to give your jobs to."

"You want us to dig up dirt on this guy?" one of his appointees asked.

"I do. Lots of it. Either that or we can all go home. I understand that the guy has lots of supporters ready to vote for him. Backing that casino for the Indians didn't hurt him a bit. Most people feel like they're underdogs to begin with so when somebody helps an underdog, like the Indians are, people feel like they're being helped too. We're going to need to hit him hard," the senator said.

"What if we can't find any?" another appointee asked.

"Hell, do what we always do, make something up. We'll let somebody else talk about it and I'll be aghast that anybody could run for office with dirty underwear like that," the senator said.

"Yeah," the appointee said.

"And we'll win," the senator said with a smile.

"You want to hit him with sex or money?" someone asked.

"Whatever your imagination can come up with. Winning is what we have to do. How isn't important," the senator said. "I like being a state senator."

"We like it too," someone said with a chuckle.

One of those in the meeting laughed and said, "I've heard that he likes little boys."

"Sounds good to me," the senator said. "Get somebody to say they heard that. Somebody write me an unbelievable reaction to anybody who could run for public office with a history like that."

One guy turned to the woman beside him and quipped. "The dude is hitting me where I live. I just bought a new car."

"Tell me about it," the woman whispered back, "We just closed on a new house."

"I'm not letting that Jackson bastard ruin me," Senator Nelson said.

She nodded her head. *Me too. Working for Nelson by just showing up every day beats the hell out of having to do real work.* Her face held a worried look.

Others in the room were mumbling similar concerns. The Senate seat looked safe and secure until Hugh Jackson reared his ugly head. All were anxious to find dirt on him or… as the senator had suggested, make something salacious up to confuse the voters.

With that, the meeting disbanded and all went their ways to see what they could find or create.

*****

Bishop and Kathy were having a relaxing dinner with music playing in the background but neither was listening. They were engrossed in talking about the upcoming fight between Hugh Jackson and Senator Aaron Nelson.

"I wonder what the incumbent thinks about Hugh eyeing his seat," Bishop said.

He couldn't know what the "incumbent" had already set in motion to fight Hugh's efforts to take it.

Kathy replied, "I've heard that he's not happy about Jackson's entry into the race but so far he hasn't done anything. He got the seat because his father had it and who, as a practical matter, willed it to his son when he died."

"He may wish he'd done more with it," Bishop said. But, he figured the state Senate was just another step for Hugh. "Who knows what he has his eyes on as his final goal?" *Governor,* he thought intuitively but let it drop. That would have to be the next logical move for a politician. And, for there who knows. It didn't much matter what he thought. What Hugh Jackson planned to do would be years away in any case. *He's going at it one step at a time. President Clinton's rise to power from a small state came into his thoughts.*

"He may not know his final goal yet," Kathy said, wisely. She also thought of Clinton. "Some people are just driven. They see something they like and go after it. They only know about obstacles and overcoming them. Usually they get rewarded if they have the skills and motivation. So far, it has worked for Hugh."

"You're probably right. He'll likely be the new senator for our county's district, and once he settles in, he'll look around to see where he wants to go next and what's keeping him from getting there. I pity anybody standing between him and what he wants. I wonder what'll happen when somebody says no and means it?"

"That'll be like that old saying, when an irresistible force meets an immovable object, what happens?" Kathy asked rhetorically.

"Have to study the Bible to get an answer to that," Bishop answered.

"Is that where that comes from?"

"I don't know. I think I've heard that, but I don't know for sure."

They enjoyed the rest of their dinner talking about pleasant things, like where they were going that weekend. Kathy favored a trip to New Orleans. They'd toured Landrum Country, a local favorite, the past weekend and thoroughly enjoyed it.

They decided to drive to New Orleans for dinner at Brennans after a stroll around the French Quarter. Bishop suggested that they stay the night at the Monteleon rather than drive back after dinner. That pleased Kathy. And whatever pleased Kathy, pleased Bishop.

*****

Senator Nelson was in his office when a couple of his appointees burst in, all smiles. "Senator," the lead man said. "You know how you told us to dig up something on the guy running against you, Hugh Jackson. If not, we were to use our imagination."

The second guy pulled at the first guy's coat and said, "Let me tell it. This is what just came in. An anonymous phone call. A man said Jackson scammed some people out of some big bucks for some land that the Freedom Tribe, wanted for their casino in Jackson's beat."

"Yeah," the senator said. "I've read about the casino. First time I've heard of it being done in Mississippi, the creation of a new tribe. I sent my congratulations. Hell, they vote."

"Yeah. Hell, I wrote it," he said with a smile. "Anyway, according to the caller, Jackson apparently got some options on the land the tribe wanted for its casino, the River Casino on the Lawton River. It's in your Senate District. Did it through a corporation, the caller said."

"I think I know that, about the River Casino. That's why I congratulated them. Pretty smart move by the Native Americans," the senator said.

"Yeah. I guess so. Anyway, when the tribe asked the corporation holding the options to hand 'em over, as apparently had been promised. You know, helping the Native Americans and all that shit."

"So, what happened?" Senator Nelson asked.

"The attorney for the corporation said the options were for sale for ... get this, worthless land in Lawton County, they wanted, in effect, six million for the land. Settled for three and a half, but that's still a hell of a lot for worthless land, like the tribe had been told before they made an application to the Gaming Commission for a casino."

"So, how does Hugh Jackson fit into that? You said a corporation had the options."

"The caller said that Jackson owned the corporation holding the options to buy the land, the caller said," the first guy coming into the Senator's office said and added. "In effect, he led the Native Americans he claimed to be helping into a financial trap."

"Wow," Senator Nelson said, "Doesn't sound at all like somebody dedicated to helping Native Americans as he claims to be doing."

"No!" Both men said. "He was just after the money."

"Proof?" Nelson asked. "What do we have that we can wave at the media?"

The men looked at each other. "Not much. Just that telephone call."

"Well, get your asses out of here and find some. I don't want to look like an idiot claiming something I can't prove. If all else fails, I'll have to let somebody else do it, but I'd like to have proof."

The two men rushed out as fast as they had rushed in. They pulled all the strings they had but couldn't nail down anything solid. So, in the end, the senator had to use a third party to claim how Hugh Jackson, contrary to his public statements, had gouged the Indian tribe out of three and a half million dollars – beginning with the five hundred thousand that was paid to him to close the deal.

All the newspapers and televisions stations carried the story, even without concrete proof to back it up. Like most folks, they believed that where there's smoke there must be fire. That was even more of a guiding force in their lives than the Golden Rule, which they often ignored when money was on the table or when it was somebody else's woman on it.

When Hugh heard the announcement he was dismayed. "Son of a bitch! Who in the hell came up with that? I didn't think they could possibly find my name. Shit."

But, of course he knew. Stuart Flint, or even some of the investors in the Lake Casino. Hell, Greenfield, he remembered, had accused him of as much – had spread money about and somehow found out that he controlled the corporation that had gouged the Freedom Tribe.

Hell, I had an attorney take the options from the people holding the land, he thought to himself. *They claimed fraud when they realized they'd optioned the land for what it was worth only to find out, somebody with more smarts than they had or ever would get, figured a way to make it worth more. The attorney wouldn't have told anybody. Hell, I could get him disbarred. Unless they paid him enough to retire. No, not likely.*

But, one man did know about his involvement with the corporation and what he was doing, the senior partner with the Mobile, Alabama, Public Relations firm, Frank Johnson.

He immediately picked up his phone, called the guy and began reaming him a new asshole threatening him with a lawsuit so big his firm would end up in bankruptcy after he got a judgment.

"What a minute Hugh. Hold on," the man interrupted to say. "I haven't told anybody anything, and I'm the only man in the firm that knew you were involved. I knew it was all an undercover situation. Hell, I don't mind telling you, as you probably know or you wouldn't

have let me handle it, I – ," he cut himself off for a
second. *Ah hell, the secretary.*

He resumed talking. "Maybelle, my secretary, she
quit this morning. Damn. When you called and told me
to wire transfer money, the five hundred thousand
dollars, to the bank in Mobile, I gave the note to
Maybelle to handle. It had the initials H. J. on it. She
must have put two and two together from the other work
we did for you and figured out what H.J. stood for. Hugh
Jackson. Son of a bitch. And she got a pay-off no doubt,
a big one. That's why she quit. I'm sorry Hugh. I haven't
told anybody anything and Maybelle was just guessing."

The man's explanation satisfied Hugh. It was just a
guess, and a guess wasn't reliable information. He could
deny it … and would. Maybelle didn't have any proof
about anything, just guesswork … and got a big fee for
sharing it.

Hugh'd had his Alabama lawyer established a bank
account for the money he would get for his options, well
the corporate options, on the land, for convenience and
also to put some additional isolation between him and
curious parties.

He'd added Frank Johnson on the account. For a fee,
he'd pull money out of that account and put it into
another corporate account. He was the only other signor
on the account.

He went to the cooler and got another beer to ponder
how he was going to respond to the accusation. When
that beer was finished, he was ready. He called Denise
back. She had called him when the story hit but he didn't
want to talk just then so he let her leave a message. He'd
told her was in the middle of writing a speech for the
campaign.

"Denise," he said. "Got your call. I think I know what it's about, someone claiming that I was behind the land deal the Native Americans had for their casino."

She had guessed that he did know but didn't say so. She knew what he had been doing from the beginning. The whole damn thing, the Freedom Tribe, the new casino, the works, had all been his doing. All behind the curtains of course so no one would know he was the one doing it. But she loved Hugh, and went along with him.

Besides, she didn't see anything illegal in any of it, just sharp business dealings she'd thought. It had been exciting to be a part of, even if just a bystander. Hugh made things happen.

"You need to make a response, a convincing response, Hugh. From what I've heard, the voters are already turning away from you."

"We'll fix that," he said.

He told her he'd be at the station the next morning prepared to give a statement. And, he was.

*****

He walked into the station holding a sheaf of papers in his hand, his face grim, a study in concentration and concern. He asked for Denise and was sent back to her office where he found her waiting for him.

"They're in the studio, ready to film your rebuttal. I assume you have one," she said with a question on her face.

He smiled. "Damn right. I plan to set the lying bastards straight." He waved the papers in front of him.

"Do you want to discuss it with me?" she asked, eyebrows raised.

He shook his head. "No. I'm ready."

He followed her into the studio and sat down at a desk in front of the camera as directed by Denise. His face was all business. His usual smile was gone. He was serious as he figured would be warranted by someone who'd been "falsely accused."

Jason was doing the filming. He was wondering if the *crooked bastard had finally been found out.* He was anxious to know. In that regard, he was like the people who would be seeing the rebuttal Jackson was about to make when it was released. And, he had a very personal reason for his interest. *If there was a public disclosure, maybe Denise would get wise and dump the bastard.*

Denise gave Jason the sign to begin taping before she walked into the frame and sat down.

She looked at Hugh and said, "Well, Mr. Jackson, I assume you've heard what somebody has reported about you. Your involvement in the River Casino."

She briefly summarized what Senator Nelson's people had been claiming to be a truthful report on Hugh's actions in connection with the Freedom Tribe's casino land.

"So you have a response, Mr. Jackson?"

"Yes, I do," Hugh said.

"I'm shocked that Nelson would make the claim he did … relying on a caller. You will note that he offered no evidence to back up the claim. Just said that a 'reliable source' had called the information in. That's low-down mudslinging and a complete lie. That's why I'm running for the office. I don't sling mud. I want to bring honesty back into politics. I don't make claims I can't back up."

At that point, he handed Denise the papers he'd brought with him. "These papers are copies of my bank account for the past month. As you can see, I have not received five hundred thousand from anybody, nothing even close. I'll authorize an audit of all my bank records. I have nothing to hide. I defy Nelson to put forth any evidence that links me, in a financial way, to the transaction involving the Freedom Tribe's purchase of land for their casino. I supported their plans and still do, but I have not benefited one dollar in the transaction."

He knew no one could ever find his Alabama bank account. He was dribbling money from that account, small amounts, nothing major, into his local account.

Denise ended the interview by asking questions which, in effect, enabled Hugh to offer more one sided rebuttals to the Nelson disclosure.

The filmed rebuttal made the evening news and from initial reports was generally effective in restoring Hugh's standing with the voters. Even so, he and Nelson, the incumbent, were about even in the polls. Incumbents always have an edge. People have already voted for them and don't like to change their minds.

Hugh knew that, and knew that he was going to have to campaign hard to win the election, but *Nelson hasn't seen campaigning like he's going to see before this race is over. The man hasn't done a thing since he took office. I've done things as a supervisor I can point to. And voters are going to know all of that before it's time to vote.*

The smile came back on his face.

I'm gonna whip his ass.

*****

Hugh drove home to relax and enjoy what he considered was a major victory thanks to Denise's support. She'd still been hinting about marriage and he'd continued to agree but for the fact that a divorced politician isn't nearly as electable as a married one.

"Maybe after this election, I'll think on it," he told her. "It should be okay then." *If hell freezes over,* he thought.

She wasn't totally happy with his answer, but there wasn't anything she could do. At least he had hinted that they could get married after the election. But, she was beginning to suspect he was just stringing her along.

I think he may be using me, she thought bitterly. *If he is ..., he'll be sorry. Damnit.*

That evening, she accepted Jason's offer of dinner. He couldn't stop smiling the whole time.

*****

The next day, even though it was early, Hugh grabbed a beer and went onto the porch to drink it and relax. He had a speech to make before an educational group that weekend. He'd written it but hadn't practiced a delivery.

Julia walked out and sat down beside him. She had a cup of coffee. He gave her a nod.

"I assume you ... lied your way out of what Senator Nelson's people claimed you did to those poor Indians you claimed to be helping. From what I've heard you saying on the phone, I know you're up to your crooked eyeballs in what they claimed. I don't know how you can stand yourself. Have you ever told the truth in your life?"

"What? You've been listening to my phone calls?"

"You bellow, Hugh. I can't help but hear. But, these days, I do move a little closer when you start talking. I enjoy listening to you lie. You can tell some big ones."

"Julia, you're a real bitch! Did you know that?"

"I think I'm a saint to put up with you, not a bitch. Just curious, why did you marry me in the first place?"

He stared at her for a moment as if trying to decide how to answer and finally said, "I'm gonna tell you, you snooping bitch. God. Your spaghetti and fried chicken. Bacon and eggs. I'm sick of that. You ever think about cooking anything else? There're cooking books you know."

She laughed and said, "Biscuits. Don't forget them."

"I hope I never have to eat another one," he said with disgust. "Like eating a lump of flour."

"So, why? Why did you marry me?" She asked again.

"I wanted this fucking land. That's the only reason. I wanted to use it. I didn't want to be poor all my life."

"My mother said as much. That's why I didn't put you on the deed. I didn't believe her at first, but when you tried to get me to deed you half, I figured she was right."

"Fuck you! I put it on my financial statement anyway."

"I know. I've seen your statement and a banker called me when you bought Riley Watson's business. I knew his family. Knew him. Still do. A good man. Comes down here and helps me when I need it. Milks the cow. He never talks about you. I don't know why not. His brother told me how you cheated him at the last minute. You lied to him. That's all you ever do.

"I didn't tell the banker anything, like a dutiful wife. I just let him run on about what a great businessman you were and let them believe you owned the farm. By the way, Riley hates your guts. I expect lots of people do."

That surprised Hugh a little but he didn't say anything. He knew people didn't like him but nobody had said anything about "hating." *Jealous,* he thought.

"Nosey. I should have whipped you. Some men would have," he told her.

She laughed. "Not in this day and time. They'd have put you in jail."

"Hell, if they knew you they'd have given me a medal. You've got about as much feeling in you as a sack of cement. Cold. Cold as hell. Worthless as a woman. I had to take pain pills to have sex with you."

She laughed again. "I've heard the way you talk to that television woman, Denise. I reckon you're sleeping with her. She probably thinks you're a stud. All the nights you claim you're out on business, I expect you're at her house. I know you are. I drove by there one night when you were supposed to be on the coast on business. Your car was out front. You lying, no good bastard. If you'll excuse my language."

"Sure as hell, I'm sleeping with her. I can barely stand being in the bed with you. Like sleeping next to a block of ice. Having sex with you almost makes me throw up."

"You haven't very often have you? By the way, you didn't do much for me either. I expect you'd stick your … dick in a tree hole if it had tits."

"Yeah, yeah. So, why did you marry me? You're not that plain. You could have married a good old country boy. Hell, they all love them biscuits and gravy."

"I thought you were better than you were. I knew you'd had a hard time when you were a kid but I thought you'd overcome that. Obviously you hadn't. Mother thought you were a con artist. I guess she was right. It took me some years before I was convinced, but I know now that she was right. I had wanted to make you happy. Make you overcome your childhood. I couldn't. You are hopeless."

"Yeah, yeah. Well, how'd you stand it? Cooking spaghetti and frying chicken couldn't have been that much fun. How'd you manage it? Living with somebody you call hopeless. I'm just curious how a snoopy bitch like you stood it," he said with disgust.

"I'll tell you Hugh. I love the earth. I love the dirt out there. It's beautiful and beautiful things grow out of it. Good things too. Things that people eat and live off of. Without that, I might have died having to live with you."

"The dirt. I guess that's why you paint those damn pictures you paint. Capturing the soul of life in the outside world! Isn't that what you say?" He said that with arrogance in every word. It was an expression he'd heard her use talking about her paintings over the phone.

Instead of replying, she said, "I'll give you a divorce, Hugh. I've decided. I won't even ask for alimony. My mother left me enough to live on. I'll take what I leant you to buy Riley's business and release my share of the business. You can even say you caught me fooling around. That'll keep your precious political career going."

I like living here in the old farm house in the country with a 'lovin' wife. Good politics. Has to mean I'm a good ol' boy and honest as the day is long. And, hell, with a wife, I have a shield from all the women I'm dickin' who want to get married. Wish I could, but I can't, would hurt my career, he thought with a laugh to himself, and said, "I reckon you're stuck with me till hell freezes over. And, if you file, I'll ask for money. You might have to sell this place to pay me off. So, you might as well forget divorce."

"Yes and I can ask for half of your appliance stores. You might have to sell them to pay me off. How about them apples? She asked with a smirk."

Damn, he thought. *She might be able to do that. I'd better talk to my lawyer to see what I can do.*

"I built the value of those stores. No court's gonna give you any part of 'em. Not even the one you made me put you on the title. My sweat and brains went into all of 'em. Anyway, what the hell would you do with a store if you had one. You don't know shit about appliances."

She didn't argue but asked, "Is that right? Well, my daddy and momma built this farm. You won't get one red cent from it."

Bitch isn't as dumb as I figured her for.

"Besides," he said, "as far as you filing for a divorce, nobody's gonna believe you were fooling around unless it was with a blind man. So forget divorce."

"You might be surprised," she said bitterly and walked away. She had thought he'd jump at the chance to leave her. She cursed to herself, something she rarely did and had never done before marrying Hugh.

Mother said he was worthless. I should have listened. Now, I'm stuck with a man I don't love, who doesn't love me and won't give me a divorce. And, if I file, the two-bit crook wants money.

Tears ran down her face just thinking about living with him the rest of her life. *I'd be better off dead.*

Hugh stared after her disappearing into the kitchen.

Has she been fooling around? Be damned. I wonder. Maybe she has one of them good ol' country boys wantin' to move in. Shit, maybe that bastard up the road, Riley Watson. Son of a bitch. Can't trust anybody these days. He laughed to himself at the thought that Julia might be getting it on with that old son of a bitch.

He called after her. "I'm going to the office to work on my speech in a few minutes. And, I doubt I'll be back tonight. Got business out of town."

"Business called Denise," Julia said over her shoulder. He heard the back door onto the back porch slam.

He grimaced. He hated to be called on his frolicking even though he knew that she knew.

Before he left for his office in town, he detoured past the living room and picked up the family album she kept on display there. If she's been fooling around, *it's likely be with somebody she knew before she met me,* he thought. *She keeps everything she's ever done, and everything her ma and pa ever did, in that damn thing.*

He glanced at a few pages but found nothing. He looked at his watch. He had to go. He left the album on the cadenza behind his desk to look at later.

Bitch, trying to manipulate me. Probably has somebody waiting in the wings. I'll find out.

He vowed that her last dig would the last time she'd call him down about anything.

He was right. He was going to town to be killed but he didn't know it.

Chapter 8

When Bishop heard the chief's car pull up outside, he shoved the small croissants into the oven to warm and turned on the coffee machine. By the time Jenkins was at the back door, they were warm and his mug was under the coffee spout being filled.

"Coming out," he shouted. "Grab a chair."

Jenkins did, and stared across the creek at Bishop's beaver pond where the furred creatures worked diligently, like robots that never tired.

Bishop slid the croissants onto a tray with butter and jam and took them to the porch table.

"I'll bring out the coffee."

"Yeah. Hell, I figured you'd have the mugs on the table by now," The chief said with a grin as he grabbed a roll and spread butter on it.

Seconds later, Bishop handed him a mug of steaming coffee and sat down with his. He also took a roll, buttered it, and added jam.

"Okay," Bishop said. "Who'd you arrest for the murder?"

"What? Oh, you're joking, right?"

"Yeah. Any suspects?" Bishop asked.

"Practically everybody he's ever dealt with over money or in politics is a suspect," the chief said between sips and bites. "Damn good," he added.

"My favorites," Bishop agreed. "Any clues?"

"Not a one," Jenkins answered. "I did bring pictures of the dead man for you to look at." He reached down and pulled out an envelope from the briefcase he'd brought.

The pictures showed the knife cut on Hugh's body. A two inch wound on the left side of his back.

"Looks like somebody knew a little about human anatomy," Jenkins said. "If he'd have been off an inch or two, he might not have hit the heart."

Bishop studied the pictures. "Interesting," he said. He frowned. "Kind of looks like the wound was made by a left-handed person."

"Is that right, Sherlock?" Jenkins said with a smile. "How do you figure?"

Bishop told him that the angle of the wound looked like somebody stuck the knife in Jackson from the left. That's why he suggested the killer was left-handed.

"Yeah," Jenkins said. "Also, it could mean the killer stepped to one side before stabbing the man. Right handed!"

"That's right. It could have happened that way, but when you're about to stab somebody, you don't do a lot of thinking. You just do. The left-handed thing just jumped out at me so I thought I'd mention it. Don't let it worry you."

"I won't and I appreciate you telling me. So all I have to do is look for a left handed person who hated Jackson enough to kill him."

Bishop twisted his head and nodded. *Yeah, I know you don't agree, Clyde, but the angle looks more like a lefty did the stabbing than a rightly.*

"So moving on, what's your plan?" Bishop knew Jenkins usually had a plan to start looking for the killer in a high profile murder case like Hugh Jackson's.

But rather than his usual automatic response, Jenkins shook his head. "Damned if I know just now, Bishop. I think I'll just have to start pulling ravels. Isn't that what you say when you're on the trail?"

Bishop agreed. "Yeah, I guess. I've done some thinking since I heard about it. You've got all those people he bought out, the appliance stores. I imagine Jackson drove a hard bargain each time he bought one. However, it's been so long, I doubt any of them suddenly got the urge to kill the man over it. Of course, murder isn't always logical, people doing the expected."

Jenkins nodded his head. "My thinking too, although I'll have to contact all of them anyway. You know how that goes. Sure as hell if I leave anybody out, that'll be the one, for some reason, who did it."

"I agree, but realistically, probably not. Anything from the scene?" Bishop was asking what the chief might have found where Hugh was killed.

"Nothing to write home about. No cigarette butts left by whoever was waiting for him to come out. Maybe the killer didn't smoke or just came on the scene when Hugh came out of the building. From his cell phone, we ascertained that he had just called, or was calling his friend, Denise Allen, the television woman. The call didn't go through. She was the one who called in the killing. She told us that her phone rang once at around nine but only once. She figured it was a butt call and ignored it. But when Hugh didn't show up at her house as promised, she drove down to see why. That's when she found his body."

A "butt call" was initiated when somebody with a cell phone "sat" on it and accidentally triggered a call. He'd made a few over the years. It was always embarrassing.

"They must have had a thing going," Bishop suggested, "if she drove down there."

"Yeah, they did. She more or less confirmed it. It had been talked about here and there but nobody knew for sure until last night. She was crying her eyes out when I got there," he said. "She didn't strike me as a killer, but I guess she has to go on the list. Maybe she found out Hugh was cheating on her like he was doing with his wife," Jenkins said. "Could be she didn't just come down there. Maybe she'd been waiting for him to come out. She would have been strong enough, from what I saw of her, to swing a sharp hunting knife. Then after killing him, she waited a bit and called it in."

"I kind of doubt it, but maybe you're right," Bishop said. "I'll be damned. I'm not surprised that Jackson might have been fooling around on the girl. Ol' Hugh had a reputation, as I recall, for putting it about."

The chief agreed.

Bishop added, "Of course, you've got the political thing. That may be the real motive for his murder. Blackledge, or somebody who had supported Blackledge's run with campaign money, most likely would be at the top of my list. No, hell, nobody would kill for that. But, maybe they would," Bishop said. "The guy he's running against for the Senate, Aaron Nelson, or some of his supporters, would be more likely suspects. They have something to lose. That power they have most likely translates into money. Nobody wants to give up the power or the money."

"Makes sense, Bishop, but probably not Blackledge. However, I'll check. I'll be dragging him in or I'll go out to his house and give him the third degree. Like, where was he last night when Jackson was killed. I don't know about the senator, Nelson, I think, Hugh was trying to unseat," the chief said.

"As you say, lots of rocks to turn over. Somebody most likely waiting for him. Had to be a long knife to hit his heart. As you said, a hunting knife could have done it. I don't suppose you found one at the scene?"

"No," Jenkins said. He was on his second croissant by that time. He got up and ran another cup of coffee into his mug.

"Glad I know how to work that machine," he said when he returned. "I've got to get my wife to buy us one of those things. She's set in her ways though and prefers to stay with our old machine."

"I can understand. It was hard for me to change. But when I got into having coffee at odd times, like now, I was glad I did," Bishop said.

"I may give her a birthday present of one," Jenkins said, smiling. "She'll have to like it and I know enough about them now to hook it up."

"Who else is on your list?" Bishop asked.

"I've been told he butted heads with Simon Oliver. The office administrator, Baxter also, but he's moved on. He was probably just doing whatever Oliver told him to do. I'll talk to Linda when I can. See what she knows. She's the board secretary. They usually keep up with the office gossip."

"I think I read that Oliver retired suddenly. Could be something there," Bishop said.

"He did. And the administrator, Baxter, quit suddenly too and went to Jackson to work. Had to move his family, uproot everything. I'll want to talk to him as well. Have to go to Jackson to do that. Oliver sure as hell, is on my list. Retiring like he did makes me very suspicious of him."

"What about the casino, the Indian casino that's going to be built on the river. The Lake Casino didn't want it but Jackson was all for it. You think murder might have gotten mixed up in that conflict? Big money in casinos. Could be enough money to motivate murder," Bishop said. "I'd look into that angle if I were you."

"Seems you've done some thinking about Jackson's murder yourself," Jenkins said.

Bishop nodded with a sip of his coffee. He was leaving the rest of the rolls to Jenkins. He'd had a good breakfast.

"Some," Bishop told him, "After you called, thoughts began popping into my head."

"They usually do. What else did you think about? What else popped into your head?" Jenkins asked. He was buttering his third roll. "Have to go for a long walk this afternoon to get rid of the calories. June's after me to go on a diet."

Bishop patted his stomach. "June's right. From the looks of your belt line, I'd say you don't get enough afternoon walks."

"Yeah, yeah. If you had my job, you'd have a stomach like mine. Somebody's always calling me. I'm always having to go to the office for one reason or another," Jenkins said as he tried to suck in the roll that poked out over his belt. "But, you're right. I need to do more. Have to make time, I guess."

"You asked if I had any other thoughts," Bishop said.

"I did. Who did it?"

"Like I'd know. I only met the man one time. I've seen his mug in the papers and on the television a few times. Somebody quoted me as saying something dirty about Blackledge in that television story the day before the election. That pissed me off. Hell, I didn't know enough about Jackson or Blackledge to say anything about either man," Bishop complained about the mud-slinging report that most likely cost Blackledge the election.

"Well, we know that was a lie. I investigated. Didn't find shit. Jackson, most likely, paid somebody to do it," Jenkins said.

Bishop nodded. "Kathy told me Jackson had a reputation for fooling around. Could be he fooled with the wrong woman. Some husband might have got pissed off about it. Hugh was too big to beat up so he knifed him. If I were you, I'd look into that possibility."

"Good idea. I don't think that occurred to me, Bishop. I can always count on you to come up with some off the wall stuff. But, it seems to me they would have used a gun, a pistol, though, not a knife. I wonder why they used a knife?" Jenkins asked.

"Don't know but I agree. Anyway, you've also got the Lake Casino as a motive. Probably won't find shit if they did it. They'd have brought in somebody. They'll all have alibis."

"Most likely but I'll check it out too. And, I'll see who ol' Hugh was dickin'. Might be able to find something there. Good idea," Jenkins told him.

He looked at the platter. All the croissants were gone. He got up for a last cup of coffee. Bishop asked him to bring him one as well.

"Thanks," Bishop told him when he sat Bishop's steaming mug on the table.

"That television woman, girl as far as I'm concerned," Bishop said when he came back. "Sure followed him around. I'd check her out. From what you said, I assume she's on your list of suspects."

He agreed.

Bishop continued. "She was the making of him, from what Kathy has told me. She aired everything he did. Like you said, she and Hugh had a thing going. Who knows what was in it?"

"Yeah. I'll talk to Kathy to get her views, if you don't mind. I'd like to hear her slant on the stories that have been going around," Jenkins told him.

Bishop told him to go ahead.

Jenkins looked across the table at him. "Uh, I just had a thought. With all those thoughts popping in your head, you could help me out. Kind of be my deputy."

"Good God, Clyde," Bishop called him by his first name for emphasis, "you've got an office full of deputies. Use one of them."

Jenkins made a face and said, "Come on Bishop. You know how governments work. The mayor calls and wants me to hire a friend. Or a councilman. I have the bodies rightly enough, but not many brains or experience. They can do what I tell them, but I don't expect much independent thinking."

"I've got contracts with banks you know. My income," Bishop said.

"Yeah, I kind of forgot. I figured on paying you, but you're busy then?"

"Oddly enough, right now, I'm not. With the economy running like it is, thanks in part to old Hugh, most loans are paying as agreed. Still, I don't want to get involved in your business."

"Just be to nose around some. Think about what might have happened and let me know. Ask around some. What could it hurt? Pay'll be good."

"You damn well will, if I take it on." Bishop leaned back in his chair then said, "I suppose I could ask some questions but hell, I'd be most likely stepping on your toes."

"Not right away. I have to drive all over the state talking to his store managers. See who Hugh bought out and who he pissed off doing it. You'd have the local area to yourself. The husbands. The casinos. Even the Native Americans if Hugh did anything to rub any of them the wrong way. Hugh's wife may know something. Julia's her name," Jenkins told him.

"I'll think about it, Clyde," Bishop said then looked at him. "No, hell, I'll help you, but I want you to announce it in the newspaper so people will know I'm official when I knock on their doors. And, give me a card showing I've got some authority."

"Of course. Damn, you don't know how good that makes me feel having you out there digging around. I might go to church this Sunday." He laughed. "The way you bump into people when you get going, you may want to go to church too. Pick yourself up a little protection from on high."

Bishop laughed. "Good idea, Chief, but I don't think I'll need any protection. I'm just going to ask questions and send you reports of what I find out. I won't be making anybody mad."

"You always say that but you always do … make 'em mad," the chief said.

"Hell then, why are you asking me to help you? I don't want some mad husband shooting at me."

"Well, Bishop, learn to be more diplomatic," Jenkins said. "Like me."

Bishop laughed.

Jenkins stood to leave. "The announcement will be in the afternoon paper. I'll have to get the mayor's approval but I don't think I'll have any trouble there. He knows what goes on in the police department.

"By the way, I have a box in the car with Hugh's personal effects including his clothes except for the shirt. Too bloody to include it. We didn't find anything of interest in the other things."

"Pretty damn sure of yourself," Bishop said with a chuckle, referring to the fact that he'd brought out the things for him to deliver.

The chief laughed. "I know you wouldn't pass up a challenge. I'll put something in the paper to give you some leverage.

"Oh, meant to tell you something. The doctor who looked at the body for us said from the coloration on his right wrist, Hugh might have been wearing or had been wearing at one time, a watch. Could you ask his wife about that? Might put a different slant on the murder if it was a simple robbery by somebody desperate for something. Grabbed the watch and got scared off."

Bishop agreed to ask.

*****

Kathy waved the newspaper with the story of Bishop's appointment as an investigator when she walked in the back door that evening. The story was on the front page. She was smiling from ear to ear. "You let him talk you into it, didn't you?" she asked.

She showed him the story, complete with one of his photos, on the second page. How Chief Jenkins had asked him to assist in the investigation of the Hugh Jackson murder.

Bishop looked at the story. "Used a photo from when I was helping Seth Campbell run for governor." He laughed. "I was younger then."

"Weren't we all," Kathy said. "Anyway, he says you'll be big help. You've worked with him before and together you have solved some major cases."

"I don't recall them, but if he says it, he's probably right," Bishop said.

They got beers and drank them on the back porch. "What are you going to do?" she asked.

"I'm not exactly sure," he said. "I think I'll talk to that Freedom Tribe guy, Martin, the one they call the eagle, and see what he knows. Jackson backed his casino and from the bits and pieces I've heard, the people running the Lake Casino didn't want it. I'll be interested in Martin's story."

"I wish you well. Just don't terminally irritate anybody, you hear me? I want you around. I enjoy our beers on your back porch."

"I agree. Chief Jenkins said about the same thing. Well, I can tell you that I'd prefer to be around … so long as you're around with me. Watching the beavers work is entertaining when you're sitting by my side," he said. "So, I'll be on my best behavior."

She smiled. "Thank you, Bishop. I feel the same way about you."

After their beers, she got up and put together a dinner for them. That was their routine. She'd make the dinner and he'd clean up. Mostly he'd rinse the dishes and put them in the dishwasher.

At one time, before the health food craze swept the country, they'd have something sweet for desert. These days, he'd peel an orange or something similar. He'd gotten used to it. Anything he did with Kathy was okay with him.

She spent the night. They had breakfast together and she went to work. He usually did the breakfast for them.

He had a last cup of coffee on the porch and thought some more about his "job."

When the cup was almost empty, he had made a decision about where to begin.

"I'll talk to Mrs. Jackson first. Get any overview she might have on Hugh's activities … and proclivities," he said with a chuckle. "Some wives know when their husbands are fooling around. Even if they don't know for sure, they suspect."

He tried to remember the old wives tale he'd heard, something along the lines of, "if they ain't gittin' it at home, they're gittin' it some place else."

He laughed. *I'll tactfully ask his wife. I bet she'll know if that applied to Hugh.*

Chapter 9

Bishop parked in front of the Jackson's home and knocked on the front door. There was a doorbell but he didn't see it in time.

He figured the house was built a long time ago. It was all wood, probably cut from trees on the property and looked like one of many farm houses around the county. It had porches, front and back, both screened to keep out the bugs. He guessed the outhouse that came with the house when it was originally built had long since been replaced by more modern conveniences.

And, likewise the kitchen, he figured. In the old days, women had to cook on wood stoves. He imagined the kitchen now had a gas stove and running water. The old wood barn at the back of the house, at the edge of the pasture, looked like it could go another hundred years.

Julia opened the door. "Mr. uh, … Mr. Bishop Bone," she said. "I recognize you from the newspaper story. You're going to investigate Hugh's … murder."

He agreed and asked if he could come in for a talk.

She invited him in and offered coffee which he refused. He felt he was practically floating in coffee as it was. In her hand was a hard cover book. He couldn't see the title.

She said, "My children are coming to be with me sometime today. My daughter is on her way. She'll stay a couple of days. Keep me company. My son has a legal problem he has to take care of first, but he'll be here later."

"That's good," Bishop said. "I'm glad. You need somebody in times like these."

She agreed.

He sat down in their living room facing her. Beside her on a table was a cup of coffee which she'd been drinking. Her eyes were red.

Been crying, Bishop thought.

"Been reading," she said, waving the book in front of her. "Fact and Fantasy. I thought it might take my mind off Hugh."

"What's it about?" Bishop asked politely.

"Not much. One thing though. The writer says the time we keep, based really on the earth's rotation may not be the time of the universe. The universe may just have begun. Who knows how it will end up? I thought that was kind of interesting."

Bishop nodded his head. "True," he said. "Who can know what's ahead for man? There may be some real problems coming. In the meantime, we have to deal with what some philosophers might call minor." He didn't ascribe a level of importance to her husband's murder. She'd no doubt call it a major problem.

It looked to Bishop like she was having to strain to hear everything he said. He figured he was mumbling so he tried to speak up and to speak more clearly. That seemed to work.

"He, the writer, also thinks there was some intelligence in the way we … mankind, was formed," she said with some hesitation, like she was unsure of the implications of what she was saying. "That the little micro-organisms that were on earth when it began its rotation around the sun were most likely on all the planets. The other planets just weren't situated around the sun like earth so the organisms could grow as they have here."

"Sounds logical," Bishop said.

"He said that whatever created us, the organisms we started from, must have thought about it somehow. The organisms developed into man and woman so they could reproduce. Some intent that we go forth and multiply. I think that comes from something but I don't remember what."

Bishop agreed. He thought it came from the Bible, but let it go. He didn't think she cared much where it came from.

Instead, he shrugged. "I hadn't really thought of it like that, but it makes sense. Something with intelligence created … us. Maybe we are something like our creator. If you're Biblically oriented, the Bible doesn't get into it that thoroughly."

"If I didn't have something to do," She waved the book again and lay it on the table beside her chair, "I think I'd go crazy. It makes me feel a little better to know that we may be some experiment that might come to an end one day."

Bishop nodded and replied. "I'm sure it would. I'd say it's good for you to have something to do to get your mind off things. Hugh's death must have been a big shock for you. Had to be. I'm sorry about it. Sorry you have to face it. It has to be terrible for you. Having your husband killed like he was."

She looked down at the floor covered by an old rug that looked worn, but still retained the original charm of the colors and the unique design.

"It was. I still haven't gotten over it," she said. "I know he had made lots of enemies. Lots of people didn't like him."

"Who, for example. If you know. If you don't mind me asking."

She shook her head. "The only one I know for sure is Riley Watson. I don't know if I'd call him an enemy but he does claim that Hugh chiseled him out of ten thousand dollars when he bought the store in Lawton. I think Hugh probably did. He was like that." She looked at Bishop when she said it. "I know ten thousand isn't much money but it was to Riley. I know Riley and his family, known 'em forever. His daddy and mine hunted together. That money meant a lot to them. Riley's the only one left now. I think too, that … it was the principal of the thing, the way Hugh did it, threatening to back out if Riley didn't take less money."

She looked away like she had a thought then said, "I think Riley liked me a long time ago. Still does, I think, from the way he comes around to help me around here. Milks my cow almost every day now. I figured he was too old for me back then and I didn't think he was right for me. My mother didn't either. She thought I should marry somebody with ambition." She laughed. "Just not Hugh Jackson. He had ambition but nothing else."

"Mothers are usually right. Has he, Riley, said anything about Mr. Jackson? Anything that suggests who might want to … well, murder him?" Bishop asked.

"Just that he hates … hated, Hugh's guts," Julia said.

Bishop made a note to talk to Watson. He got the man's phone number and address from her.

"Is he in good health?" he asked. "Watson?"

She shook her head. "He gets around, but I don't think he could run a foot race with anybody."

"Anybody else?" Bishop asked. "Anybody else … hate his guts? Hugh's?"

He figured most people did, but was hoping she could give him some names.

She frowned. "I'd guess lots of people from what he talked about. He didn't tell me much, but I heard him talk on the phone now and then and it sounded like he was always in a pickle or a fight with somebody."

"Any names, specifically? I'm trying to track down who might have killed him."

"Let me see," she said and rubbed her chin. "I think I heard him talking to somebody … Stuart somebody, I think I remember, about the casino the Indians – I guess I should say Native Americans these days – want to build. Stuart didn't want the casino to be built. I think that's what they were arguing about. I only heard what Hugh was saying. Hugh told him he had no say in what the Native Americans did. In the end, Hugh just hung up on the man. He hadn't changed his mind. He was still going to back the new casino. That's what he told the newspapers and that television girl."

"Did Hugh say anything else about the new casino?" Bishop asked.

Julia stared at Bishop a second or two before answering. "I think he … well, from what I heard him saying on his phone, I guess he was behind the whole thing from the start. I know he denied it on the television but the whole thing was his idea from the start."

"His idea? You mean he was secretly backing the casino?"

She nodded her head, yes. "I mean he was the one who started the tribe, the Freedom Tribe. It was all his idea but he kept it a secret. The land on the river, the casino, everything. He didn't even know that I knew, but I'd taken to listening in when he got on the phone. I also read his emails when he was gone. He deleted everything when somebody claimed he was behind it but I'd read them already. He got money from it, lots of money. Over a million. I couldn't hear how much, but when he was talking to somebody he said millions. I think he was asking for five or six million for the land they wanted for the casino."

She paused as if collecting her thoughts then added, "From all the arguments I heard him having on the phone, I don't think he got nearly that much though. I don't know if he even got any. If he did, it never made it into the house. There was also that television story about the money. Hugh went on the air and denied it but he probably would have gotten some, if he had lived. That's the way he was. If there was money to be had, he wanted some. And he usually got it."

May be why he was killed, to keep from giving him anything, Bishop thought.

"Damn. Lots of money," he said. "Wonder what happened to it." He answered his question, "It may not have been due until the casino was built and up and running."

She nodded her head. "I hope. I think I have enough to last as long as I will, but I can't be sure. If it's legal, I hope he has some coming and I get it."

"Yeah, I understand." He laughed to himself, remembering when Hugh went on television to deny any involvement in any of it. That was after he'd announced his run for the state Senate.

I wonder how that race would have come out. It was going to be close, but I bet old Hugh would have pulled it off. The guy he was running against hadn't done a damn thing while he was in office and I imagine before the race was over, everybody in the district would know about it in spades.

"Somebody must have found out," Bishop said. "There was a television story by the guy Hugh was running against."

"I saw it. Hugh did too. It upset him, but he calmed down and had that reporter girl he was seeing record his rebuttal." She shrugged. "I saw it. Have to say it was convincing."

"Girl? You mean Denise Allen?" Bishop asked.

"He was sleeping with her. Got to where he'd stay with her. They'd go out of town together."

"How could you stand it?" Bishop asked.

She grimaced. "I didn't mind so much. We never had much of a love life if you get my meaning. I didn't mind that either. I had my paintings. He just married me for this farm. I didn't give it to him. Mama said he was a crook. I guess he was. He put it on his financial statements anyway. The banks never checked. That's how he got started ... buying the stores 'n all. Running for supervisor. He was always thinking ahead."

"Maybe he was stringing the girl along? So she'd help him." Bishop wondered.

"I reckon you're right. Most likely are. I don't think he ever loved anybody but himself. His mama and daddy never got along much, he told me that one time back when we were still talking. I don't reckon he ever learned what love was. I thought I could teach him to love but I couldn't. If he learned, he never told me."

"I've heard it said that if a child doesn't learn it early on, they never do. Some figure out how to get along. Some do like I suppose Hugh did, they just love themselves."

"He did that," she said. "Nothing else mattered to him but what he wanted. And I don't think he was ever satisfied."

"Did he say ... let me ask it this way, did he have any long range goals? I doubt the state Senate was going to satisfy him."

She shook her head. "I don't know. He never talked about it to me or on the phone. If there was a king, I'd guess he would want to be king, but he never said."

Bishop laughed.

"Excuse me for saying so, but it does seem like he had a massive ego problem," Bishop said.

"I guess. He'd had some problems. First his parents were divorced. Then, his mother ... died. I don't think that did him any good. He was pretty messed up from what I could see."

"That may be as good an evaluation as any," Bishop agreed. "How'd his mother die?"

"She, uh, committed suicide a long time ago. She had a love affair with a married woman who didn't want to leave her husband was the way Hugh told it. They kept up the affair even though she wouldn't divorce her husband. That hit Hugh pretty hard though he never admitted it." She paused to wipe away a tear.

"As I said, he was pretty messed up inside. I think his quest to always win was the way it came out. He may be better off dead." She paused again, then added, "I think the world is. He was like a dangerous storm."

Bishop nodded his agreement and said, "You may be right, but somebody killed him, and I appreciate your helping me find out who. Has anybody been threatening him? Running around like he's been doing, I'd be surprised if a bunch of people didn't want him dead."

She shrugged. "Maybe. One day when we were talking civilly, he said somebody threatened him. That Stuart guy from the Lake Casino. I already knew it from listening to his phone calls, but he told me anyway.

"He wanted Hugh to quit pushing the River Casino 'or else' was the way Hugh said he put it. Hugh took that to be a threat."

"I would have too," Bishop said.

"Oh, and Hugh got a couple of … maybe you'd call 'em hate letters. Somebody put 'em in our mailbox. No names on 'em."

"Too bad. What'd he do with them?" Bishop asked.

"I don't know. Last time I saw them, they were on his desk where I read them. He might 've thrown 'em away."

"Can we take a look?" Bishop asked.

He followed her into the room Hugh used as an office. It was just a converted bedroom. He'd bought a desk for it and a couple of chairs for people visiting.

She walked behind the desk and twisted his in-box toward Bishop so he could look. The first two sheets were the letters. Both typed. *Probably printed. Yep, computer,* he thought as he picked them up and read them.

The first one he read dealt with Hugh's support of the river casino. Basically it said he was to quit immediately or risk injury.

"I assume this one came in before the River Casino was approved," he said, looking at Mrs. Jackson.

She nodded. "As best I can remember. The other one came in after he announced he was running for the Senate."

Bishop read it. It said, "You'd better learn to sleep in your own bed. If you don't, you may not wake up one morning."

Julia said, "I think somebody's husband was giving him a warning."

"Any idea whose?" Bishop asked.

She shook her head. "Could have been anybody's. If a woman offered and she had all the right parts, I don't think he ever turned 'em down. I don't know for sure, but that's what I've been told. And that girl. He's been sleeping with her lately. I offered to give him a divorce if he wanted one. I was tired of it, frankly."

"What'd he say?"

"He laughed at me. He wasn't going to give me a divorce. Let me see if I can remember what he said. He said if I filed, he'd ask for money. He figured the farm had gone up in value since we were married. Primarily because of his name and all he'd done. So if I filed, he'd force me to sell my farm to pay him off. He knew I'd never do that, so he said I was stuck with him till hell froze over." She wiped more tears from her eyes.

"If you'd rather stop," Bishop offered.

"No, it's okay. That was what we talked about before he was killed. It kind of puts Hugh's attitude into focus if that's what you're after. If a divorce would make him money, he'd jump at it. If not, forget it. Frankly, I think, looking back at it all, he probably wanted to stay married so he'd have an excuse when one of his women, the latest for sure, that Denise girl, wanted to get married. He could say he was married and I wouldn't give him a divorce or something like that."

"Yeah, sounds like the man. It did seem like he was kind of laughing at you," Bishop said.

"What really hurt me was what else he said before he left. It's crystal clear in my mind. I had told him he could file and I'd tell the court I'd had an affair. That wouldn't hurt his political ambitions. I was tired of him. You know what he told me?"

Bishop shook his head.

"He said, 'Nobody would believe you were fooling around unless it was with a blind man. So you can forget divorce. That made me cry. To think he had no respect for me."

"Can't say I blame you."

"I walked away but my insides were all torn up. I still can't believe he thought so little of me. I don't guess it matters now." Tears ran down her face.

Bishop figured it was time to wind up the interview. He sighed loudly and thanked her. "You've given me some stuff I can use, Julia. It'll help us find out who killed him. Did you tell Chief Jenkins any of what you've told me?"

"No. He just came out to tell me Hugh had been killed. I was too upset to tell him anything and he didn't ask. I'm glad you came by, and I'm glad to get it off my chest. As I said, Hugh was one ... screwed up man. Maybe he's finally at peace. And he can quit running for something now."

She looked away. Bishop assumed she was still ruminating about Jackson's insult when she offered him a divorce.

"I like that thought. He can quit running," Bishop said. "If you think of anything else, would you let me know? Do you have anybody who can stay with you till you ... get settled. Relatives?"

She shook her head. "Just my children, but they'll stay with me, off and on, as long as I need them. I was the only child my mama and daddy had. All their relatives are dead. I'll be okay. I've learned to take care of myself, living with Hugh. He's never been here for anything. And Riley, my neighbor, comes down to help me with the farm. Don't worry about me."

Bishop nodded. He didn't doubt it, knowing as much about Riley as he did. He obviously liked Julia.

He noted the computer on Hugh's desk and said, "I'll want to go through his computer files as well if you don't mind. You never can tell what you'll find. Did he have a password? I can't log in on mine until I feed it my password."

She said yes and told Bishop she thought the password was Hugh's birthday. He kept it in his desk drawer. The key to that was under his desk pad.

On the credenza behind his desk, partially concealed under papers, was an album. Bishop moved the papers and touched the album with his hand. He asked, "Is this his family album. I might want to look through it."

Julia appeared to become flustered. "No. That's not his. Goodness no! Not at all! It's mine. My mother started it and I kept it up. I don't know what Hugh was doing with it. I usually kept it in my closet but had taken it out to look at and left it on the coffee table. It had little to do with Hugh but he must have wanted to look at it for some reason. Our wedding pictures are in it, but I doubt he cared about them."

She reached over and took it from Bishop. "I'll put it back where it belongs."

Bishop promised to be back in a day or two. That'd give her time to get settled some.

She thanked him.

"I have his personal things, things he had on him … that night … in the car. I'll bring them in if you'd like. Do you mind? Or I can bring them next time I come out."

She said he could bring them in.

"Oh, I also wanted to ask you a question. Chief Jenkins said your husband's right wrist looked like he wore a watch? Do you know if he did?"

She appeared puzzled and said, "Of course. He always wore his watch. Was it gone?"

"Yes. Looks like whoever … anyway, looks like it was taken."

"Somebody robbed him?" she asked.

"Looks like it. Was it expensive?"

"It was. Hugh only wanted the most expensive things. I bought it for him. Had little diamonds put around the rim of the watch. Wedding present. Cost almost three thousand dollars with the diamonds. He wanted a leather band."

"It was taken," Bishop said.

Could point to a simple robbery, he thought. *Somebody killed him and got scared before they could take more than the watch. Had to unhook the strap. Damn. Could have taken his wallet easier but the diamonds might have caught the killer's eye.*

He went out and got the box the chief had put Jackson's things into and gave it to Julia.

"Do you see anything else that's missing?" he asked.

She picked up his wallet and looked inside. The bills hadn't been taken. Likewise the credit cards. Nothing but the watch had been taken.

She thanked him for bringing the things to her.

"No problem. The chief had to look at everything first. He didn't find anything suspicious ... other than the missing watch."

"Hugh always wore it," she said, sadly.

He gave her a card with his number on it. "When I come back, I'll want to look through his files including what's on his computer, to see if there's anything that'll point to his killer. I'll set aside some time for it. Might take a few hours. I'll have to do the same thing with his office in town, where the supervisors meet. I understand that he has one ..." He didn't finish. He had a sudden realization that that was where her husband was killed. He cursed himself for not being more considerate.

She promised to leave everything in the office there as it was, sniffing as she said it.

Shit, he thought, *I didn't think. She'll probably go back to the book she's been reading and drink some more coffee. I hope it works.*

As he turned to leave, he noticed the original oils and water color paintings on the hall walls. He was so interested in seeing Hugh's office he hadn't seen them before. The walls were decorated with over twenty of them, most were two feet square but some were larger and there were some miniatures.

Paintings! Ah, that's what she was talking about before. I somehow missed that she was talking about hers. She's good, he thought.

"Beautiful," he said as he strolled past and looked. "Wow!"

"They're mine," she said proudly. "It's what I do... what I've done with my time while Hugh's ... while he was out beating the bushes for whatever he was after. I may have said. Hugh didn't care for them. My children love them.

"They didn't much get along with their dad. He wasn't what I'd call a caring father. He thought if he threw money at their problems, that was the equivalent of love. I think he used us as his excuse to go out and make as much money as he could. He could give us money but not love. He never caught on. A smile is worth more than a thousand dollars. I tried to tell him that for the first three years of our marriage. I couldn't and finally gave up. I'm sorry I failed."

"Some people can't change. They never realize they should. Hugh probably never learned how to love, based on what you told me about his childhood," Bishop said.

"I reckon." She looked at the paintings and said, "I'll give you one of them, if you like. I haven't tried to sell any ... yet. I may now. I need something to do to help put it all behind me. I haven't sorted out my money situation. Hugh controlled the check books."

"I'll pay you," he said. "How about that? Can I buy two?"

She agreed. A smile replaced the sad frown on her face.

He picked a misty morning looking through the pecan orchard with corn stalks growing in the field under the trees. The other was a misty morning or perhaps a misty day after a rain, of a pond partially surrounded by green shrubs, some blooming and larger trees, all covered in a gray mist.

"These go on my hall wall," he told her. "How much do I owe you?"

She hesitated. "I don't really know. I've never had anybody look at them before. I just painted to keep from going crazy living with Hugh."

"Well, how about three hundred. That's probably not enough so if you find somebody who says they're worth more, let me know and I'll give you more."

She agreed, smiling, obviously pleased that somebody liked what she'd done. She helped him take them from the wall.

Bishop gave her a "smiling" goodbye hug when he left.

*****

Immediately after getting back to his cabin, he hung the paintings in a prominent place on his hall wall.

"Beautiful," he said, standing back for a look. He knew Kathy would love them as well.

After that interlude, he went into his office and emailed the chief a report of what he'd found out.

"Somebody will figure out how to get it to him," Bishop said, knowing the chief was likely on the road.

In the report, he noted that Jackson's wife had, living with Jackson, picked up a pretty good understanding of the relationship between men and women.

Unfortunately, Jackson never did. "She's actually quite intellectual," his report said. "And, she was right handed." He laughed when he wrote it and bet the chief would laugh when he read it. He'd watched her hands while they talked. She always seemed to favor her right hand.

Bishop also reported what Julia said about the watch and the implications, real or an attempt to point away from some other motive.

He tentatively figured his next stop would be the Lake Casino for a visit with Stuart Flint. That would change after he'd thought about it some.

Might need a flack jacket for that one. Flint sounds like he is used to getting his way. Makes him a prime suspect in my book. However, somebody took the man's watch. Was that robbery or somebody trying to make it look like robbery? He wondered, as he thought about his report to the chief.

"I guess we'll have to keep an open mind," he said, continuing the dialogue he was having with himself.

He thought about what Mrs. Jackson had told him. Although all of it was worthwhile, he found the most intriguing thing she said was her insight about her husband.

"He was all messed up because of his childhood. He didn't understand how to love and nothing she did could ever change that. All he understood was his next challenge. Like winning that would somehow mean that somebody loved him. His children had to suffer like she did. He needed to reach out and hug them. Tell them he loved them. They could love him back. He never learned. A cold man, Jackson.

I wonder how many movers and shakers have that same problem. Searching for something to take the place of a love they never had. No wonder he pissed everybody off. He wanted what they had and they somehow sensed that he was going to try and get it. No surprise that somebody killed him. The only surprise is that it didn't happen sooner.

He'd learned enough from the conversation he'd had with Jackson's wife to put the new casino squarely on the table as motivation for anybody involved in either casino to kill him. Hugh'd made both sides mad enough. And the money was big enough to motivate anybody,

He wondered more about the money. Julia said she'd heard Jackson talking about it. *Millions. Didn't make it into their personal account, she said. Did he get any? If he did, where did it go?*

As he thought about seeing Flint, he decided it might be better to talk to Denise Allen first. Hugh might have told her something he could use when talking to some of the others he had on his list. One of those was Riley Watson. *Apparently hated Jackson's guts, if Julia was quoting him right.*

He shook his head and thought, *I don't see him as a murderer though based on ten thousand dollars, but who knows what triggers murder.*

Martin, the chief of the new Freedom Tribe, and Flint at the Lake Casino probably had reason to hate his guts too. It looks like he screwed everybody. One way or another. *I'll find out more when I talk to them. I'm not so sure about Martin though. I think he made out okay.*

"Hell, I also need to interview Oliver Simpson. Why'd he suddenly retire? Blackmail? Must have been.

The chief will probably take care of Baxter since he'll be on the road talking to Jackson's appliance managers. I imagine Jackson did a number on both Simpson and Baxter," Bishop told himself.

"Blackledge has to be on my list. Jackson sure as hell made sure he didn't win that election. He had to be the one behind that last minute smear that cost Blackledge the election. But first I'll talk to Denise Allen."

*****

Kathy called to tell him that the chief had stopped by the library to talk to her on his way out of town.

"Wanted to know if I knew anything. I told him I only knew what the two of you had talked about when he was at the house. I gave him my opinions. Not worth much but that's all I really had to give him that he didn't already know."

"Right. Sometimes opinions trigger thoughts that help out. He's going to talk to Jackson's appliance store managers to see if anybody had been threatening Jackson," Bishop said.

"In my report, I asked him to see if anybody knew anything about Hugh's involvement in the River Casino. I bet Hugh did some behind the scenes work to get a gambling license for it."

"Probably did. Clyde also wanted to know about the television girl, Denise Allen," she said. "Wanted my opinion about that. I told him all I had was an opinion, but it looked to me, from the way she followed Hugh Jackson around, reporting on everything he did, that they must have been at it hot and heavy."

"I think she admitted it the night she found Jackson's body. She told the chief that they'd had a relationship going for some time," Bishop said. "His wife also knew about it. Apparently she didn't mind or was so used to him fooling around she'd quit caring."

He told her the rest of what Mrs. Jackson had said, including her observations that most of Jackson's actions probably came from a childhood without love between his parents. Without that, Bishop told her, Jackson must have substituted acquiring things and the status that came with what he'd done to give him the satisfaction love didn't.

Kathy said she was impressed that the woman had that much insight. "I'll tell you this Bishop, if you had fooled around like he did, I would have let you know in spades," Kathy said. "In the hospital, you wouldn't have been in any condition to acquire anything." She laughed.

"I don't blame you," Bishop replied, adding a chuckle. "I guess I'll have to be careful."

"Careful isn't the word I'd have used."

He laughed. "Right. How 'bout I won't fool around. I have the best already," he said.

"That's more like it,"

She said she'd be out later and bring tamales for dinner. Bishop promised margaritas.

Bone headed out to see Denise Allen. *She probably knew more about what Hugh was doing and to whom he was doing it than anybody. Hell, he was sleeping with her according to Julia and what she told the chief. Even Kathy suspected as much.*

"Hmm, I wonder if she had a boyfriend? If she did, jealously could be a motive. The boyfriend might have decided to get rid of the competition. The problem might be getting her to tell me anything," he said. "She most likely still has feelings for the man. Loyalty hangs on even after death. I may have to be a little tough with her."

Chapter 10

He decided to see her at the television studios, where she was the news anchor. He knew she'd be inclined to use the status of her position at the station as a kind of shield from his hostile questions if it came to that, but that was a hurdle he'd just have to overcome. Bishop wasn't inclined to wait to interview her.

He walked into the offices and told the receptionist, "I'm here to see Denise Allen. Police business." He flashed the card Chief Jenkins had given him.

"Yes," the young woman said. "I saw your picture in the paper. I'll call her."

"No," he said. "If she's in, I'd rather not give her an excuse to be busy, if you know what I mean?"

She smiled. "Yes. I understand. Police business takes priority over everything, especially if a murder's involved."

"Yep."

She told him how to get to Denise's office. It was at the back wall of the studio, overlooking a garden.

Bishop didn't know Jason, but passed his desk on the way to her office. Jason recognized him from the newspaper story but also knew him from past television reports of other cases he'd had. He gave Bishop half a wave. Bishop nodded in reply.

He saw Denise sitting in her office studying her computer screen. Her door was open. Bishop walked in and stuck out his hand. "Bishop Bone, I want to ask you some questions about Hugh Jackson," he said.

She appeared startled. "I didn't get a … no one told me you were coming."

"Thought I'd just barge in. I was in town and Chief Jenkins insisted that I speak to you since you and Mr.

Jackson were on … well, as I understand it, close terms. Having an affair to be accurate. He told me you'd pretty much said as much the night you found Mr. Jackson's body."

She stared at Bishop for a couple of seconds, took a deep breath and said. "That's right. I guess I did. I was upset."

She got up and closed her door.

"Let's make this private," she said.

He nodded.

He started with a general question to let her say what she was willing to say. "Tell me what you know about the man. Some people say you were the making of him. I tend to agree even though I don't follow politics that closely. He did come by my place when he was running for the supervisor's seat."

"He said he was going to visit every voter in the beat," she said. "I think he did. He was a man of his word."

Yeah, Bishop thought. *With every word designed to get him something somebody else already had.*

But, he didn't say that. He just nodded for her to continue.

"I'd say he was very ambitious. Very. He always said he wanted to help the people and people in public office are the only ones who can really do that. That's why he was running for the Senate seat. The incumbent hadn't done anything since he … inherited the office from his father who hadn't either."

"From what I hear, he had a good chance of winning," Bishop said. "Although there was the claim that he'd scammed the Freedom Tribe over the land. I think the station aired your interview with his rebuttal."

"The incumbent said someone called his office to report that Hugh … Mr. Jackson was involved in

formation of the River Casino and the newly formed
tribe. Mr. Jackson rebutted that," she said.

"But I've heard from a very reputable source that he
was up to his eyeballs in all of it," Bishop said, recalling
what Hugh's wife had told him. "My source said he was
to get a big pay-off for the land the Freedom Tribe
wanted for their casino on the river."

Denise looked away. "I don't ... I didn't know ...
well, Hugh never told me the details, nothing about any
big money, but I guess I knew from what he did tell me
that he was the driving force behind it all, the new tribe
and the casino. I'm not surprised about the money
though. Especially in light of the story the incumbent
was probably behind. Politics, as you probably know, is
a dirty business.

"Frankly, I firmly believe that Hugh never did
anything for anybody unless there was something in it
for him. So, he probably was getting a pay-off and it
probably was more than anybody bargained for."

Bishop agreed with a nod of his head and said, "You
ever consider your relationship in that light. He sure as
hell got a lot out of his affair with you. His wife knew
about it. She thinks he was stringing you along."

She looked down at her desk for a moment then said,
"Yes. I suspect ... began to suspect anyway that he was.
I love him though. Still do, although now that he's dead
and I've had a chance to think about it, I realize that
maybe he was stringing me along. Other people have
told me that. He kept stalling about getting a divorce
from his wife."

"She offered to give him a divorce," he said.

Her face showed surprise. "I didn't know that."

"The night he was killed, she told Jackson that she'd
tell the court that she'd had an affair. That way, she

figured his political career wouldn't be hurt," Bishop said. "I'm not sure she was thinking clearly, but that's what she said."

"What'd he say?" she asked.

"He said nobody would believe she'd had an affair unless it was with a blind man."

"What a rude thing to say," Denise replied. "But, thinking back at some of the other things he'd said about people he didn't like, I don't doubt that he said it."

"It hurt her. She thinks he didn't want a divorce because as long as he was married ... well, I guess I'll tell it like she told me. She thinks as long as he was married, he had an excuse not to marry anybody else."

"He didn't tell me any of it," she said. "I'd talked to him earlier in the evening. I think Hugh's wife was right though. Every once in a while, as I just said, I got the impression that he was using me."

"Maybe he was saving it as a surprise, her offer to divorce him," he said, but didn't believe a word of it. "Could be he was going to do it but didn't want her to know. You never can tell with someone like Jackson. I got the impression that he would say or do whatever pleased him?"

She nodded with a skeptical look on her face. Obviously she didn't believe Jackson ever intended to get a divorce either.

"Did he ever talk about being threatened by anybody?"

"I think somebody from the Lake Casino got after him for supporting the River Casino," she said.

"Stuart Flint?"

"Yes, that's who it was. Also, everybody pretty much knew he was behind the mud-slinging that cost Blackledge the election. Blackledge would have won if that man hadn't come in and claimed he'd been forced out of his teaching job at JC."

"Why didn't you check out the story before running it?" he asked.

Again, she paused. "That's right. I should have. I ran it without checking. Hugh needed something to cut the lead Blackledge had. I … well, I let my personal feelings get in the way of my professional judgment and ran the story without checking it out. The election was the next day. If I'd taken the time to check it out, it would have been too late. That's rationalization, Mr. Bone. I know that. I knew it then but ignored it. As I said, I was in love and knew the story would help Hugh win, so I ran it."

"I don't imagine it made Blackledge very happy," Bishop suggested.

"No, he called the station and complained. Even had a lawyer threaten us. I heard that he'd made threats against Hugh but I don't know if he made them directly or was just shooting off his mouth. It would have made me mad if I'd been him."

Bishop agreed. "I understand that the chairman of the board appointed Blackledge to replace Baxter. That must have irked Mr. Jackson."

"Oh, it did. He cursed Mr. Oliver. Said he had to go."

"How'd he do it? Get rid of Oliver? And, how about Baxter? Did he get rid of him too?"

She agreed with a shake of her head. "I don't guess it'll hurt to tell the truth. Hugh told me that Oliver and Baxter were taking bribes, kickbacks really. He bluffed Oliver into forcing Baxter to get another job … in Jackson. Then, to get rid of Oliver, he told him that he had a videotape of him taking money from a contractor. Henry Hankins."

"Did he?"

"No. It was all a bluff. Hugh was good at that. If he wanted something, he didn't care what he had to do to get it."

"He sounds like he was corrupt to the core," Bishop said. "Unscrupulous may be more accurate. Hell, even that may be an understatement."

"I guess he was all that, now that I step back and take a serious look. Looking at it through glasses coated in love, I just thought it was all fair game. In politics it seems that everything is okay. What he did, his actions were the actions of a man who was clever enough to win. That's what I thought. I think that's partly why I fell in love with him. It was thrilling to watch, thrilling to be part of it. I hate to admit that, but I am… well, was anyway. Makes me feel a little better confessing. I had a position of public responsibility. I should have done more with it. I hope you're not going to tell everybody in the world what I've been saying."

"No need to, I guess. I'm looking for a killer, not somebody who acted out of love. Love shades your common sense and your sense of duty," Bishop said. "Money does too."

He was saying that from his personal experience.

"Hugh paid for everything when we went out," she said. "At least he didn't leach off me. He was a gentleman. Well, seemed to be."

"As you said, he did what he had to do to win. He obviously wanted to keep you on his side. You made him a winner."

She nodded her head in recognition. "I think you're right, now that I can look at it fairly."

"Did he tell you about anybody else threatening him?"

She thought about it for a second or two. "I think the people who sold the land thought he was behind the funny business with the land that was sold for the casino and cursed him for it. I don't know if they threatened him, but they were pretty upset, Hugh said. Also, the people investing in the new casino might have threatened him. It was their money he supposedly was taking. He never said anything about it, but part of the story we aired talked about it. That's most likely the money your source told you about. I'm trying to remember the guy's name who accused him of double dealing. Oh, I remember, I think. Greenfield's the guy's name. I don't think Martin, the guy elected to be chief of the new tribe, cared one way or the other. He didn't have any money in it. Hugh said he was just going to be a figure head but he was going to hire mostly Native Americans to work there."

"Good idea," Bishop said. "They need a break. I think our ancestors took their land from them. From what I've read, they still haven't recovered. I assume from what you've said that Martin didn't make any threats."

"No he didn't. I agree with you about the Native Americans. They need all the help they can get. Our influence in their lives hasn't helped one bit."

"Yeah. Anybody else come to mind?" Bishop asked.

She looked at him pensively and said, "None. If they do, I'll call you."

Bishop had given her one of his cards when he sat down.

"I guess that's all I came to find out. You've been up front on everything. I anticipated some stalling and double talk. You didn't do that. I'm impressed."

"I decided it was time to tell the truth. With Hugh gone, there's no reason to continue the charade. He was a wheeler-dealer, I guess," she told him.

"I think he was. I don't know if he broke any laws, but he was as corrupt as any man I've known in a long time." He stood to leave but paused and asked, "I need to know if you had a boyfriend. Boyfriends can get jealous enough to kill."

She looked surprised. She shook her head. "I didn't. I've had friends, but I wouldn't call any of them boyfriends." She did quotes with her fingers.

He thanked her and said goodbye.

She shook her head as he left. Tears ran down her face. She was wiping them away as he left.

Like Mrs. Jackson, Denise hasn't gotten over it either. I guess even con men can get love even if they can't give it.

*****

In the hall, Bishop headed for the outside door but stopped when he heard his name. He stopped and looked back. Jason was hurrying toward him.

As he came closer, he introduced himself. "Jason Garcia. I'm the cameraman who followed Denise around reporting on everything that crooked bastard Hugh Jackson said and did. I just wanted to tell you, in case she didn't. That man was a crooked, two-bit con man who'd used anybody and everybody to get what he wanted. That included Denise. He conned her into falling in love. Just snowing her. Hell, he only loved himself. I don't know all the details, but from what I heard, I'd say he screwed the Indians, Native Americans, I guess I should say. And the landowners where the casino is to be located. He also screwed Blackledge who was running against him for the supervisor's seat. And he sure as hell would have come up with something against the sitting state senator, Nelson."

Bishop knew all that, and Denise had just confirmed most of it, but he let Jason continue to talk. He usually learned more if he let people talk.

"Ever hear anybody threaten him?" Hugh asked.

"I heard Denise say the people who ran the Lake Casino were pretty mad at him. Hell, everybody he ever dealt with ended up hating him. That was because he always had to come out ahead of any deal he was in."

Bishop said that was what he'd heard as well.

"What's your relationship with Denise?" he asked. He figured with feelings as strong as the ones he obviously had, he must like her very much.

Probably more than just like. The boyfriend? Would he have killed over her? For her? Why not? He's not all that big, but how big do you have to be to shove a sharp knife into somebody's back?

"Just a working one as her cameraman really. I guess I'm her friend. Maybe her only true friend. Now that that con man is out of the way, I hope to be more. She had the policeman call me the night he died ... to come over. That made me happy."

"You know I'm working with Chief Jenkins to find Jackson's murderer."

Jason said he'd read the story. Also, Denise announced it during her local news report.

"So, I'm obliged to ask where you were at nine. That's the time Jackson was killed."

He said he was at his apartment in town watching a PBS program and gave Bishop the name of the program and what it was about. Bishop checked later and that part checked out. That didn't mean he hadn't killed Jackson, just that he had an alibi that wouldn't stand the light of day.

I'll mention it to the chief if I don't find somebody else who looks better for it. He could search the guy's apartment for a knife.

Bishop thanked him and left. He went to his cabin and typed up a report of all Denise had told him and the corroboration Jason added. He couldn't tell for sure if either person was left-handed, but Denise appeared to be right-handed, the way she picked up paper nervously while they talked. He planned to rub it in a little since the chief had made light of his suggestion. He guessed he'd done enough rubbing it in though and would give it up with that report.

He suggested that the chief send somebody out to question the people who sold the land to the Freedom Tribe for the casino, the people Hugh had, as somebody had said, "screwed."

Afterward, he called the chief's office to get Greenfield's full name and phone number. Also, his office address.

He walked onto his porch and sat down to do some thinking.

"Okay, what have I learned?" he asked, talking to himself, and then let the answers to his question come into his thoughts. Stuart Flints' name came up twice. Once from Jackson's wife and once from his mistress, Denise. "I guess I can call her a mistress. That's what she was."

He stared out at the river and continued his conversation with himself. "So, that makes Flint a bad guy. I'll sure as hell want to talk to him. What else?"

He knew that three people had told him what a crook Jackson was; his wife, his mistress, and someone most likely jealous of the man, Jason. Three people also confirmed that Jackson had absolutely no scruples.

"So, it shouldn't have been a surprise that somebody decided he had to go."

But, why kill the man with a knife? Why not just shoot the bastard? Well, gunshots make more noise for one thing. Taking the watch was smart. Makes the killing look like an interrupted robbery. But, that's the first thing an incomplete robbery looks like to an investigator. And that tells an investigator, me to be specific, to keep revenge and hate on the table as a motive for the killing.

Greenfield sounds like he was pissed enough to have a motive to commit murder. Jackson must have cost him several million dollars. That's plenty of money to motivate murder. Greenfield's not likely to have done it himself so I'm not likely to get much more out of him than an impression, but every rock has to be turned over, like the chief said.

He wondered what his next step should be. Greenfield? Flint? Hell, even Riley Watson. *Hell, I can't even leave out the Native American guy, Martin.*

Any of them could have killed the bastard. He cautioned himself for passing judgment on Jackson. He'd only met the man once but he figured that was enough to form an opinion. Besides, even Kathy agreed, and she wasn't nearly as judgmental as he was.

"Blackledge isn't likely to be the kind of guy who'd commit murder. But Oliver … hmm. If blackmail forced him to retire, he could have been afraid Jackson might use it again should the need arise. Both men should be relatively easy to interview." He laughed to himself as he wondered what Oliver would say if Jackson told him he wanted an endorsement from him as he ran for the senate seat.

Anyway, that's how he decided on his next step. He'd interview Blackledge and Oliver. Then, he'd get to the big hitters, Flint and Greenfield. He'd work Martin in sometime. He wasn't certain about Watson. Ten thousand dollars may have been enough to motivate murder, but it was hard to believe.

"But Watson did say he hated Jackson's guts. That at least gives him the mindset to kill. I kind of doubt it's enough of one, but I'll have to keep him on the probable list. I'll pay him a visit later too."

*****

He parked in front of the board's offices and walked into the building. The first person he saw was Linda working at her desk. Her name was prominent on the desk plate. He showed her the card the chief had given him to establish his official status and asked to see Blackledge. She pointed to the man at a desk.

Secretaries know everything that goes on in an office. I should talk to her too. It's almost lunch. I'll invite her to lunch, he thought as he headed toward the man's office.

Bishop noted that Blackledge had a few years and a few extra pounds on him, but otherwise looked healthy and in good shape.

He walked in and introduced himself and gave a one sentence statement about why he was there. Blackledge stuck out his hand, looking somewhat confused.

"I understand you and Mr. Jackson didn't exactly see eye to eye. I believe the consensus is that he more or less cheated you out of the election for the supervisorial seat. I'd guess that didn't set very well with you?"

"There was never any proof, but most people believed Jackson was behind it. I think it's fair to say that I didn't like him one bit. Simon appointed me to take Baxter's place. I suspect he did it because he and Jackson didn't get along either but I'm not one to look a gift horse in the mouth."

"I understand. Why do you think Baxter quit," Bishop asked. "He was settled in pretty good here."

Blackledge grimaced and paused but finally said, "There was some talk that Jackson threatened to make public a claim, that's all it was, I understand, a claim, that Baxter had taken kickbacks from contractors. Baxter and Jackson didn't like each other somebody told me."

No doubt. And, Simon Oliver had to retire probably for the same ... claim.

"Any particular contractor? Or were there more than one?"

"Uh, I don't know," Blackledge said.

"I'd guess you hated the man for ... in effect, accusing you falsely, like people say he did."

"I don't know if I'd go that far, but I don't think I'd offer him a cup of water if I ran into him in the desert."

"Do you have an alibi for the night he was killed?" Bishop asked bluntly.

Blackledge stared at him with an angry scowl, but said, "Yes. My daughter and her children were visiting. Since my wife passed on, they come up to stay a few days now and then."

He gave Bone her name and phone number. "I have her address in Gulfport if you need it," he said.

Bishop shook his head. He'd give the information to the chief's staff for a follow up.

He thanked the man for his time and headed for the door. Blackledge closed his office door behind Bishop, loudly.

I must have pissed the man off, Bishop thought, with a laugh. *Some folks are thin skinned.*

When Bishop headed for the door, Linda was picking up the phone. Her face took on a frown. Bishop glanced over his shoulder. Blackledge was on his phone as well.

Linda was saying, "I'm sorry, Sir. Yes sir. It won't." She hung up and sighed as Bishop walked past.

On a whim, Bishop stopped and said, "I was just going to grab a bite of lunch, Linda. Would you join me?"

She smiled and said yes.

They went to a place in town that served "old timey" food like collards, turnips, potatoes, black eyed peas, snap beans, cornbread, even biscuits, fried chicken, fried pork chops; all dishes most folks around town grew up eating from their gardens. And on each table was a bottle of homemade pepper sauce to flavor the vegetables.

News about the health benefits of eating well was turning older folks away from hamburgers and fries.

Bishop got a bit of everything including a thinly sliced pork chop and found an empty table. Linda joined him with her plate. They talked about how good everything tasted.

"Coffee's good too," Bishop said as he sipped from his cup.

She agreed.

"Well, how is it, now that Hugh Jackson is no longer around?" he asked.

She wagged her head. "I know most people didn't like him and he was full of it, if you know what I mean, but he invited me to lunch a few times. Sent flowers for my birthday. I liked it. My late husband used to do that."

"He ever ... you know, make a move?" Bishop asked.

She laughed. "No. I think he liked 'em young, like the television reporter. One time when we were having lunch, just before Thanksgiving, he did talk about bringing a bottle of wine to the house, but he never did. That's as close as he got to a … move."

Bishop smiled. "Sounds like what I've heard about him. Ever hear any arguments in the office that had anything to do with him?"

She looked at Bishop for a second then said, "Since Baxter has moved on, I'll tell you something if you tell me it won't go any further."

He promised. Bishop figured the scolding she'd gotten from Blackledge for letting Bishop burst in without warning didn't hurt him a bit. She probably enjoyed a bit of retaliation even if only psychological.

She told him about the shouting match Henry Hankins and Baxter had had about the bids on Indian Creek Road. Hankins was mad because Baxter hadn't called him to "look at the other bids, like in the past" before putting in his bid. He was cursing Baxter and Hugh. He said Hugh had promised him the contract and he was pretty mad that he might not get it.

"Mr. Baxter said Mr. Hankins and Hugh were as crooked as rattle snakes. Something to that effect. He said that was what Mr. Oliver said."

"The road was paved. I thought I saw one of Hankins' trucks out there."

"Oh yes, Hankins got the contract. I think Mr. Hugh did something. I don't know what, but it wasn't long after that contract was let that Mr. Baxter left."

Be damned, Bishop thought. *I guess old Hugh paid a visit to Oliver and told him to let Hankins look at the other bids like he always did. Sounds like Hugh knew what had been going on and threatened Oliver and Baxter. Blackmail. Well, well.*

"Don't tell anybody, Mr. Bone," Linda said. "I shouldn't have told you, but …"

"Don't worry, Linda. I'm only interested in who killed Jackson. I kind of know how the system works anyway."

"Thank you," she said.

"Ever hear anything about Jackson and Oliver?" Bishop asked.

"I know they didn't like each other since Hugh ran against Oliver to be the board chairman."

"I bet," Bishop said.

"I heard Mr. Oliver tell somebody over the phone that he figured Hugh was behind all the mail the board got in support of having Indian Creek Road paved. I think the board turned it down, but a few days later they voted to go ahead with it. Hugh was smiling when it was announced so I knew he had done something to make 'em do it."

"Looks like some in-fighting on the board," Bishop said.

"Mr. Oliver and Hugh got into it almost every meeting," she said. "Until Mr. Oliver retired and Hugh became chairman."

She thanked him for lunch.

Bishop promised they'd do it again.

*****

That lunch was worth the money, Bishop thought after dropping Linda off back at the board's offices.

Can't say Blackledge told me anything I didn't know. He has an alibi, but Linda told me plenty. Hugh was probably behind Baxter's move and Oliver's retirement. So, both men had reason to kill Jackson. Revenge. I'll have some ammo when I talk to Oliver. And, I'll let the chief know so he can squeeze Baxter when he talks to him. Hankins got the contract so I can't see him carrying

*a grudge against Jackson. If another contractor had
been awarded the contract, I'd say Hankins would be
near the top of my list. I'll still talk to him to make sure.*

He drove to his cabin and called the chief so they
could fill each other in about what they'd each learned.
So far Jenkins had found nothing of interest, nothing to
suggest that any of Jackson's managers or the restaurant
buyer had anything to do with Jackson's murder. "Only
thing I've got since I've been on the road is indigestion,"
he told Bishop. "I ate at the restaurant Hugh sold."

Bishop laughed.

But the chief was very interested in Bishop's info
about Baxter and Oliver. "I'll sure as hell talk to Baxter
about that. Threaten the hell out of him."

Bishop said he'd do the same thing with Oliver, talk
about his confrontation with Jackson. And he'd be doing
that next.

Before he hung up, Jenkins said he should be back in
Lawton late the next evening. Thanksgiving was coming
up and he had to be home to help June get the turkey
ready. He promised to invite Bishop and Kathy to dinner.
Bishop said they'd be delighted. He'd tell Kathy. They
could pass on buying a turkey and wondering what to do
with the leftovers.

Bishop told him, "I'll turn over the investigation to
you the day after Thanksgiving."

"Not so fast," the chief protested. "There's still
enough work for both of us. Your banks haven't been
calling have they?"

Bishop told him all was quiet. Apparently all the
borrowers were doing well.

"Okay, we'll struggle along like we're doing. You
handle the hard interviews and I'll … drink coffee and
handle the paper work."

"Yeah," Bishop said, and hung up chuckling.

The next day somebody from the chief's office emailed Bishop a report with the information he'd requested on Greenfield. He was renting a house in Lawton while he more or less managed the development of the River Casino. The heavy equipment was already out, cutting down trees and getting the site ready for the new casino Hugh Jackson had set in motion with his greed. Included in the report was where Martin was living. It was on the casino site.

The report from the chief's office said the casino people wanted to have their grand opening during the Christmas holidays when people prayed before going out to gamble and eat a ton at the casino's buffet before their annual vow to go on a diet.

Bishop thought about who he should interview next. He had planned to talk to Oliver next but with the chief coming back sooner than he'd expected, he re-thought that decision. *Oliver will deny any involvement in Jackson's murder and will likely have some kind of alibi anyway. He'll be a rock turning exercise.*

Bishop decided he should see Stuart Flint before the chief got back. *Knowing him, he'd want to do that one himself. Probably angle for a free beer, maybe dinner on the house. But, he doesn't know the guy like I do … at least from what I've heard. I'm thinking Flint might be my hardest interview. From what everybody is saying, he's a tough nut. The chief wouldn't be ready for that. Hell, I don't know if I am. I don't even know the guy. He may be seven feet tall and all muscles. Maybe I'll drop by and talk to Martin first. He may know something that'd be of value to me when I talk to Flint.*

*****

Bishop drove down a gravel road to the casino site, where Martin's trailer was located. "Pretty big," he said when he saw the thirty-two foot rig. Heavy equipment was all around, working, and more was being delivered as he parked. There was a temporary power pole near the rig along with a septic tank and propane gas tank. A pickup truck was parked near the door to the trailer.

They're getting ready to move some more dirt, Bishop noted. Most of the trees had already been cut down to clear the land enough for the casino and all they needed to support the casino's operations.

He knocked on the door of the trailer. A thin, dark skinned man opened it.

"Joe Martin?" Bishop asked. And as he always did when meeting somebody for the first time, he evaluated what he saw. What he saw was a man who looked to be in good shape, but had a few lines in his face. He stood a few inches under six foot and was dressed in work clothes like he was ready to go out and help with the work. He appeared to be an honest man as far as Bishop was concerned.

Bishop flashed his police card. "I'm Bishop Bone. I'm investigating the murder of Hugh Jackson."

"I've been expecting you since I saw the story in the newspaper. Come in."

Behind him Bishop saw a woman at a table. She was also dark skinned and, like the man, had dark hair. Her face was what he'd call plain but honest. *Maybe sincere,* he thought.

She introduced herself as Martin's wife. She gave a name but Bishop didn't understand it. She had a bit of an accent.

Martin asked Bishop to sit down and motioned toward a small living area with chairs. That's where they sat. His wife disappeared into their bedroom.

"I've heard Jackson stuck it to you on buying this land. I've also heard that he was behind forming your new tribe. Any of that true?"

Martin concurred. "He contacted me about forming a new tribe. I welcomed it. It was a way for Native Americans to do something for ourselves. I didn't know he was only doing it to make money. When we got ready to close on the land, we found out that he – well, it was his corporation, we found that out later – wanted six million for the land. We finally settled for three and a half and gave the corporation five hundred thousand to start. Our investors weren't happy at all. Mr. Greenfield looked like he was going to have a stroke."

"Did you do anything about it?" Bishop asked. "Like stab the man in the back?"

"No, I didn't. Mr. Greenfield asked me about it, the money. I told him that was between him and the investors. All I wanted was for the casino to be built so the people in the tribe could have jobs."

"You never found out for sure that Jackson was behind it, did you?"

"Mr. Greenfield said he was. I believed him. But no, I guess we never found out for sure. I didn't try to find out for myself. I wouldn't have known where to start."

"Where were you the night Jackson was killed?"

"I was here with my wife. I'd been supervising the clearing of the land. We had to put in a road too."

He called his wife who came into the room. She'd changed into a jogging outfit. Before, she was wearing what looked to Bishop as pajamas.

"Tell Mr. Bone where I was the night Mr. Jackson was killed." He looked at Bishop and said, "Mr.

Greenfield called me the next morning to tell me somebody had killed him. It was a shock to me … and my wife."

The woman looked at Bishop and using his Native American name said, "Talako and I watched shows on PBS from after dinner until time to go to bed."

"He didn't go anyplace?" Bishop asked.

"No, sir. We were here all day and night. Talko helps with the clearing during the day. I cook and keep house."

"Weren't you upset when … somebody said you had to pay millions for land that wasn't worth nearly that much?" Bishop asked Martin.

Martin shrugged. "Sure I was, but what could I do about it? Besides, Mr. Greenfield was running things by then. We had a gaming license and the approval of our new tribe. Mr. Greenfield promised jobs for the tribe members. Our lawyer said we, the Freedom Tribe members, were kind of a partnership. I suppose I was the president. The investors, the money people, bought this trailer for me. They give me some money each month to watch out for the equipment and to help out."

"Anybody threaten you?"

"A Mr. Flint called me. He basically offered me money if I'd pull out of the project. I told him it wasn't up to me but if it was, I'd have to tell him no. I told him to call Mr. Greenfield.

"Mr. Greenfield told me later that Flint had called him and sounded mad over the phone. Said the area didn't need another casino. Mr. Greenfield said Mr. Flint was just afraid of the competition and told him they were going to build the casino and develop the property with commercial buildings and houses."

"Well, I'll be talking to Mr. Flint. I know what to expect. The man sounds like a bully."

Bishop thanked them both and put all that was said in his report to the chief when he got home. His closing statement was, "I didn't find shit. Martin has an alibi, his wife, but what wife wouldn't back her man?" As he'd decided, he said nothing about whether Martin was left or right handed, but it looked like he favored his right.

I'll see Flint next, Bishop told himself as he punched the "send" button to send out his email.

Chapter 11

Bishop wore his dark suit with a tie for the meeting with Flint. He parked in front of the main building of the Lake Casino. It was an impressive structure with contemporary styling featuring a huge multi-colored rainbow, both with lights and coloring, ending in a simulated pot of gold. A flashing sign along the front of the casino displayed the words – Here all your dreams can come true.

They'll come true sooner if you keep your money in your pocket, Bishop thought as he headed for the entry door.

He didn't call for an appointment to see Flint, assuming he'd "be busy" if he had. He figured he'd just storm in and "nicely" ask for an interview. He wasn't sure how that would go as he walked toward what appeared to be the administrative offices just off the entry lobby into the casino area.

He stopped at an outside desk and asked the young lady which office was Stuart Flint's. He'd flashed his "Lawton Detective" card so she didn't argue, just pointed toward a closed door with a name plate he could see that said "Stuart Flint" as he came closer.

With a questioning, amused, look on her face, the young lady watched Bishop approach the door. Bishop saw it with a backward glance and laughed to himself. *Apparently Flint scares the hell out of his staff,* Bishop thought. *We'll see if he scares me.*

He took a deep breath, opened the door and walked in. Music played in the background. Something classical, Bishop decided. *Good taste in music, anyway,* he thought.

Flint, staring at papers on his desk looked up with an angry frown. He covered the papers and opened his mouth to protest but Bishop interrupted him, showing his official investigator's card and saying, "Bishop Bone."

He is a big son of a bitch. Probably outweighs me by 20 pounds and got muscles all over. Shit, I hope I can get out of here alive. I'd better come up with a plan. And almost right away, a plan to survive popped into his thoughts. He hoped it would work.

He explained that he was there to ask him some questions about Hugh Jackson's death. "I understand that you and Jackson exchanged hostile words and that you threatened him if he didn't quit backing the River Casino the Freedom Tribe was developing."

"Who in the hell did you say you were? Wait a minute, I know you, heard of you anyway. You're not a cop. You're nothing." He looked at the card in Bishop's hand.

"Phony bullshit! What'd you do, have somebody dummy you up a card to get in here and harass me? I know Chief Jenkins and Mayor Roosevelt of Lawton. Both of them. If you don't get your ass out of my office NOW, I'll call security and throw you out. I remember reading something about a problem you had with some dumb shit cotton farmer and his son. You think that entitles you to barge in here and interrupt my work? I'm sick and tired of dumb shits like you and the damn Indians telling me what I should do."

"If you'd shut your mouth, I'll tell you why I'm here. And, it's not to tell you what you should do. A couple of questions and you can get back to your work."

Flint shoved out a hand for him to go ahead. The angry scowl stayed on his face however.

Bishop explained how the chief was a bit shorthanded and asked him to investigate Jackson's murder while he was out of town. "The chief and I have worked on other cases together. And, if you read the whole story about the plantation owner and his son, you'd know that the chief was backing me up during that confrontation."

"I don't give a shit. Just get the hell out of my office. As far as I'm concerned, all you are is a stupid debt collector throwing your weight around for a bunch of greedy assed banks. Next time, call for an appointment. Get out."

That pissed Bishop off, but he didn't respond directly to the insult. Instead, he scoffed and said. "So your secretary can tell me you're busy until next year? You threatened Hugh Jackson and he ended up dead. I think your exact words were, 'quit pushing the casino or else'. Sounds like you were threatening the man who ended up dead. That's why I'm here. Call the chief if you doubt my authority. Hell, call the mayor if he's your good buddy."

Flint sighed with a frown. "Okay, asshole, I didn't threaten the man. I asked him politely if he'd quit backing the other casino. The county didn't need two casinos. A second casino would cut into our business and put people out of work. I discussed it … nicely with Jackson. I also had a meeting with him and some of the other supervisors. He promised to consider what I was saying.

"Turns out the bastard, through some dummy corporations, had options on the property and was the moving force behind that new fuckin' Indian casino. He was a smart son of a bitch and I spent a ton of money to find that out. In the end, I did … by kind of an accident. I wish I had killed him but I didn't. He deserved to die. Screwing everybody he came into contact with."

"I assume you have an alibi," Bishop said.

"You can assume up your ass. I didn't threaten the man and I didn't kill him. You're barking up the wrong tree. You don't have shit for evidence that I even spoke to the man except for that one meeting I had with them. I told you to get out. This is private property and you're bothering me. I won't call security, I'll throw you out myself."

"You mumbled something about proof. Old Hugh was pretty smart. Smarter than you, it seems. Did you know he recorded your phone call ... the one when you told him to back off or else. How about that for proof of a threat? I think I could drag your ass to the police station and question you there. Threatening a man who was killed not long after – "

Flint practically jumped to his feet and hustled around his desk toward Bishop, both his fists clinched. No doubt what his intentions were. Time for talk was over. He stood.

Shit. Well, I hope this works or my ass is grass and Flint's gonna cut it, Bishop thought and adopted his stance.

He braced himself with his left hand on a chair next to him but otherwise did nothing to indicate he planned to do anything. Flint didn't look like he cared one way or the other. He was taking a back swing with his right hand to knock Bishop into next week.

As he did that, and was only a stride away, Bishop let fly with his left leg, his plan. His shoe hit Flint's crotch, where it'd hurt the most.

"Agh," Flint cried out. His face immediately turned red and he instinctively bent over. When he did, Bishop lashed out with his right elbow and hit Flint in the jaw, knocking him to the floor, half conscious.

Bishop looked around. The secretary who'd showed him Flint's door was standing in Flint's doorway watching. The amused look was still on her face.

"What's going on, Mr. Flint? Do you want me to show this policeman out?"

Flint heard her and nodded. He looked at Bishop and said. "You'll hear from me again, asshole."

"I'll bring something stronger next time," Bishop replied.

He decided it was time for him to go before the security force arrived to throw him out and create an incident. Bishop was a paid member of the Lawton police force so if anybody threw him out they could end up in jail.

He left. As he was going out the door, he saw a number of uniformed men running toward Flint's office.

"Well, they'll find him. My plan to save my ass worked," he said to himself as he hurried to his car.

He went back to his cabin and typed up a report of the meeting for the chief, including as many of Flint's threatening remarks as he could remember. He said that Flint was a bully and accustomed to getting his way, but he doubted he killed Jackson. "He would have had imported labor do it and I doubt they'd have used a knife. However, if I turn up dead, I think you should question the man … if you can get an appointment."

Within the hour, Jenkins called him. "Can't you ever smile when you're dealing with hard cases like Flint? He called the mayor. His lawyer's already threatening to sue the city. Our lawyer told his lawyer to go ahead. Maybe the two of you should have a beer sometime."

Clearly Jenkins hadn't read his report yet, so Bishop explained what had happened including the name of the secretary who witnessed his confrontation with Flint. Like most, her name was on a plaque on her desk.

"Besides, I was in front of the man's desk. He had to charge me to end up where he did. Hell, chief, he was going to beat the shit out of me."

"He said he was just standing there and you kicked him in the balls," the chief said with a laugh in his voice.

"Hell Chief, when a two hundred pound gorilla charges you, and you don't have a weapon, you have to think fast. All I could think about was aiming my shoe at his crotch. I got lucky." He didn't go into the fact that he'd anticipated being attacked by Flint and had planned his response, the kick in the balls.

"Listen, Bishop, I know about what happened. You asked your blunt questions and it pissed the man off. He lives with a short fuse as it is. I imagine, knowing you, that you lit it when you pushed your way into his office."

"I can't argue any of that," Bishop said. "I pissed him off when I wouldn't leave before I could ask what I came to ask. He told me he didn't kill Jackson. I'm inclined to believe him but that's not a totally satisfying inclination."

"I get you, Bishop. I just think you should avoid the Lake Casino for awhile. Maybe a few years. You and Kathy gonna be over to turkey tomorrow?"

"If I'm alive, we'll be there."

"I'll do the public relations bit and call Flint. I understand he had to be driven home. You must have steel toed shoes." He laughed. "Frankly, I've seen him around and don't blame you a bit for taking action to keep your head on your shoulders. I expect he had in mind separating it from your body."

"At least," Bishop agreed.

"By the way," Jenkins said, "I talked to Baxter at his office a while ago. After I more or less promised him immunity, he confessed to taking kickbacks from Hankins. Said Oliver did too. Jackson forced him to resign or risk exposure. If it had come out, Baxter's working days in any public office would have been over. No doubt Oliver retired to keep his reputation intact."

"I'll be mentioning that to Oliver when I interview him. I had suspected as much. I'll be nice, before you even tell me to."

"I doubt Oliver would charge you. You're bigger than he is. I can't say that about you and Flint."

"Hence my foot to the rescue."

"Yeah," Jenkins said. "At least you can still drink coffee and eat a croissant. If you hadn't stopped him, you might not have any teeth and your face would have been rearranged."

"No doubt."

Bishop told him goodbye. "See you tomorrow night."

*****

He had to repeat the story for Kathy when she came out that evening. It was all over town how Bishop Bone had attacked Stuart Flint at the Lake Casino.

"I doubted that was the full story," she said. "I know you don't attack anybody without provocation."

He assured her that the Flint confrontation was totally the consequence of the man's short temper because he'd barged into his office unannounced and without an appointment.

"I pushed him some when I said Jackson had recorded the threat he'd made against the murdered man. I think that's when he jumped up to tear me a new one." *Nobody's said anything about that threat I made. Wonder why?*

She laughed and said she never thought otherwise. "You never back down and you push whatever point you have."

"We all have our crosses to bear," Bishop said with a laugh.

*****

Thanksgiving at the Jenkins was spent eating all the turkey delights including mashed potatoes, cranberry sauce and especially the pumpkin pie Kathy contributed. They had wine with dinner, a gentle rosé, and classical music played in the background. Bishop was a little surprised at the music, knowing the chief, but assumed it was June's doings.

During the evening, Jenkins said that Flint considered the casino his own. He made over a million a year managing it. He wasn't a lady's man but was known to import prostitutes frequently. He'd been married a couple of times. Both ended in divorce with the wives claiming he'd physically abused them. He'd had no children.

"I think I see a pattern," Bishop said. "Why waste time talking when you can get faster results with brute force."

Jenkins agreed.

"His association with the casino is probably why he got so excited when Jackson pushed for the second casino to be built," Bishop said.

Everyone agreed.

"His lawyer called the city attorney and asked that you not contact his client again. He had no objection to answering questions, but preferred that they be asked by the chief of police or the city attorney. He'd have his attorney present," Clyde said smiling. "Gotta learn some public relations, Bishop."

"Yeah. I have some when I'm dealing with reasonable people," Bishop said. "But, I won't go near the casino unless you ask me, Chief. I guess I'll have to pass on their belt-bustin' buffets."

"Good," Clyde said. "I don't want to visit you in the hospital … or the morgue."

"I share that wish."

Bishop told them that Flint had somehow found out that Jackson was behind everything involving the River Casino, including the formation of the new tribe, the river property, and the gaming license.

"How?" Clyde asked.

"I'm not sure. I gathered it was via something unexpected. He evidently paid out money to find out but wasn't successful. Jackson's wife heard most of what Jackson was doing by listening to his phone conversations and probably reading his emails. She may have told somebody but I doubt it. I'll ask her next time I'm out there. I want to look over Jackson's computer. Julia, that's Jackson's wife's name, knows enough about computers to read his email. She may have deleted something but I doubt she's computer literate enough to know about how to delete files."

I'll drop by after I talk to Riley Watson, Bishop thought.

"I guess we need to meet, me and you, privately," Bishop told Clyde.

"When I get settled in good. I've been on the road, you know," the chief told him. "Write me an email."

"I'll do that so we're not bumping into each other in this investigation. However, you may not want me

involved anymore, considering the flap I made with
Flint. You want my badge?"

Jenkins laughed. "No, I want you involved. When
you make flaps, you usually are finding stuff out. But,
you're right, I need to know what you have in your
pipeline. I'll work around you for now."

Bishop promised to keep sending him email reports
of what he was doing and what he planned to do.

"However, could you send some of your minions out
to see if anybody heard cars or trucks on the road the
night Jackson got it?" Bishop said. He was thinking
Riley might have decided to make a trip into town.

He said he would.

"Crazy world," June said. "People stealing and
killing. Who would have thought it'd happen here?"

Everyone agreed.

And that was how the evening ended.

*****

While Kathy was getting into comfortable clothes to
watch a British murder mystery, Bishop sent the chief an
email outlining his plans for the next couple of weeks so
they wouldn't end up doing the same thing. He also
reminded the chief to check the people along the road
from Riley Watson's home to the highway. The road
they lived on was known as the Leaf Road which ended
when it merged into the highway.

Riley, Bishop knew, lived about a mile on the other
side of Julia's old farm.

*I need to talk to Oliver, but I think I'll see what Riley
has to say first. As far as I know Riley's wife died and he
doesn't have a live-in, like some of us do.*

Kathy walked in wearing her comfortable night wear. Bishop took one look and said, "Hell, Kathy, we can watch the murder mystery another time."

She smiled.

*****

The following Monday morning Bishop got dressed to interview Riley. As he had with Flint, he decided to just drive out, not phone ahead and give him a chance to say he was busy or had a doctor's appointment.

Wonder how old the guy is? Bishop asked himself. *Julia said he was considered too old for her. She has to be approaching fifty. He must be at least sixty. Not too old by California standards if money's around, but probably too old for a more conservative culture like we have here.*

Bishop located Riley's driveway off the Leaf Road. It was gravel and flanked by huge trees, some evergreen, some not. The "nots" had already shed their leaves for the winter. Dead leaves covered the ground.

Probably was gravel when they built the house and probably will stay gravel. People learn to live with what they have in our neck of the woods.

He parked in front of an old log cabin with front and back porches. The back porch had been screened in to keep out the mosquitoes.

His parents must have built it a hundred years ago. Cut down the logs and fitted them together. I wonder if ... hell, they must have added bathrooms as soon as they became fashionable. Likely have propane for heat and cooking. Must have been hell in the old days when people had to burn wood for everything. And, the boys had to cut and split it. Plus bring the water from the well. I imagine everybody out here has city water now. Julia's house looked completely upgraded.

He almost thought "Jackson's house" but realized that Julia still owned it.

From where he'd parked, he could see behind the house at the fields and pastures. Directly behind the house was a pecan orchard. The field had been plowed and was probably planted during the planting season. It showed no weeds.

He could also see pastures with cows grazing. The way it was fenced, Bone figured the man rotated his pastures so the cows could graze on while the other recovered. That's how the good farmers did it.

Bishop got out of the car, walked to the front door and knocked. Nothing happened so he punched the doorbell button. Within a few seconds, an older man opened the door and asked, "Who are you. I'm not buying anything."

Maybe more than sixty, Bishop thought.

He began closing the door but Bishop stuck his foot in the space and said, "Riley Watson?"

The man stopped closing the door and said he was Riley Watson.

Bishop told him who he was, showed his "official" card and asked if he could talk to him a few minutes about Hugh Jackson's death.

"That crooked bastard. I'm glad he's dead," Riley said. "I didn't do it if that's why you came out here, but I'm glad somebody did. And, I don't have anybody to cover for me. So, we're both up shit creek. You're wasting your time and mine. I guess I could give you a cup of coffee." He had a mug in his hand.

Bishop smiled. "I've had enough coffee, but would like to ask you a few questions."

Riley made a face as he waved Bishop inside. Bishop heard him mutter, "Shit fire and save matches." He'd heard it before. It was a commonly used expression. He laughed to himself.

Bishop followed him to the living room and sat in a padded chair that looked like it had seen a few years. He took note that the man walked with a bit of a limp but otherwise seemed in good health.

On the table in front of the sofa was a stack of photos and an album. It looked like Riley had been putting pictures into the album.

"Your nickel," Riley said with a wave in Bishop's direction. "Make it snappy. I ain't got all day."

"Okay, I'll get to it. You hated Jackson –"

Riley interrupted to say, "I sure as hell did! He cheated me out of money I needed. I had a wife dying and had to pay for around the clock help. I had … to watch … her die." He choked up and had to wipe tears from his eyes. He drank some coffee until it passed.

"Did you kill him?" Bishop asked after the pause.

"Already told ya, no! I wish I had. Maybe I could sleep better knowing I did something to revenge my wife."

"Think carefully, Mr. Watson. I'm expecting you to tell the truth. Chief Jenkins is asking people along Leaf Road, between here and the highway, if they heard any traffic on the road before nine o'clock the night Jackson was murdered. Stabbed in the back. So, my question is – did you go out that night?" Bishop wasn't sure if the chief had begun investigating the road traffic that night yet or not, but would check, and remind him to do so if not, as soon as he got back to his cabin.

"You're accusing me of killing the man? What bullshit! I remember very well what I was doing. That was the night somebody gave me a Christmas present early, killing the crooked son of a bitch. I went to the convenience store where the road meets the highway and bought a six-pack of beer. I was out of beer, a sin as far as I'm concerned. The store closed at nine. I got there just before they closed. I drink a bottle before I go to bed. Makes me have to get up and piss at three in the morning, but it helps me fall asleep."

Doesn't mean you didn't have time to drive into town and stab Jackson in the back. It'd be tight. Hell, how would he know where the man was? I'm grabbing air.

Bishop said, "I see you keep an album. Julia Jackson does too."

Riley sighed. "Julia. Damn, I loved Julia a long time ago. I wanted to marry her. But, hell, her mamma said I was too old and not likely to amount to a hill of beans. I guess she was right, but I still think about her. Hell, if I was going to kill Hugh Jackson, it'd be because he hit Julia. She has to wear a hearing aid in her left ear these days to hear people good. That's because the bastard got mad and hit her upside the head. Broke her ribs another time. She had to wear a brace for a month."

"I hadn't heard that. Julia didn't tell me. Why did he hit her?" *I thought she was having trouble hearing me.*

"Now and then she'd get sick and tired of him fooling around and complain. Julia can complain loud when she gets mad. He'd hit her to shut her up, was what Julia told one of my cousins."

"You ever get down there to see her? Feeling like you do?" Bishop asked. He knew he did but wanted to hear it from him.

The man twisted on the sofa nervously. "Yeah. I go down there and help her. Do handyman work. Milk her cow. But I haven't …. you know, said anything to her about … anything. I'm still too old for her. I just try to be her friend. I figure she could use one."

Bishop didn't argue the point.

Bishop felt the interview was about over. He didn't really get anything new, assuming Riley's alibi held up and he didn't doubt that it would.

He leaned forward and touched the pictures on the coffee table. "These your family?" They were pictures of people doing things.

Riley perked up a bit with the change in Bishop's questions. "They are. I've been meaning to put 'em in the book for my children and what's left of the Watsons."

There had been six children. He was the only boy left. His two sisters lived out of state but came back now and then for a visit.

He picked up one picture and handed it to Bishop. "Here's one of me and Julia after my Papa and hers had killed a deer when they went huntin'. Used to be lots of deer in the woods behind the place. All killed out now. That's me and Julia standing by the deer they'd killed. It was hanging from that pecan tree out's younder." He pointed to the pecan orchard in back. "I sell the pecans. Cows too. It's how I make a living these days. I spent every dollar I had trying to save Mary Anne and I don't regret a penny of it."

Bishop looked at that the picture. Riley and Julia stood on opposite sides of the deer. Julia's hand was touching the deer's stomach.

"We're getting ready to clean it, my papa and mamma. We'd eat deer meat for a month after they went huntin'," he said proudly.

Bishop stood to leave. "Well, I'll let you get back to it, Mr. Watson. I don't know if I'll see you again. I'm sorry your wife died. I can understand how you feel. I wish you the best with your life. Maybe you should say something to Julia when she feels better."

Following Bishop, he said, "Yeah, I might. I ain't worth a damn as a man these days but I could take care of her. I thank you for your kind words, Mr. Bone. I'm sorry if I came on strong when I saw you at the door. I didn't know who you were exactly and didn't feel up to being bothered."

Bishop said he understood. The man waited in the doorway until Bishop drove away, trailing road dust.

Chapter 12

"Well, I guess I have time to search Jackson's office and go through his computer files. See if Mrs. Jackson has anything else to say." He shook his head in disbelief. "Jackson beat her for complaining about his screwing around. Somebody should have done the same to him."

He laughed. *In a way, somebody did. Riley was right. Jackson was a son of a bitch.*

Bishop parked in front of Julia's home and got out. "Wonder if she's home." Somebody, he assumed Jackson, had added a garage with a door. It was closed so he couldn't see a car.

He walked to the front door and pushed the doorbell. The door was slightly ajar. That bothered him. He called her name. No answer. He pushed the bell button again. When there was still no answer, he went inside and called her name again. It was a one-story house and not that big so she should have been able to hear.

He chanced a look through the back window. There she was, patting one of her old cows. *Still has a few. Maybe a good thing. Kind of like friends, her cows,* he thought.

He let out the nervous breath he'd been holding and relaxed. "Damn, I was afraid somebody had … killed her too."

He walked onto the back porch and called to her. "Sorry about barging in, but your front door was open. I was afraid something had happened to you."

"I guess I left it open," she said, as she walked toward the porch steps. "Old age catching up with me, I suppose."

Bishop smiled and said, "I was just talking to Mr. Watson. He speaks highly of you, by the way. Seems like he has a good heart. He didn't much like Mr. Jackson, I don't mind saying."

"No. Hugh cheated him. Riley's wife was sickly and finally died. He tried to save her but couldn't. He comes down to see me now and then. Helps me. One of these days, I'm going to cook dinner for him. Our families were close. His dad and mine used to hunt deer. We'd dress 'em out and divide up the meat. We all got involved with each other, one way or the other."

"I gather. He has a bunch of pictures he's sorting out. Good idea, about the dinner. He could be a good friend for you."

She nodded and said, "Mamma took pictures after a hunt to put in our album. She gave them copies for theirs too."

He noticed the photo album she'd retrieved from her husband's office. It was now on the coffee table in the living room. He was so anxious when he came in, he hadn't noticed it.

"Apparently he treasures them, like you do yours," Bishop said, pointing to her album. "If it's convenient, I'd like to rummage through Mr. Jackson's desk and check out what he may have on his computer."

It was convenient and he followed her to Jackson's office.

Once they were in her husband's office, she booted up the computer and typed in the password. "Have at it. Just holler when you're done. The desk is unlocked."

Bishop began his search looking through Jackson's desk files. Mostly reports from his appliance stores, IRS filings, and information for speeches he'd made or planned to make. He also had files for his newspaper clippings. But of interest was the checkbook he found in one of the desk's drawers. The checks bore the name of a corporation – Moving Ahead, Inc. No entries had been make in the register. *I'll ask Julia about it.*

He found a couple of telephone numbers on a piece of paper way under the desk pad. He knew from calls he'd made to Mobile in the past that both numbers had Mobile area codes. He wondered who Jackson was calling in Mobile and made a mental note to call the number and find out.

After he'd finished that search, he began going through Jackson's computer files. He had a bunch and it took a while. Some were speech notes. *Probably stole 'em from someplace or somebody, knowing him,* Bishop thought.

In the end though, except for the telephone numbers and the checkbook, he'd found nothing that pointed to who might have killed him.

He found Julia in the kitchen. "I'm finished," he told her. "Frankly, I didn't see anything of much value."

He looked at her left ear. *Be damned.* She was wearing a small hearing aid. *I may be slipping or she wasn't wearing it last time I was here.*

"Riley said that Mr. Jackson … well, he … beat you. Is that true?" he asked.

She turned and stared into the pasture at her cows. She only had a couple left.

She sighed and said, "He did. Maybe I deserved it. He was always fooling around with other women and I complained about it. He'd get mad and knock me about. Now I can't hear so good out of my left ear. I quit complaining. Just accepted that he was going to fool around. That's when I started painting. I guess that's about the time we just gave up on having a marriage. We just lived together, nothing more. Painting has kept me from … killing myself."

"You do some beautiful work," Bishop said.

"After you were here last time, I took some to a gift store in town. Mrs. Cooley said she would be glad to have them in her shop. She's already sold half a dozen. Wants me to bring more."

"Congratulations! I knew I liked 'em," Bishop said. He almost hugged her but caught himself in time.

He was about to tell her he wasn't likely to see her again, but remembered the checkbook and asked about it.

She looked puzzled and said, "I found it too. Not only that, a man from some kind of outfit in Mobile called me. Called it a firm." She shrugged. "He said he'd heard that Hugh had been killed and wanted to talk to me. Frank Johnson was his name. He left his phone number. I was shocked at what he said. Hugh had money in a bank over there. The bank for that checkbook you found."

"I called the bank but they wouldn't tell me anything, even though I'm, or was, his wife. So, I called the attorney who probated my mother's estate and asked him what to do. He filed papers to ... probate Hugh's estate and got an order that will transfer the money from the account to my account here." She gave him the attorney's name and number.

"I'll be glad to get it. I'm not hurting but I could use a little extra now that Hugh's not bringing any in."

Bishop said he'd see what he could find out.

*****

Later, Bishop would match the bank's number she had called with one of the numbers he'd found under Jackson's desk pad. The other number was an attorney's number. He admitted representing Hugh Jackson but wouldn't tell him more because of client confidentially.

Bishop called the attorney probating Jackson's estate and asked if he'd get an order authorizing Hugh's Alabama attorney to tell him the extent of his representation of Hugh Jackson. Julia had told him he could tell Bishop anything he asked about.

"He may have formed a couple of corporations for Jackson," Bishop told the probate attorney. He gave him the corporate name he'd found on the checkbook. "His attorney probably formed the corporation for Jackson's casino land deal. Ask what he knows about it and find out what he knows about the money Jackson, well, Jackson's corporation, was to receive from the sale of land on the river."

*****

Bishop drove to the supervisor's offices to look through Jackson's desk for anything else relevant to what Hugh had been doing. Chief Jenkins had told Linda to keep it locked until he told her otherwise, but she unlocked the office for Bishop since he was "the police."

In Jackson's desk he found a copy of the agreement Greenfield had signed agreeing to pay Jackson's corporation the three and a half million. *Answers one question I had. I'll tell Julia's probate attorney not to bother about that,* Bishop thought. *But, I still need him to find out about the up-front money Jackson was due.*

He'd fax her attorney a copy of the agreement. The attorney would be told by Jackson's Mobile attorney that his corporation had indeed been paid the five hundred thousand specified by the agreement and was scheduled to get another million by mid-year. The attorney would notify Greenfield that all future payments under the agreement should be made to Julia Jackson.

Julia's attorney was also told about the second corporation Jackson was using for the money after it had been paid to the first corporation.

Bishop recognized what Jackson had been doing. *Using the second corporation as a conduit for the money. It'd be cleaned of any connection with the Freedom Tribe by the time it passed through the second corporation.*

When she heard about the money and what Hugh had been doing, Julia would ask her attorney to close all bank accounts her late husband had opened except for the one she had in Lawton. All the money if Hugh's other accounts would go into the Lawton account.

She didn't understand all that had happened, but from what she did understand, it sounded good. She was more than pleased. She could call the vet out to look at her cow. It seemed to be ailing. She'd been holding off doing it.

Bishop notified Greenfield to make all future payments directly to Julia Jackson but her probate attorney had already done it.

Bishop made no pretense about Jackson's relationship with the corporation that sold the property. It was Jackson's corporation and although Jackson had worked a scam on the tribe, it looked legal to Bishop, but if he wanted more information he could call Julia's probate attorney.

Her probate attorney would also include the chain of appliance stores in the probate. He got a court order approving the sale of the chain. That would bring another million into the estate.

When Bishop finished his investigation, he would tell himself that Julia wouldn't have to limit herself to two cows. She could buy a herd. *I wonder how old Riley will like milking a herd of milk cows.* He knew that wouldn't be case, but it amused him to think about it.

*****

Bishop drove out to Julia's farm to see if she had any questions about anything. Julia answered his knock and took him into the living room. He saw Riley sitting on the sofa. They had been reading everything her attorney had sent, trying to understand it all.

Riley and Bishop exchanged greetings.

"Thought I might try to wade through all this legal rigmarole Julia's been getting. See if I could make sense out of it. From what we've read and what Julia knows, I'd say old Hugh left her in good shape with his flim-flam off them Indians. She's gonna git a shit pot full of money."

"I think she will. I just came out to see if she had any questions, but I guess you have answered them already," Bishop told the man. Then said to Julia, "I'll be talking to a man called Greenfield who represents the investors in the new casino pretty soon. My questions will relate to your husband's murder, but may get into the money end of what Mr. Jackson had been doing. If I find anything that you might need to know, I'll call and pass it on."

"Thank you, Mr. Bone. You've been a big help."

"You are welcome," he told her on his way out. He'd given Riley a nod.

At least all that is on the table, Bishop thought. *Pretty clear, there's enough money involved to motivate murder. I don't know what I'll get out of Greenfield, but I'm curious about what he's going to say.*

*****

Bishop decided to wait until the next day to see Greenfield. It had already been a long but fruitful day and he needed to send a report to the chief about his interviews that day. And equally important, he was already thinking ahead about enjoying a cold glass of wine with Kathy who would be getting off work soon.

She showed up fifteen minutes after the library closed. They had wine on the porch even though it was getting cold. Leaves on the trees around his cabin and in the woods on the other side of the creek had already begun to turn orange and yellow. When the late afternoon sun passed through the trees' canopies, it created a magnificent sight.

Kathy took pictures of the foliage with her iPhone. She promised to give Bishop copies.

Bishop caught Kathy up on all he found out and what was being done by Mrs. Jackson's probate attorney.

The next morning she felt enthusiastic enough to cook waffles for them.

"I didn't much care for waffles until I met you," he told her. "Now, I love 'em."

She thanked him.

*****

Kathy had gone to work and Bishop was ready to visit Greenfield when he heard a car pull up outside. It was Jenkins.

"Damn, what's he doing out here? He usually comes out at beer time," Bishop said.

He was at the door before the chief could knock. "Come on in," Bishop said. "Coffee's ready."

"Good. Any croissants lurking about?" he asked.

Bishop told him he'd rustle up a couple just for him. They'd have to have the coffee inside however. It was in the low sixties outside.

"Okay," Bishop said as they sipped their coffees. "What brings you out so early."

"Ah, well, you said we should get together and sort out the rest of our responsibilities. Here I am," the chief said.

"Hell, I was half way just making small talk, and I did send you an email, but hell, let's talk. I'm down to a meeting with Greenfield and a final report, frankly. If we don't see who's on first after that, I'm going to wrap up my investigation and call it a day. No, I still have Oliver to see. Unless you want to take over now."

"No," the chief quickly said. "You stay with it. Greenfield and Oliver. Go get 'em. But, seriously, do you think old Oliver could kill anybody?"

"I've seen him on television. He looks frail but I'll eyeball him and ask directly is he did," Bishop said.

"Yeah."

"Greenfield is a more likely suspect. He and Jackson had a confrontation about the land one of Jackson's corporations had sold to the tribe. Jackson denied he had anything to do with it, but I think somehow everyone involved in the transaction, including Greenfield and Flint, found out. They threw enough money at the problem to get Jackson's name."

"I saw the rebuttal Jackson made on television," Jenkins said. "Looked like he was telling the gospel truth."

Bishop laughed. "Don't all con men? It's all out in the open now. Everybody involved knows how Jackson scammed them. So, do you take on Greenfield or do I?"

He shook his head, no. "I agree, based on what you've found out, that Greenfield is the most likely suspect. However, I'd just as soon you take him on. You're into the investigation and have all the questions ready. I don't think he'll be like Flint, ready to do battle at the drop of a hat or question, but I don't think he'll back away from a challenge either. I'd rather you be the bad guy. I'll have your back if you need it," Jenkins said with a slight smile.

"Yeah, I figured. So, what about you? What are you going to do?" Bishop asked.

"I reckon the first thing I'll do is sit down and read all your reports including the ones you're going to send me after you've talked to Greenfield and Oliver, if you're still alive to make a report. Greenfield may just shoot you."

"No, he'll just try to give me some loud bullshit. I don't see him as the shooting kind," Bishop said. "But, if he does shoot me, you can figure he didn't kill Jackson since Jackson's killer used a knife."

The chief laughed. "That's one way to look at it. I'll make a note in case you don't show up after you meet with him."

"Right."

"Anyway, to answer your question about what I'm going to do. I'll read your reports and see if anything hits me. You haven't found shit officially to date, but maybe you've said or will say something that'll point me at somebody to go after for the killing. Who knows? If not, I'll drive back out here for beer or coffee and bitch about your failure."

"Yeah. I might do some bitching too. This has been a bitch of a case. I like your plan though. Beats the hell out of working," Bishop said with a laugh. "Send me out to do the dirty work and you can bitch about what I didn't find out."

"Leaders don't work, Bishop. You should know that by now. We delegate, like I'm doing with you."

"So, that's your plan."

Jenkins laughed. "You got it."

They finished their coffees and left Bishop's cabin. The chief went to his offices in Lawton and Bishop headed to the address he had for Greenfield.

*****

Greenfield's office was in an old barbershop in an almost vacant strip center. The red and white barber pole was still in place. The sign over the space read 'The Freedom Tribe's Offices, Donations Appreciated.'

They don't miss an opportunity, Bishop thought, getting out of his car. He walked inside. The barbershop chairs had been removed, replaced by regular waiting room chairs. The mirrors were still on the wall.

The young girl behind a desk, a Native American from her appearance, Bishop figured, smiled and asked if he was there to make a donation. He shook his head, showed her his police card and told her he wanted to talk to Mr. Greenfield. The smile left her face. She picked up the phone and said, "Mr. Greenfield, there's a Mr. Bishop Bone here from the Lawton Police Department to see you." She paused, obviously to listen, then told Bishop to go on back.

A youngish, wiry little man sat behind a desk covered in papers. He wore glasses and had dark hair. He'd been studying a stack of papers when Bishop walked in.

Sure as hell doesn't look like a killer, Bishop thought.

He looked up and asked, "What are you doing here? We have all our permits and we're underway. I'm reviewing contracts now. Eileen said your name was Bone. Ah, I remember now. You're working for the police department trying to find out who killed Jackson. It was in the papers."

Bishop agreed. "I am. I'd like to ask you some questions."

"Go ahead."

"I know you and Mr. Jackson had words. I believed you accused him of scamming the Native Americans backing the new casino out of money, as I guess he did as it turns out. But, as a lawyer, I think it was perfectly legal. I doubt he'd get elected to a public office after it was found out, but that doesn't matter to him now, does it?"

Greenfield frowned but agreed.

"We found out what the crooked bastard had done. After the tribe had its gaming license we asked the attorney for the corporation holding the options for a price. The Tribe had been told the land was practically worthless. The attorney quoted us a price of six million dollars. I can tell you that didn't set well with the investors I represent or the Tribe, not to mention the landowners. They felt they'd been scammed as well."

"At that point, it looked like Jackson was acting as the Beat 2 Supervisor where the casino was to be built. No scam."

"We suspected he had an iron in the fire. So I spent some money and found out he was behind everything, the corporations, even the Tribe. He set that in motion. He was the kingpin, pulling strings so could get a big pay-off. I don't know who killed him. I didn't, but I'm not sorry the crooked bastard is dead. And we're still having to pay, our attorney says."

"I agree with your attorney. Where were you the night he was killed?"

"You can't believe I killed him. I just told you I didn't."

"Jails are full of people who've said the same thing."

"I was here. Working. I quit around nine thirty and went home. I'm renting a place in town."

"Jackson was killed around nine. That'd mean you could have driven to his offices, killed him and then gone home." But, Bishop didn't like the theory. Looking at Greenfield's face, he thought, *how in the hell would he know where Jackson was?* He answered that thought with another. *Could have taken a chance that he'd be working late, at the board's offices, I guess. But why knife him? Same reason, no gunshot to alert anybody. He would have been smart enough to take the watch to make it look like a robbery that had been interrupted by something.*

"You living alone?" Bishop asked.

"My wife and I have a home in Savannah. I fly home every chance I get. And, she visits when she can so we see each other. She was not here though when Jackson was killed."

"When will the casino be finished?" Bishop asked. "I've read that Native Americans will be employed exclusively. Is that true?"

"You're asking if we're going to screw the Indians like Jackson screwed us? I don't give a damn what you call them. They're still Indians to me."

Bishop nodded. "To lots of people, it seems. It crossed my mind that you might be intending to … screw them. I thought I'd ask."

"Hell no! My only interest is getting the casino built and operational. We'll hire as many of them as we can!

We're not screwing anybody! We just want to make some fucking money!" He came out of his chair.

Bishop took note of the fact that he was not much taller than five and a half feet. He laughed to himself. *Guess I won't have to use my shoe strategy on him.*

It wasn't necessary. Greenfield sat back down. "Do you have any more questions?"

"Just the one I asked. What is your completion date?"

"Oh, I missed that when you asked about the Indians, the Freedom Tribe. We expect to have slots in place before next Christmas, Thanksgiving if possible. And as many as want jobs will get 'em."

"You going to run the place? You personally?"

Greenfield stared at Bishop a second before answering. "I don't like your tone, Bone, but I'll let it go. I represent the people putting up the money for the casino. We're also going to develop the remaining acreage over time. Whether I'm the manager or not depends on the investors. Right now, I'm managing the development. I've done it before. I've also run companies. Directly as a major stockholder, and indirectly as a consultant. And, I didn't kill anybody while I did. Does that answer your questions?"

"I guess it does. But I may want to talk to you again," Bishop said and walked out of his office.

*****

Bishop drove back to his cabin, had a late cup of coffee and booted up his computer to type his report for Jenkins. Once he'd finished that report, he typed another one, summarizing what he'd learned from his investigations thus far. That took longer than the Greenfield report because he wasn't sure he'd learned anything. He wouldn't send that one until he interviewed Oliver.

In the summary of his ending preliminary report, he said that three people wanted to kill Jackson and none had fool proof alibis. He still had Oliver to interview, but that'd end his investigations. He'd amend the report to include that interview and his investigation would be over.

*****

Bishop drove to Oliver's home and parked within steps of the front door. Knowing Oliver was the last person he had to interview, he felt happy and relieved. He didn't like the fact that he hadn't found a killer yet, but there wasn't a damn thing he could do about that.

He was impressed that the house looked in pristine condition. "Being a supervisor must have paid well," he said under his breath. Of course, his reaction was similar to Jackson's but he had no reason to investigate why, like Jackson did, and frankly didn't really care. It wasn't his problem. He slid out of his car, hurried toward the door, and pressed the doorbell button.

Within seconds, a gray haired lady wearing glasses and an apron opened the door and asked, "Yes, sir. What is your business here?"

Bishop almost laughed. It was obviously the maid answering the door. A voice came from the rear. Both Bishop and the maid twisted a bit to see who was speaking. They could see Oliver walking towards them down the hallway. As they turned back, a shot was fired from the road. It hit the maid in the shoulder. The shot, obviously meant for Bishop, came so close to his head, he felt the heat of the bullet.

He dropped down and pulled the maid with him. She was crying in pain and bleeding. A second shot passed less than a foot or so over their heads. Bishop's car prevented the shooter from aiming any lower.

Bishop heard an engine start up and the sound of a vehicle driving away. He couldn't see what it was, a car or truck. However, he assumed it was the shooter driving away.

Oliver rushed to help Bishop, who was examining the maid's shoulder wound. Oliver's wife, Pauline, appeared in the hall and began running toward the front door.

"Call an ambulance," Bishop told Oliver, and asked Oliver's wife to bring a towel to press on the wound to stop the bleeding.

Oliver grabbed for his phone to make the call.

His wife returned with two towels. Bishop pressed one against the woman's bleeding shoulder. Fortunately, it was a flesh wound and the gunshot had hit nothing vital. Nevertheless, it had bled quite a bit before Bishop could stem the flow with the towel.

Within a few minutes, an ambulance arrived and took the maid, Kay, to the hospital for treatment. Bishop stayed behind.

Watching the ambulance drive away, Oliver looked at Bishop and said, "I recognize you from the newspapers. You're helping Chief Jenkins find who killed Hugh Jackson. If you're here to interview my wife and me, you'll have to come back tomorrow. We're going to the hospital to check on our maid. Somebody must have been shooting at you and hit her."

"I can't imagine who," Bishop said, but Flint popped into his thoughts almost immediately. "In law enforcement, you're everybody's target. I don't know who I've made mad enough to take a shot at me. Somebody though."

"I'd say. Lucky for Kay I called out to her. Turning like you both did must have saved your lives. That made the shooter miss you and hit Kay. Thank God, his shot only grazed her."

"I agree," Bishop said.

Oliver turned and shouted for his wife, "Come on, Pauline."

"You'll have some time, the doctors will take an hour or so to patch her up, but suppose I come back around ten in the morning."

Oliver agreed. "I doubt you'll find anything from me, but I'll see you then."

With that, Pauline and Oliver walked away and Bishop got into his car and drove away behind them.

*****

Bishop went home and wrote his report to the chief. His bottom line was "Although I have no usable evidence that Flint was behind the shooting, I'd put money on it. However, I imagine if you call the casino, you'll find that he was in sight all morning." He scoffed.

That was the case when they called.

However, the chief and Lawton's mayor made a conference call to Wallace Scott, the president of the corporation that owned the casino. The mayor had given his full support to the casino when it was proposed and had become "friends" with the president.

After the usual introductions and "how are you doing's" the mayor explained why they were calling. Someone had tried to kill one of their police investigators. He asked the chief to explain.

The chief explained that Bishop Bone, as his investigator, had interviewed Stuart Flint recently. Flint became angry during the questioning and attacked Bone.

"Defending himself, Bone kicked Flint in the groin and disabled him. Flint said Bone hadn't heard the last of him. We have absolutely no proof that Flint was behind the shooting, but he is known to have a short fuse and did threaten both Bone and the late supervisor, Hugh Jackson. Jackson was publically supporting the new casino on the river."

Scott sighed loudly in the phone. "So, I assume you're complaining about Stuart."

The mayor said that was the case. "I didn't back a casino with the notion that it'd bring violence into our town. Flint sounds like a bully who is used to getting his way and when he doesn't, he lashes out."

The man sighed again and said, "Frankly, we've had other complaints about him. He's attacked guests and other employees. He's a good manager when he's not angry, but he can't control himself."

"That's how I see him as well," the mayor said.

The chief agreed. "Next time, the shooter may not miss. I'm sure Flint will have plenty of witnesses who saw him at the casino when the shooting took place."

Scott agreed. "Assuming it was Flint. As you say, you don't have any proof other than the alleged threats Flint may have made."

The chief said, "Flint's threats were reported by people I trust."

"I take your point. I'll call a board meeting and see what we can do."

A week later, Stuart resigned as manager of the casino and left town.

It was rumored around town that a few days before he left, Flint had tried to kill himself by taking bottles of

Ambien, Xanax and pain pills he'd had various
employees get for him. A secretary found him barely
alive, but got him to the hospital and on a respirator in
time to save his life.

Chapter 13

Driving to the Olivers' late the next morning, Bishop made damn sure nobody was following him. And he looked around carefully to see if anybody was pointing a rifle at him as he got out of his car. He saw nothing. Oliver answered the door and ushered him back to their living room.

The chairs looked to be covered in leather and were soft to sit in. An expensive rug covered a planked floor and the ceiling showed old wood beams.

"Your house is wonderfully decorated," he told the man. "Impressive."

I guess being chairman of the board was worthwhile, Bishop thought.

"Pauline did it." He nodded in her direction. She was waiting to see if Bishop wanted coffee. He didn't. He just wanted to ask his questions and be done with it.

Oliver continued, "We love the house. Had to rehab it. It was her parents' home. They left it and the land to her. We sold ours and moved in … about ten years ago, now. Pecked away at remodeling it."

"Well, you did a good job," Bishop said. *The chief should have been here. I couldn't get more tactful than that.*

"Okay. Why'd I come? You and Jackson didn't like each other. I won't go into the details, but I know everything. Understand?" He was talking about the blackmail.

"I figured it'd come out sooner or later. Is it public knowledge?"

"No. My investigation is Jackson's murder. However, the way he "forced" you to retire, gave you a pretty good motive. That's why I'm here. I'll ask now. Did you kill him?"

Oliver let out a loud breath of air and said, "No. I'm not the killing type. Can't you see? Hell, I've never killed anything in my life. My mother used to ask me to kill a chicken for dinner. I just couldn't do it. She'd say, 'All you have to do is wring it's neck.' I just couldn't do that."

"All we need is some proof that you didn't wake up one morning with a change of attitude. Jackson did force you to retire. Forced Baxter to get another job. That's plenty enough for a motive."

"I guess you're right. Hugh Jackson was the most corrupt man I've ever known. Totally without scruples. I don't know if he ever took money from anybody, though it's said he likely swindled that new Indian tribe out of money or screwed them out of it. I don't know that as a fact, but I do know that he was the crookedest man I've ever run across in my life. He'd do anything he had to do to get what he wanted and didn't care who he hurt in the process. He deserved to die!"

Taking kickbacks would put you in the same league, Bishop thought, but kept it to himself. He doubted Oliver would want to talk about that anyway, and he was being diplomatic.

"Proof is what I'm looking for. Where were you the night he was killed and can you prove it?" Bishop asked.

"That's easy, Mr. Bone, I was here. My wife and I were watching a British murder mystery with my granddaughter. She'd just lost a child at birth and we invited her to stay with us while she recovered. The show ended at nine." He gave Bishop the ending, then reached over, picked up a pad, wrote her name and phone number on it and gave it to Bishop.

"Call her. She'll verify what I just said." He called his wife in and asked her what they were doing the night

Jackson was killed. Since he hated the man, his murder was talked about extensively for days afterward so the night would never be forgotten.

"Nothing says you and your wife are lying. Add your granddaughter. You know the drill. You can lie to the police. Every criminal does. Nothing wrong with that."

"Yeah, I get your drift, but I don't follow that drill, Mr. Bone. I try to stick to the truth."

Except when kickbacks are involved. That's what he thought. What he said was, "I don't think I'll get into that with you."

Oliver knew what he was implying.

Pauline came into the room. Simon said, "Would you tell Mr. Bone where I was the night Hugh Jackson was killed."

She gave Bishop the same story Simon had given him, including the presence of their granddaughter.

Bishop thanked them and left. He'd call the granddaughter from his cabin when he got home. She'd confirm their story.

"Well," Bishop said as he drove away, "unless they're all lying, which is always a possibility, Oliver didn't do it."

For lunch, Bishop stopped by a small Mexican café and had a tamale and coffee. Too early for beer. He thought about the case and what he'd learned.

Not a hell of a lot when you boil it down. I don't have anybody I can point to with any certainty. Damn!

He finished his lunch and drove home. After he called the Olivers' granddaughter and verified what Oliver had told him, he cranked up his computer and emailed the chief the report of his visit, closing with the comment he'd made to himself about discovering nothing of value.

The chief called minutes later. "So, where does that leave us? Flint's gone. We got rid of him for you. You owe me for that."

"Yeah. Thanks," Bishop said without conviction. "Look at it like this. You don't have to investigate my murder along with Jackson's."

The chief continued. "The man left town barely alive. Terminally depressed. He'd lost the only thing that meant anything to him. He didn't look like he had any fuse left. He came by to say how sorry he was and asked that I give you his message and apology."

"Well, I hope he learned a lesson. You can't attack somebody because you disagree with them and you sure as hell don't try to kill them later."

Jenkins agreed.

"Well, I'll wait for your final report and recommendations if you have any."

"I'm still thinking about it," Bishop said. "I imagine I'll send you something tomorrow. Right now, I'm thinking about Kathy coming out. We're having pork chops coated in fennel with wine. Don't you wish you were going to be here?" Kathy sliced the pork chops thinly. They were Bishop's favorite.

He did. "You lucky bastard."

"I am that."

*****

He and Kathy had a delightful evening beginning with a cold beer on the porch watching the creek flow past and the beavers at work in their pond. It had been a somewhat warm day in South Mississippi. And, the dinner was excellent. She'd brought bread pudding for desert.

"What's the occasion?" Bishop asked. "I love you for it."

"That's the occasion," she said. "I love you too, and knew what you liked and how hard you'd been working on the Jackson case. I figured you could use a good dinner."

"I did, and I had the best woman in the world preparing it," he said.

For breakfast, while she showered and got ready for work, Bishop fried up some bacon and eggs to go with their coffee and toast.

After she'd gone, he sat down at his computer to see if he could be creative enough to write the chief a decent report, with recommendations that'd mean something.

He sat staring at the screen for fifteen minutes then began to type his final report.

He typed: "Almost all the people I've interviewed could have killed Jackson. And, almost all have alibis that are somewhat questionable. Flint would have been my main suspect but the way he reacted, tried to beat me to a pulp for suggesting it, leads me to believe he didn't do it. Greenfield has the balls for it and a reason to kill him, but I'm held up by the fact that he wouldn't have known Jackson was in his office that night. Unless, of course, if you want to reach, he could have had somebody following Jackson around. I wouldn't hang my hat on that. So, I can't really look at him as a viable suspect.

"The Olivers, well Simon, has a good alibi. Their granddaughter was watching television with them. The show ended at nine, about the time Jackson was killed.

"So, who does that leave? Riley Watson. Riley hated the man, but the convenience store manager remembers he was in there around nine. I guess he could have raced to town and killed Jackson but like Greenfield, but how'd he know Jackson was working late?"

Something nagged at his subconscious but he was too tired to see if he could find it. He continued his report.

"I suppose Jackson's wife has to be a suspect. She did know where Jackson was and did have plenty of reasons to kill him. But, I can't see her stabbing Jackson in the back with a knife.

"So, unless I come up with a sudden revelation, I don't have anybody I can point at as the killer. I'm sorry I drew a blank. Cost the city money and don't have a damn thing to show for it."

That ended his report, which he emailed to the chief. He received no reply. That didn't set well with him, but he was not surprised. It wasn't often that he failed on a case, but this happened to be one.

He went outside and did some pruning and weeding. After he did that, he sprayed some stuff he'd bought from the gardening center on his fruit trees. Mostly though, he thought about the case. *What the hell did I miss? Was there a suspect I overlooked? Did I miss something during the interviews? I may have to leave town. I doubt the chief will ever ask me to help again and hell, I don't blame him.*

He stewed all day, hoping, he told himself, to come up something brilliant he could tell the chief. He knew Clyde had to report to the mayor.

"I bet he dreads that call," Bishop said to himself. "I would. I dreaded sending Clyde the report. He's probably looking for his razor blades." That was how Bishop described somebody who might be looking for a way out.

Mid-afternoon, Bishop's phone rang. It was the chief. He sounded glum when he said he'd gotten Bishop's last report.

"You call the mayor?" Bishop asked. "Or look for the strychnine?"

"I wish I had some. That's how damn low I feel. I've never had a case this frustrating. No, I didn't call him ... yet anyway. I've been doing what you say you do, ponder. I've been pondering what the hell I should do. I've read all of your reports twice and can't see anything else we can do. I could go out and cover the same ground, but I doubt I'd find out any more than you did."

"Yeah. I feel the same way. We haven't had many cases we couldn't crack, but this is one."

"I think I'll come out for a beer. Would that be okay?"

"Come on. It's about time. It's warm enough to sit on the porch. If you hurry. It gets cold when the sun starts to set."

He'd be right out.

*****

They sat in the cushioned chairs Kathy had bought for the house. She had said she was tired of bruising her bottom on the hard things he'd bought. Neither man said much. Now and then one or the other would say something about the case, but it was mostly to bitch about their failure to find the killer.

"I'll call ... no, I'll do what you did and send him a report. He can read that before he asks for my resignation."

"Surely not, chief. Some cases just can't be solved. I hate it as much as you, but I have to admit this may be one."

"But, you and I don't have to run for office. The mayor may think he has to show the public that he'd doing something ... like getting rid of an incompetent police chief."

"He's not that dumb," Bishop said.

"Maybe not, but he's a politician and he wants to keep his job. You don't keep a job unless you can show you're doing something. Why do you think I hired you to help. I figured you'd find the killer and I'd be a hero and maybe even get a bonus."

"Sorry."

"Maybe June and I can buy a piece of land around here and build a shack to live in. We could still fish and drink together."

Bishop laughed.

Kathy came up the steps. She was early and had an angry look on her face.

"What happened?" Bishop asked. She was rarely angry about anything.

"Oh, I had a bad day. I had to fire an employee. A young girl going to JC. She did something stupid. I didn't have a choice but to let her go."

Bishop and the chief asked what the girl did that was so bad.

She explained that the library had bought some new books. They were on a table to be put into the shelves the next day by genre. Kathy used the list that came with the books to decide which books went where. She found out that one was missing. She knew it was there when they unpacked them. The girl had unpacked and put them on the table.

They searched the entire library for the book, even called the seller who assured her that he'd personally compared the books he sent with the list when he was putting them into the box.

Kathy had the entire staff search the library again. They found nothing. Well, she remembered seeing the girl fooling around with the books before she went home so she called her into her office for a "talk."

It was what she called a "hard talk." The girl seemed reticent to talk about it at first. But Kathy practically accusing her of doing something with the book.

"It wasn't the money. And we could re-order it. It was more about solving the mystery of where it went. Well, to make a long story short, the girl admitted that she'd taken the book. No logical reason. She wanted it and took it."

"And that's why you fired her?" Bishop asked. "I don't think you had a choice. She should have admitted it right away and brought it back."

"She gave me some kind of Mickey Mouse excuse. She wanted it for herself. She'd read it at JC and loved it so much she wanted it."

"I'll be," Clyde said. "Funny how things happen. You looked all over for the logical places it could have been and it turned out to be something you couldn't possibly have logically deduced."

"I'm sorry."

"Me too. I put everybody through hell searching where it might have been."

Kathy went into the kitchen for a beer. Clyde knowing it was the "happy hour" for them, said goodbye.

"I'm going home, Bishop," he said. "If you get any revelations during the night call me. Don't worry about the time. I doubt I'll be sleeping."

Bishop agreed. "I doubt I will be either." He knew the Jackson case would keep him awake, searching for the clue he missed.

He and Kathy had a beer. By then, it was too cold to sit outside so they had the beers at the breakfast bar. They commiserated more about the poor girl.

"I may call her back. I don't know. It made me so mad, I felt like I had to fire her."

"Think about it," Bishop said.

They didn't talk about it any further. Bishop figured it was best. Kathy had good judgment and if she wanted to call the girl back, she would.

They had a great dinner, enchiladas with beans and rice. Bishop whipped up some Margaritas to go with them. They had cheesecake for desert.

During the night, Bishop did what the chief accused him of, he pondered. Around three he woke up with a thought, a damn enlightened thought, and the thing that had nagged his subconscious while he was typing his last report hit him.

Damn, now it all makes sense, he thought.

He started to call the chief but decided to ponder it the rest of the night to see if he'd overlooked anything and call him in the morning if he still thought it had merit.

Over coffee the next morning, he told Kathy what he'd come up with. "You planted the seed in my mind when you talked about the missing book and it sprang up during the night," he said.

She said his thought sounded like it may be the answer. "It's better than anything you've found so far."

Bishop said he'd call the chief after breakfast and get his reaction. He would wait until Kathy had gone to work before calling.

"I don't want to mix business with being alone with you," he told her. "You make life worth living. I don't want to spoil it with business unless necessary."

She kissed him and repeated it when she left.

Chapter 14

Bishop sat and stared out the back for a few minutes, then went to his computer to type an addendum to his final report on the Hugh Jackson murder that he'd sent to the chief the day before. That addendum would, indeed, be his final report on the murder. As soon as the report was on its way, he punched in the chief's phone number.

"Hello, Bishop," he said in his early morning gruff voice. "You've solved the case right?" He asked facetiously.

Bishop laughed. "Not my job anymore, Chief, but I did have a thought and a recommendation for you during the night. I've just sent you an email, but figured I should call you to discuss it."

"Well, hell, don't keep me in suspense. I may have to go back to bed. Do you know who did it? Not the mayor, I hope."

Bishop laughed again and told him what he'd come up with during the night.

"I'm recommending that you get search warrants for both Riley Watson's home and for Julia Jackson's home. I recommend that you lead the search. You'll be looking for a hunting knife at Watson's place. That's what was used to kill Jackson. It'll most likely be in the barn where his family dressed out whatever game they'd shot. I image there'll be all sorts of hunting and cleaning stuff down there. Check the knife for Jackson's blood. I'm betting you'll find it."

"How the hell did you come up with him. You said he had kind of an alibi."

"He does, but it wasn't fool proof. He had a few minutes to kill Jackson. I'm counting on that. By the way, remember my thought when we first talked about the murder. How I thought a left-handed person stabbed Jackson. Well, last time I saw Riley, he was using his left hand for everything. He's the lefty."

"Okay, you were right again. I'll learn one of these days. Proceed. Let me have the rest of it."

"When you search Julia's home, you'll be looking for Jackson's watch. I'll talk a little more about that in a minute."

"Damn, you did do some thinking. I hope you have something, other than the fact that the man was left-handed, that backs up what you're recommending."

"I'm not sure. You'll have to talk to the DA about it but, if you can get the search warrants and can find what I've just said, you'll have your back up."

"Give me the rest of your thinking," Jenkins said.

So Bishop did. He described what he'd thought of during the night. Kathy's experience with the young girl triggered the thought.

"We've been thinking somebody took Jackson's watch as part of a robbery or to convince us it was a robbery. I didn't think much of it when Kathy told her story, but during the night, when I woke up, I asked myself, what if the taking of the watch was some kind of psychological thing. As in a wife taking back an act of love made when she thought she could fix the flaws in Jackson's personality ... from his childhood. She'd given him the watch. Taking it back might have been her way of de-bonding with Hugh, if you don't mind my description."

"Makes sense Bishop, psychologically, I guess, but how does Riley fit into that equation?"

"All right. I had to push and pull but I finally came up with a theory."

"I hope it's a good one," he said.

"Whether it is or not will be up to superior minds," Bishop said.

Jenkins laughed. "Hell, Bishop don't bullshit me. We both know nobody has a mind superior to yours when it comes to crime. That's why I asked you to give me a hand. So, talk."

"I think, after Julia and Hugh had their 'come to Jesus' talk the night he was killed, she was very upset, in particular at what he'd said about only a blind man would have an affair with her. No woman wants to hear that, and especially a woman who'd tried as hard as she had to teach Hugh how to love. And, there she was offering to go to court and admit infidelity so he could get on with his life and he, in effect, laughs at her and belittles her in the process.

"I figure she then calls the only person she considers as a friend, Riley Watson, and tells him about the talk. Remember, Riley already hates the man, and he still … loves Julia, I'm assuming. So when Julia tells him what Hugh said, he's enraged and tells her he's going to town to have it out with him. He's already mad at Hugh because of the money Hugh had cheated him out of and because he'd beat Julia when she complained about his fooling around."

"That fits together, Bishop. How'd they do it, stab Jackson?"

"I'm thinking that Julia went along for the satisfaction of seeing her bully of a husband put in his place. Lord only knows how she expected Riley Watson to do it. He was much older than Hugh, and not in what I'd call fighting shape. Hugh wouldn't take a dressing down lightly.

"So Riley, knowing the same thing, took his knife in case he needed it. They stop for his beer and his alibi and hurry into town. They park in the supervisor's lot so they can watch the door into the building and Jackson's car. But Riley is fuming, more or less stepping into Julia's shoes. So when Hugh turns off the lights, Riley hurries over, knife in his left hand, and when Hugh walks past, he stabs him.

"When Julia sees the knife in his hand as he waits for Jackson, she gets out to stop him from using it but she gets there too late. Jackson is dead. She sees the watch and had a sudden impulse to take it, her psychological way, whether she thought it or not, to divorce herself from him."

"You put all of that in your report?"

"I did."

"I'll read it over. If it still makes sense, as what you've just said does, I'll take it to the DA and ask him for search warrants."

"I hope I doped it out right," Bishop said. "I did a lot of imagining, a lot of guessing. Mostly it's my gut feeling triggered by Kathy's experience with her employee."

"I know, Bishop, but you know human nature better than anybody. I never doubt your guesswork or gut feelings. If it works, I'll take credit. If it doesn't, I'll blame it on you. Just kidding. I think it makes more sense than anything else we've come up with."

Bishop said he'd sit in a dark place and wait to hear what happened.

Jenkins said he'd call as soon as he had anything definitive to tell him.

*****

It was late afternoon before Bishop found out anything. The chief drove out to see him. Bishop looked out the window to see if he were smiling or frowning. He couldn't tell. He went to the door to let him in.

"I've come for a beer," Jenkins said. He was smiling.

"First tell me. Were you a success? Did you find what I said?"

Jenkins patted him on the back. "That's from me, the DA and the mayor. It'll be in the morning papers and on tonight's news. I'll give you the details when I get my beer."

They went to the living room and sat down with the beers they'd detoured past the refrigerator to get.

"I'll tell you what happened. We found the knife in Riley's barn, along with the hunting stuff you told me to look for. There was what looked to me like a stain of some sort on the blade where it connects to the hand guard. I read him his rights and arrested him."

"Have you analyzed it, the stain?"

"That's why I'm late. An hour ago, the lab confirmed that the stain was Jackson's blood."

"Damn, we cracked it! But what about Julia? How'd you do at her house?"

"We found the watch in her bedroom. She practically showed us where it was. She's still pretty upset about everything. It was pretty much the way you said. She'd called Riley for some emotional support and when he said he was going to confront Jackson, she went along. Instead of a confrontation, Riley stuck a knife into his back. She tried to get there in time to stop him but didn't. Like you said basically. Also, she told us Riley is left-handed.

"Riley told us the same thing she'd told us. He took all the blame. All she did was come along for the ride, he said."

"Works for me," Bishop said. "What about charges against her? She was there. Possible accessory."

"The DA is willing not to charge her if she testifies at Riley's trial. That made it easy. But, there won't be a trial. He'll plead guilty. I doubt he'll ever spend time in prison in any case. A cousin called and told me Riley has cancer. Prostate I think she said. Advanced. That's why he took the knife and choose to use it instead of just telling Jackson what a bastard he was for hitting Julia."

"Thanks for coming out to tell me," Bishop said. "I've been wondering what happened all day. I was afraid the DA had turned you down and you were still working on it."

"Had to. I wanted to see the look on your face when I told you. I haven't seen you smile in a long time."

"Cases like that one can destroy a smile."

"I imagine the television girl, Denise Allen will be out to interview you. That'll be hard to take, right? After all you've put up with trying to find the killer."

It was.

Just then, they heard car noise out front and looked to see what it was. Indeed, it was a television crew coming to film a story for the evening news. The chief became part of it.

Bishop noticed how happy Jason appeared to be. *He must have moved into the place Jackson held with Denise before he was killed. He'll treat her right instead of using her like Jackson did.*

When Kathy came home to tell him the news about the development in the case, how they'd arrested Riley Watson and charged him with Jackson's murder, Bishop pretended not to have heard it, but made sure they saw the late news when the story aired.

When she saw Bishop on the screen, she laughed and walked over to kiss him.

"He was a natural," she said, "but so are you, Bishop Bone, a natural at keeping me in suspense."

The End

Made in the USA
San Bernardino, CA
06 February 2020